I0671381

Cellar Door: Words of Beauty, Tales of Terror (Volume Two)

Stephen Cooney

James Ward Kirk
PUBLISHING
2 0 1 3

ISBN-13: 978-0615907536 (James Ward Kirk Publishing)

ISBN-10: 0615907539

Contents

Poetry   8

Alex S. Johnson Essence of Ebon, Preserved   9
Mathias Jansson Smoky bottles   10
Dona Fox The Door   11
Dona Fox Me and My . . .   11
Dona Fox Magur   12
Dona Fox The Wonder Cave   13
DJ Tyrer A Darkness in the Cellar   14
DJ Tyrer Cellar Door   14
DJ Tyrer Foundations   15
Robert E. Petras The Soul Worms   15

Flash Fiction   16

K. Z. Morano Wooden Lips   17
Essel Pratt Dalliance   19

Short Stories   22

Dale Hollin The Last Eulogy   23
Mike Jansen The Angel's kiss   29
Neil Baker A Late Summer Afternoon on Cranberry Farm   33
Michael Thomas Knight The Gates of Lament   40
Dona Fox Forevermore   56
Greg McWhorter Sempiternal Denouement   64
David Eccles The Esoteric Espial   72
Matt Cowan Numen   76
M. J. Sydney Ellensburg Blue   84
David Perlmutter Little Pony Ride   95
Lee Forsythe Karni Mata   102
Justin Hunter Geisha White   108
K. Trap Jones   A Soul's Lullaby   117
Lori Safranek Angels Behind Glass   121

Suzy Saylor A Halcyon Panacea   132
Patrick Lacey Last Words   142
Kevin Rodgers The Scent of Jasmine   153
Matthew Wilson Video Nasty   163
Michael Randolph Leannan Sídhe   167
Gary Murphy Horrorwerk   175
Adam Blampied Buried   181
Jason WolfgangGehler Scarecrow Fields   184
Author Bios   195

Dedicated to Karin Ruijmgaart

Poetry

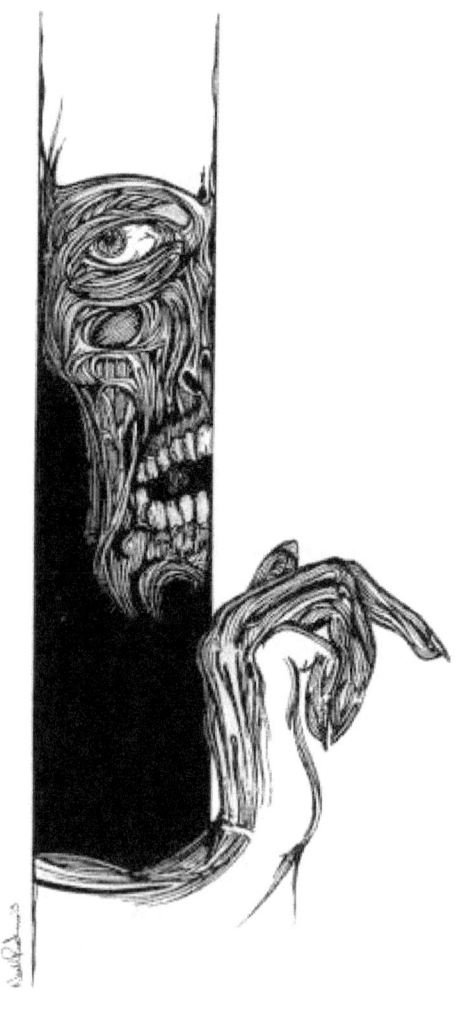

Niall Parkinson

Alex S. Johnson
Essence of Ebon, Preserved

What squats shackled
behind the cellar door, a goblin
with inky skin and all the appetites
of Caliban, feeding with loathsome eyes
on the fair Miranda, her pale virginity
preserved by magic seals?

With luminous eyes and corkscrew claws
the creature bulks a chest of dream-slaughtered jewels
as the heart that thunders, dull and hollow
presses suit to generate
new breeds of nightmare, incubus
spawned from slavery, legendary force
enchained, a family's shame—
dark mirror of the other horror
burning in the attic, shorn of voice,
without a name
essence of ebon, preserved.

Mathias Jansson
Smoky bottles

My grandpa left me the house on the hill
an old mansion filled with kitsch and trash
cheap souvenirs from around the world
book shelves filled with ghost stories
a legacy barely worth to feed to the fire

Then I found the cellar deep down under
a single bulb revealing the secret room
filled with bottles on rotten shelves
a wine cellar worth a fortune I believed

Disappointed I examined
bottle after bottle filled with smoke?
Old handwritten labels saying
Canterville 1887 and Helsingor 1599

What a strange collection I thought
gazing into the smoky bottle in my hand
when suddenly behind the glass
a terrifying sight appeared

Horrified I drop the bottle on the ground
stumbled backwards with fear
into the rotten shelves behind
to the sound of thousands of bottles
shattered on the stone floor

Behind the closed cellar door
no one heard my scream of horror
when I discovered my grandpas
ancient collection of ghosts

Dona Fox
The Door

Quivering her parted lips on mine
she fed me the bread of life
and I passed through that awful door.

The time between I could not enjoy
for I dwelt on her return.

Now she calls to me as her lovely
corpse crawls into my bed.
She covers me with her hair
and inhales my breath
in a final, bloody kiss.

Dona Fox
Me and My . . .

Stealthy as a spider,
Stalking me since childhood,
He lingers at my footsteps,
Dancing in the wind.
Testing, always testing.
He curls around my ankles,
Insidious, unpryable.
I dash into the house – he hides,
The light comes on – he leaps.
I know he's with me in the cellar,
I feel his trembling bites
grow rougher and I scream
But no one hears
for he presses the darkness
to my face . . .

Dona Fox
Magur

The beast, larger than several lives,
haunts the night-black cellars of your town,
Lurking beneath your treasures,
waiting for an innocent treat.

Pray that should his red hands grasp you,
pray that he will chew you well.
The crushing pain of mastication,
the easy out – to die quickly,
Huge green tongue rolling you
between the rancid yellow molars –
Sweet oblivion as he cracks your spine.

But should he toss you to the darkness
of his throat, swallow you
Whole as a bitter pill,
Your hell has just begun.

To the gutter wash of his belly, Afloat
in rancid wine, Waves of juices
lick and eat your skin.
Release to putrid, twisting chambers,
Squeezed and leached until the sucking,
Sloshing, gurgling world falls silent.

And you land upon the ground,
Crawl from the cellar to the light
of a day you knew you'd never see –
just another tramp with death drunk eyes.

Dona Fox
The Wonder Cave

My spirit has found no peace
since the night I went to sleep
and passed through the cellar door
into the wonder cave.

A feast was spread; cool water flowed,
the coverture glowed clear and crystalline;
And there within the brilliant jewels
of crystal shone my friends and foes.

I could change their circumstance or place
as I felt it should be;
My friends could wait for first I longed
to deal with my great enemy.

I focused on her figure then
and harsh within the crystal spires
in the magic of the wonder cave –
she stood and focused in on me.

The cave turned dark, and damp and cold;
Creatures slithered at my feet;
Wings fanned the air about my face,
teeth bit into my cheek.

I began to fall through chilling dark
sure the end was soon to come.
As faces leaped and nipped at me
I landed in a fire –

A fire so hot my skin was cold.
I felt that I could stand no more
And I found my body deep in ice –
Ice so cold it burned.

Then I woke to the alarm
and time to go to work where
my enemy met me at the door
grinning with delight,

Tonight, she said, tonight.

So make a pot of coffee,
my spirit will find no peace,
for I fear to go to sleep.
And pass through the cellar door
Into the wonder cave.

DJ Tyrer
A Darkness in the Cellar

Beyond the cellar door
There is darkness
A darkness more solid
Than darkness has any right to be
Coiling and flowing
More like oil than shadow
Taking brief form
Only to melt away
Before your beam of light

DJ Tyrer
Cellar Door

Cellar door shut tight
What does it conceal?
Intended to keep you out
(Or to keep something in)
It is less a deterrent
Than a challenge
An invitation to the curious

DJ Tyrer
Foundations

Climb down beneath the house
In secret spaces long unseen
Foundations from antiquity
Far older than you'd expect
With strange carvings
Hinting at elder times
Long forgotten

Robert E. Petras
The Soul Worms

The wind wails...
only dead branches clawing the house,
you say, trying to abate my fear,
but through the cracks of the boarded windows
I can see
the dead trees, their Medusa limbs growing
under the beard-clouded moon.
Already they are downstairs.
I could hear them days ago
inside the secret room,
the one you deny. They came
from the cellar sewer, didn't they?
Squirmed their way up from
the bowels of the earth.
They can squeeze
inside every little crack, small as a
dime.
Did you not often tell me?
They get inside everything. Everything.
There—behind the cellar door—
I can hear them, creeping, crawling, wriggling.
There is nowhere to go now.
Nowhere.
Don't look at me that way;
it runs on your side of the family.

Flash Fiction

Mike Jansen

K. Z. Morano
Wooden Lips

The cellar door is a wound, a break on the earth's skin. It is a gash in the ground where malignant thoughts trickle like blood into the cesspit of my filthy brain. The cellar door is a mouth... the wooden lips of a whore whispering obscenities into my ear, sticking her spectral tongue into my acoustic tunnels and to the roof of my skull to caress murderous designs into being.

She tells me what she wants me to do...

She tells me what I want to do.

She speaks to me even with her lips tightly shut, bolted with heavy metal.

The cellar door is hungry. And her cries follow me even to my sleep... soft fragmented sobs that swell into angry screams as midnight approaches and the moon's fat face pales from the anticipated terror.

I try to fight her, I swear... every single time.

But then there's the scratch... the sound of sharp fingernails raking against the door, creating deep cuts into the sensitive sheath of my sanity.

Feed me, she says.

I can hear the seismic growling of her empty belly, persistently reminding me of my duty. I walk towards the door... that other door. I turn the knob cautiously as if the monster were on the other side. The rusty joints creak to reveal the sacrificial lambs, their eyes floating towards me, terror blanching their faces.

I have learned to ignore their fright. It is merely a job that must be done. I pick one... a little boy, this time. As I free him from his shackles, a tiny whimper of protest issues forth from dry cracked lips. But he comes with me, nevertheless... the beautiful bleatless baby sheep... with his skin smooth and tight over his fragile skeleton.

I take him to the kitchen where I carve off that skin. I do it with a blank face... with studied precision. Then I stare into my work-- that amorphous figure of glistening pink flesh. Peeled of all pretensions, he is nothing but meat--a sexless, lifeless substance... her evening meal. I take his flayed body outside where stars always oversprinkle the sky... falsely festive, my co-conspirators, for they have witnessed me doing this for years and years...

I unlock the cellar door, cautiously... reverently... Now that her lips are parted, I can hear her voice more clearly, murmurs, sounds of pleasure sliding back and forth her muddy throat. Her malodorous breath reaches my nose--the smell of the earth's intestines, the stench of digested matter... of pulped flesh... of decaying bodies.

The meat sticks to my flesh, clings to me as if seeking protection. I drop it into the cellar door, into that gaping mouth and into that throat... that tunnel stretching into eternity. It may take a while to satisfy her... yes, it may take a very long time. And I have devoted my entire life simply for that purpose. I replace the locks on her lips... those wooden cellar lips, knowing that she'll be quiet, pacified for now.

Often, I wonder what would come of this... sure that someday, they--all the children that I have fed her--will return, resplendent in their new skin. Will they come for me then? Will they be grateful? Or will they exact their vengeance? Only time will tell.

How long, I wonder, will the locks be able to hold the door?

How long before they come crawling out of her pestilential hole?

My sleep becomes plagued with all these thoughts, my pillows always bloody like butchered sheep. I wash my hands often... over and over, until they are raw. Right now, there is only one thing I know. I serve that voice in my head... the voice of whatever unutterable monstrosity that dwells beneath the cellar door.

Essel Pratt
Dalliance

I've always heard that a normal person locks their skeletons away inside a closet, securing them behind neatly folded Egyptian cotton towels or seldom used golf clubs. I don't have fancy towels, nor do I play golf, I guess that is why I have opted to hide mine within my musty cellar, locked behind the wooden door. Never had I imagined the stigma of my demons would weigh so heavily upon my heart, and upon my mind.

Misguided deeds have a way of creating penance within one's self, I am no exception. I loved my wife and the child she was expecting. The key word is "loved", I guess love is a one way street and my wife drove the car that smashed into my heart. When I arrived home from work early to surprise her with a box of chocolates and fragrant red flowers, to celebrate her eighth month of pregnancy, I never expected the love that was meant for me was lustfully being loaned to a complete stranger. Apparently, someone she met on line in a forum, someone hungry for her gravid affection.

Both perceivably enjoyed the experience, they did not hear me arrive over the penetrating screams of ecstasy. My heart died in an instant, so did the fully erect Spanish man as his last thrust provided a rush of nirvana to both that played the game. I can still remember the warm gush of blood that spilled from his neck, mixing with the seminal fluids splashed upon my wife's sweaty chest.

Her screams of ecstasy turned to horror as her Japanese eyes opened wide, soaking in the view of my rage above her. Her horror became anger as she cursed me for my deed. Obscenities mumbled from her, most of which I was deaf to until they climaxed with admission that the child in her womb was not mine. I lost control, grabbing her by the throat, and tossing her to the floor. Blood spilled from her head as the nightstand's corner ripped through her skull. Convulsing upon the floor, next to her adulterous lover, their blood mixed within an eternal caress.

As her life faded, deadly contractions forced an unexpected birth; before me, on the floor, lay an innocent human being born of lustful demons. Picking up the knife, I cut the rubbery umbilical cord and lay the innocent child upon the tainted bed. My attention turns to the bodies on the floor as I drag the man towards the cellar. His body is heavy and still warm, but I manage to manhandle him down the dusty stairs and prop his corpse in a dark corner. I repeat the process with my wife, spilling no tears as her last breathe exhales. Almost immediately I feared their afterlife embrace, their eyes looked through me, knowing all of my dirty secrets, I feared their escape. Like a child, I ran up the stairs and to the garage where I found some old chain and sliding locks, which I quickly affixed to the cellar door, locking the evil within.

I tried to care for the baby, I really did. Love was lost within his chaotic creation, so I ignore him. His life was short. Grabbing him by his tiny leg, I unlatched the cellar door and tossed him within. The limp body bounced upon the withering steps, until he came to rest on the concrete floor below, where pillows of dust cradled him. Although he was dead, his cries seemed louder than ever before, mixed with the damning obscenities from the lustful corpses below. To silence the noise, I retreated to the living room where I downed two pints of Dragon's Milk Stout, and half a bottle of whiskey. Never had I slept so peacefully.

When I awoke this morning, the screams were back. They didn't come from behind the cellar door, not any longer; the skeletons below had found their way into my head, their bony fingers scraping the insides of my skull as they reminded me of my wrongdoing, ignoring their own. For the past five hours, their incessant poking inside my brain has released me from the stigma of the horrible deed. I am no longer afraid of their hidden agendas. Not as I sit here, with a bottle of Jack in hand, tequila and vodka at my feet. The spirits in the bottles chase away the demons in my head, as their screams retreat to their prison behind the tenable cellar door.

Although muffled within, their screams endeavor to penetrate my thoughts. I feel the need to end this farce now, ignoring sanity and madness, opting for relief. I pour the vodka upon the floor, and throw a shot of jack upon the door, to cleanse the infectious evil. I down two more shots of Jack, and a mixer of Jack and Cuervo, to numb the pain that I will surely endure. My shaky hands struggle to strike the match that will cleanse my soul with hellfire. After six broken matches, I finally succeed and stare at the flame before my eyes. I let it burn to my fingers, ensuring I feel no pain, and drop it to the floor. The liquor ignites with a passion for destruction, as it works its magic to free me. Paint bubbles on the door; the flames dance on the floor, the beauty is mesmerizing.

I welcome the warmth as the flames caress my flesh and burn away my clothing. My eyelids melt, allowing me to see my skin melt away revealing the skeleton within my body. The voices below, behind the cellar door, fade from within, leaving quietness for the peaceful sleep beneath the blanket of fire that consumes me.

We all have skeletons, not all are in our closets, I keep mine locked behind the cellar door, burnt and charred, as I retreat within my personal purgative pyre.

Short Stories

Niall Parkinson

Dale Hollin
The Last Eulogy

"I want another kiss," he said.

He began to feel warm as her face moved slowly forward. The last touch of her lips upon his seemed an eternity ago. A cool, plush softness brushed his mouth like an autumn breeze and he craved the pale contours of her throat.

"Michael, I'm not leaving you. I never really have."

The long, dark hair seemed to lift and cascade across her shoulders in the still room. He reached to grasp it with his fist, but couldn't quite take hold of her. It felt to him as finely spun black glass dissipating into vapor. Her eyes moved to the open window across the room. The first

2.

tendrils of dawn wisped dark shades of violet in intervals along the Eastern horizon. Her face became slack and withdrawn.

"I have to go for now. The other will be near soon. He mustn't know I've come here."

Michael inhaled deeply as she moved slowly from atop him, her eyes never deviating from the window. He wondered vaguely about this "other". She had spoken of him before, but he had rarely asked her for any details about his meaning or status to her. He only knew that she still came to him in the nights, and that was all that mattered for now; that she came to him at all.

"I will wait for you again," he said.

She looked at him, her face still slack, but somehow paler than before.

"I will be here tonight, when he releases me."

He watched as she drifted sullenly to the window. She placed her head and upper body outside of its frame and fell forward into the early dawn. *She's gone again.* He never questioned why she wouldn't use the door. It had been months since she had walked through the rest of the home. She seemed content to remain confined to his bedroom at night. The clock on the wall above the mantle read 5:09. She always left at exactly this time. It seemed ritual to him, for some reason; as if the numbers themselves were a painted portrait, speaking volumes in a language not conveyed through simple words.

He rolled over and pulled the pillow over his head to close completely the dim light of the rising dawn. He thought how blissful the walls of sleep would be in this hour, but knew these walls were illusions. If ever he did sleep now, it was an experience he carried no memory of. Not

3.

since...the parting. Not since "the other" swept his love away like so much magic dust under an old and frayed rug.

He smiled lightly beneath the enclosure of the pillow. It was as if his face were wrapped in a soft tomb. He blinked his eyes and stared into the darkness. *Danielle.* Her once smiling face, from a time past, materialized within this created tomb. *She was once happy here.*

"Time to crawl out of here," he whispered to himself.

He threw the cushion to the floor beside his bed and sat up. His mind felt awash in vertigo and he covered his face with his hands, peeking through his fingers until the room leveled. He uncovered one eye and glanced at the half empty bottle of Chianti still set on the bedside table. *Ahhhh...breakfast is served.* He poured the draught into the stained glass set beside the bottle. The wine looked to him like liquefied garnets, swirling a toxic sheen through the fine crystal stem. He lifted it to his mouth as if holding and inhaling a delicate red rose. *Danielle.* He drained the glass and stood.

He heard a door open and shut somewhere in the house. There always seemed to be a door opening somewhere when he was alone. What did it matter? He used to wander the rooms and corridors, searching for strangers or possibly her. No sign of a soul could he find. Just doors and the myriad of photos hanging on the walls. He grabbed the stem and chianti and walked to his desk in the front room.

He sat in his chair and glanced over at the TV in the corner of the room. It was cold and dark. It hadn't been turned on since the parting. He had a gun and often thought of shooting it

4.

just to hear the glass break. It would seem such a more decorative piece, he thought, without the constant and dusty reflections held in that glass. He could gut the box after he shot it and place something pleasant to look at within. Like a picture of her. Perhaps the one of her dancing to the beautiful and droning sound of the cicadas when they once camped by the river. He had always loved to watch her dance. Within the gutted box, she could dance eternally for him.

The wine flowed again and he smiled at the thought of it. He turned his attention from the TV and stared at his monitor centered atop his desk, gently running his fingers across the keyboard. He had grown tired of writing these eulogies for people and families he had never known. It was what he seemed to do best, though. Prominent mortuaries across the tri-state area paid him well for this service. Since the parting, he had taken to infusing certain blasphemies into the sermons for his own personal amusement. His last eulogy was written for a locally famous Jewish woman who had died of emphysema. He had purposely inserted a line which was a direct quote from Mein Kampf towards the end of it. Hitler's words intertwined and fit beautifully within the rest of the memorial. No one seemed to notice. No one cared.

His newest corpse to memorialize was a partner with a major law firm in the city. He died of heart failure. So many attorneys did die of heart problems, it seemed. Probably because they had so little heart to sustain anyway. He scanned through his personal life details quickly. Father of four. Divorced twice. Involved in various civic and community organizations. Fairly generous in his monetary charitable donations. All useful to him in regards to the eulogy, but meaningless otherwise. He stared for a moment at the man's photos. One an obvious high school senior

5.

photo, one a wedding photo with his second bride, the last one a more recent photo taken recently before his death. All of them shared in common the same set and plastic grin most people wear as a kind of mask when posing for pictures. He wondered how the people at his service would react if the mortician would sew his lips in place to mimic this same grin in the casket and almost laughed at the thought of it.

He pushed the photos aside. He couldn't think of this man now. Him or his petty life accomplishments. He could only think of this "other". This man who had stolen his wife, as if she were some golden trinket he could possess when the sun had risen. Could she only come to him while he slept? There had to be a reason she only saw him on such a precise schedule. He would find out. He would find this man and release her from his bondage. He knew he would have to kill him. He raised his head and glared at the ceiling. *Danielle. I will save you from him.*

The screen of his monitor drew him forward. A eulogy. Yes. He would prepare for the death of this other by writing his eulogy even before his demise. The man should be grateful. Generally only the very wealthy and elite were privileged enough to have him write their final memorial. A problem was he really knew nothing of the man's life. Knew nothing of his accomplishments, besides of course, having the exceptional talent of taking what was his. Yes. A thief. A very skilled thief he was, and he would receive a thief's memorial.

He opened a new file and stared at the screen. He had to pay this other homage, no matter how much he hated him. He had accomplished what no other could. He had purloined his beloved's heart. The man was probably a fairly handsome chap. His wife was an extraordinarily beautiful woman and would surely not accept an other not fair in appearance and charming in the

6.

extreme. He closed his eyes and tried to visualize him. He couldn't do it. He decided to place a mask on the other much resembling his own features, but with lighter hair. Maybe a better physical build. Better dressed. He opened his eyes and began to type.

Today, we gather as friends, acquaintances, and loved ones of the other. Not in mourning. For no man's life should be truly mourned; but in celebration of having held the privilege of knowing and experiencing his intervening presence. He came to us not through an extended invitation, but from his own bold and perceptive heart having heeded a call from each one of us. Each one of us who has held the longing and necessity within our own hearts to lose everything so that we may find strength within ourselves.

We may compare this man to the Sainted Patrick of Ireland who had the divine grace to lead the serpents from the plush and green land of his people, so they would know the serpents amongst them no longer. For these serpents were within their hearts then and ours now; and today, we celebrate this other who has freed us from them, so they may strike at our heels and poison our souls no more.

Although I have only known this other for a short length of time, his grace and wisdom have gathered the snakes which had coiled around my feet and soul and led them into the far away Netherworld where such creatures dwell. With my serpents followed my transgressions, and with my transgressions followed.....

7.

Michael glanced above the monitor as the slim figure of a shadow passed across the wall. He turned quickly around in his chair. No one. Always no one. He slowly turned to the dark screen of the television. Danielle's reflection stood still and staring back at him. Her image sometimes materialized in the black glass, but she was never there. She was with him. Always with him until the sun closed its dimmed scarlet eye and the night fell upon his bedroom window like an old and tired companion. He closed his eyes and wished her reflection gone. He hated the television. Hated the dark glass which tormented him when he looked within it. He opened his eyes and she was gone. All that stood there now was his own image staring back.

He opened the drawer of his desk and pulled the blued 380 caliber revolver from it. He pointed it at the screen and fired. The sound was deafening. It angered him that he wasn't able to have the pleasure of hearing the glass shatter. He ran over to the television and began kicking the rest of the glass in with his bare foot. Again and again his foot went through the screen until his own blood began staining the carpet and plastic frame of the set.

"Michael!!! What are you doing!!!"

He felt hands and arms pulling him to the ground. He sat there stunned for a moment and looked up to where the scream had come from. It was her. *Danielle.* He glanced over to the window, scratching down the side of his face. He glared at her.

"What are you doing here, Danielle. You don't come till night. You're not supposed to be here till night. You're supposed to be with him. Your "other". Where is he? Is he here? Maybe I have a little something special for him, too. Maybe I'll shatter him the same way. WHERE IS HE????"

8.

She covered her eyes and began sobbing.

"Michael, there is no other man. I have always been here Michael, but you don't see me. I bring your food and your wine, but you don't see me. Sometimes I stand behind you while you write these god-forsaken eulogies, but you don't see me. There is no other man, except you. You are the other, Michael...AND YOU DON'T SEE ME!!!!!!!"

He scratched into the side of his face deeper and stood up, moving towards her.

"Bullshit, bitch. Every morning at 5:09 AM you leave out my window. Every morning. You leave me here alone to be with your other. You said so. You said you return when he releases you. Your words. He releases you at night. Your words. Now where is the bastard?"

She wiped the tears from her face and looked at him sullenly.

"No, Michael. 5:09 is when you leave me. I am in this house all day long and you don't see me because YOU ARE THE OTHER!!!"

He snorted laughter and shook his head. He wanted to kiss her, but he knew better. She was his now. This other's. He pictured the soul of a woman and saw an image of a desert filled with beautiful reptiles, writhing and mating in a wasteland of refined white sugar and jewels.

"Leave, Danielle. Go to your other. Go see him. When night falls, you come to my window. You are my beloved. Always. Just go."

She turned and fled, weeping. He went to the television and carefully cleared the remainder of the glass from its gutted frame. He looked above the set to where their wedding

9.

picture was hung on the wall. He stood and removed it, placing it carefully within the empty space he had created within it. He smiled at the photo in the television. The faces in the photo smiled back at him.

He sat back in his chair and stared at the eulogy. He had to finish it. He would finish it for her. She loved this other as she loved him. He knew this now.

....my beloved. I will heed the wisdom of the other. For he has shown me the way. He has shown me that it is my duty. My honor. My love to release her from his bondage. *Danielle.* **And release her I now must do.**

He slowly picked up the gun and placed it to his temple. He smiled.

"My beloved Danielle. Your other is no more."

Mike Jansen
The Angel's kiss

Your face is hardly visible behind the respirator, only your golden hair reminds me that it's you sitting on your high throne, pillows supporting your frail limbs, soft gurgling coming from the machines at your side that keep you alive. Your eyes are vivid though, blue gray, the dark ice that first attracted me to you all these years ago, when you gave me your stern look, the one with the promise.

This is a ritual we perform, once in a while. A matter of time really, before you either die, or get cured, although a cure seems years away, years you normally would not have. I cannot live without you. I decided more than a year ago, no matter the cost.

You never asked me about the medicine I provide and I never volunteered. That's my own cross to bear. I am not a killer, but I will go to any length to protect the one I love.

Right now, in these halls of the sick and dying with the Gods in their white jackets dispensing medicine and protocol, I expect an Angel of Mercy to walk past the thrones of all the Kings and Queens. Perhaps it is my hope, a decision taken without me, for I am just as much at the mercy of my own desire to see you alive a little longer.

I could not believe that you, we, would one day end. A strong belief is a gift, it is conviction, a power of will that drives a man to extremes to attain goals that some would call improbable, if not impossible. And with a little help of the Ancients my will has so far overcome the obstacles of your disease, although it gets harder every time to obtain the essence needed to make you live a little longer.

Looking into your eyes I see the need for release, and end to it all, but I shake my head. It's not your time yet, no, not yet, I won't let you go. A God enters and looks at some papers. He shakes his head and leaves, not feeling the daggers my eyes plant in his back, not noticing my hand that is in my right jacket pocket, holding onto the scalpel that I swiped from one of the trays outside the Sterile Kingdom.

I hold onto your hand for a while and cry while making up my mind and hardening my resolve. I mumble something about a bathroom and promise to return, soon. Your eyes follow me as I leave the room. There are tears. I know there are. I feel them in my eyes, too. Yours' are for your situation and your loneliness. Mine are for the life I'm about to end.

The halls of the kingdom have many doors, some open, most closed, some with red lights, some green. Some lights are off; an absence not only of light, but of the soul that once occupied the few square yards of the throne inside. When I round a corner I see one of the Gods leave a room, gloves still on, carrying a tray with a syringe and a little jar with a rubber cap that I know contains a heavy sedative. I know this is my sign, my omen and I'm not one to ignore the hand that fate deals me.

Looking around I slide into the room, keeping my right hand clutched around the handle of the scalpel in my pocket. I feel my hand trembling and a cold shiver runs down my spine. Always I feel reluctance, an almost tangible resistance against what I'm about to do, the tithe I'm about to deliver to Gods other than the ones roving these halls. We can all be Angels of Mercy if the moment is upon us and with great clarity I realize such a time has just arrived.

Soft snoring reaches my ears. It's not a healthy expression of life. Rather, it's the struggle of a sick body to retrieve oxygen, to keep its heart pumping, to keep its organs from failing. And for what? All to maintain a disease the body doesn't even know is there. We are such pitiful creatures, bound to our earthly forms without regard for the world around us, not understanding that we are all part of a remorseless cycle that will grind us all to dust given enough time. Because time we don't have, something people residing in these halls know all too well, despite the reassuring susurrations of their white robed Gods.

The low light of the room focuses on the throne. Yellow skin, limp hair nearly all gone, the man is frail, his skeletal form only partially covered by a thin white sheet. I slide up to his side; observe the slow, labored rhythm of his breathing, the thin line of his life clearly visible, floating above him.

The aspect of the Angel of Mercy is upon me, obviously. Every time I have seen the line, was when someone needed to die, so that my love could live a little while longer. My prayers follow the patterns of the yellow man's breathing, synchronizing, making me one with the room, the situation, the need to create the perfect moment for his departure and the collection of the remainder of his energies.

I cut the stopper that kept the sedatives from flooding his body and observe the clear liquid enter his body. At first his breathing seems to stop and I hope, I pray this one will go quietly. But then his eyes fly open. They are blood shot on yellow and I see the fear inside, the knowledge that Death is upon him and that his time is up. He tries to open his mouth and I see his blotchy tongue, all swollen, a slimy worm that writhes and attempts to escape, which, of course, I cannot allow.

Using a piece of cloth I grab his tongue, pull, and then slice it clean off using the scalpel. I quickly wrap the tongue in the cloth, then push the man's mouth closed and lean on his jaw until the sedative rushing through his veins gets a good grip on him. His eyes roll back and he loses consciousness. Blood gushes from his nostrils and he drowns in his own blood, leaving me with a trophy, the vessel the Ancients require to carry living essence back to a loved one.

Careful to leave no trails, I leave the room. The light above the door has turned red, a sign that Gods will converge on the hapless soul within, to snatch him back from the doorstep of oblivion. The light in the bathroom is ice cold and the mirror shows my face, ashen, with lines I never noticed before. *A line for a line* shoots through my mind, although I know it is nonsense to think like that. I look down at the bloody cloth in my hand and drop it in the sink before turning on the water to wash away the blood. The piece of tongue is a light pink color after all the fluids have dripped out.

The flesh is soft, salty, with a bitter aftertaste, reminiscent of the scents that float around the halls of this kingdom. Warmth suffuses my body, a rapturous elation floods my brain, making me at least the equal of the white robed Gods, wielding power they never could, bestowed by the aspect of the Angel of Mercy. With near narcissistic delight I dispose of the piece of cloth, wash my hands and face and check for spatters on my clothes. I'm good to go, ready for my love.

Past Gods and demi Gods that rush through the halls I make my way back to her throne. She rests, fitfully, her golden hair spread around her like some ancient crown. I sit beside her and hold her hand, feeling a deep satisfaction, knowing that once again I can prolong her existence, keep her with me. Whatever it takes, however long it takes, I will do what the Ancients required. As I bend over her hand to give her the kiss of life, she pulls back.

Surprised I look up, straight into my love's dark ice eyes. There's no love there now, no anger, no determination, no guilt, no fear. I recognize resignation and somehow it fills me with despair. She pulls the respirator aside; her hollow cheeks are yellow, like her hands, her arms. She whispers: "No more. Enough."

I hold the metal bars on the side of her throne and squeeze. "I have been an Angel of Mercy, my love, for you. Please, do not deny me. You are all that stands between me and murderous insanity."

She smiles at me. "It's ok. I forgive you." Her hand comes to rest on my hand and I lay my head on it, feeling the cool touch of her fingers.

"You were always the strong one," I murmur into her flesh.

"Be my Angel of Mercy," she whispers.

I look up at her. "I cannot do that. Do not ask this of me."

"This is your cross to bear, my love." Her breathing is labored and she replaces the respirator to regain some strength. After a minute she looks at me with tears in her eyes and whispers through the mask: "Release me."

Slow, the realization occurs to me that this moment in time is her final act of defiance, the final spark of strength that drives her to choose the time and manner of her passing. For me it is a moment of satori when the thought of using the power I have acquired through the taking of a life can also be used to take another life, even if that life is so very dear to you. To Hell with the careful balance the Ancients sought in the giving and taking of life.

The aspect of the Angel of Mercy descends upon me and I feed it, not only with the fires of the rage within me, but also with the sparks of life I so carefully hoarded over the past months, until its black wings stretch to infinity and darkness descends upon the room. There's a price to pay, there always is, but I gladly comply to spend moments that seem eternities with my one true love, feeling our energies mix, our souls intertwine, until a red light comes to life.

Neil Baker
A Late Summer Afternoon on Cranberry Farm

If there is one good thing to say about inter-dimensional portals, it is that they are punctual.

The portal that liked to materialize beneath the oaken boards of Cranberry Farm was indeed punctual, turning up every Tuesday in the same place at precisely 4:53 pm for exactly one minute and forty-two seconds. However, that was the extent of its positive attributes.

Margo Nakogee appreciated punctuality. She appreciated her quiz shows coming on at the same time every day. She appreciated the roar of the FedEx truck as it thundered past the farmhouse at 10:34 am sharp every other day, reminding her that there was a world outside her cross-beamed confinement. She relied on the regularity of her self-medication, her time for pill popping announced by the hourly *ping* of an apple-shaped egg timer. However, she did not appreciate the regularity of the five violent knocks on the front door at two minutes past midnight, every night, when Roger would return from another miserable day in the office, followed by an equally miserable session in *The Wolf Paw* where he would bemoan the lingering state of his useless wife while fuelling his hatred with whisky. No matter how frail she was feeling at night, despite how much her legs ached or her throat burned with the bitter memory of a day of vomiting, Margo had to be there to let him in. Five thumps on the door, each one louder than the last. She would struggle to raise herself up and depress the latch, rolling out of the way as her husband barreled in, tossing his door keys onto the side table, kicking off his loafers and then stamping into the kitchen for one last shot before dragging himself upstairs to sleep alone, as he had done since his wife's cancer had left her unable to walk three years ago.

Of his hatred for her Margo was in little doubt, but the extent of his hate came as something of a surprise one day when she discovered that he had been tampering with her medication, reducing the number of pills in one bottle, swapping out others for generic vitamins. This had coincided with Roger canceling their landline, rendering her phone and laptop useless, and the

---

location of Cranberry Farm, thirty kilometers east of Thunder Bay and at least ten from the next homestead, left Margo trapped. A prisoner in an open field. For these reasons, it had been somewhat of a mixed blessing when the monster first revealed itself to her.

Margo had very quickly deciphered the pattern to the scraping noises that interrupted her TV watching at the same time every Tuesday and after a few months she had decided to break from routine, forsaking her favorite shows. The sounds always came from beneath a hideous bearskin rug sprawled across a square trapdoor, which led to the cellar. She had previously descended the wooden steps just once, before the illness had robbed her of the ability to do so, and knew that the space beneath the floorboards was vast, full of unopened packing boxes and machine parts. Now it would appear that it was full of vermin. Curiously punctual vermin. Armed with a fearsome broom, Margo waited, watching the clock above the mantle, counting down the seconds until seven minutes to five. Immediately, the scraping began. She had already slid back the bolt in anticipation and, with considerable effort, Margo hooked the end of the broom through the circular iron handle and heaved the door open, ready to crown any rats that dared showed their pointy faces. Nothing emerged and she wheeled forward until she could peer into the hole in the floor. This was not the cellar she remembered. Gone were the wooden steps leading down to cold cement and colder memories. Instead smooth, stone steps, black as pitch, spiraled down into a hazy fug that wafted up, assaulting her senses with a cloying stench that reminded her of decayed squash. She had no time to process this sight before a shape emerged from the gloom, scaling the steps with the serpentine sway of a lizard as it crawled out into the yellow glow of the living room. Margo wheeled back in terror, upending her chair and spilling to the floor as she hit the couch behind her. The creature was pewter-gray and hairless, its translucent skin pulled taut across a sinewy mass of muscle and bone. It had six limbs, each one ending in a trio of stubby digits, which in turn tapered into crystalline points, and its head hung low between the forward shoulders. It possessed no face to speak of, just a gaping maw filled with blanched needles and a collection of pinched scars to suggest eyes, ears and nose. It heaved its bulk across the floor until its front limbs were upon her and then leaned in, flopping out a thick, purple tongue with which it tasted her, starting with her head and working its way beneath her gown, across her chest, between her legs, down to her knees. Margo wanted to cry out, to move away, but the warmth of the fleshy appendage as it probed her inside and out, the sickly sweet smell of its breath, erased all thoughts of self-preservation. On the contrary, her initial revulsion had been smothered by an overwhelming bliss and she decided to give herself entirely to the beast, no matter how it might end. Suddenly the creature paused with its tongue wrapped around her left calf. It licked her right leg, then reared up with a disgusted snort. Threads of saliva looped from the upper rows of teeth in the giant mouth as the creature squatted low, turned and scuttled back into the hole in the floor. She dragged herself over to the cellar opening but, by the time she reached the edge, the stone steps and smog were gone. In their place were wooden planks and the faint smell of damp. Margo rolled onto her back and started to sob, confused by the feeling of rejection that overwhelmed her. Then she coughed, the spasms turning to laughter as she righted her wheelchair and heaved herself into it, knowing full well that it was the tumors in her legs, the poison in her bones, that had prevented her from being eaten. Bad meat.

For several months Margo tried to cajole the creature from its temporary domain, using each brief slice of the realm's existence to entice it with various meats and liquids, once even her own, naked flesh, but the monster showed scant interest in anything she dangled before it. Then, one fresh April day, a small field mouse happened to dart across the room just as Margo was opening the trapdoor for her stubborn guest. The speed with which the monster scuttled from its hole, scooping the tiny animal with its wonderful tongue and crunching up the rodent like a cheese puff, had taken her by surprise, but also showed her how to keep it happy. There was no shortage of small mammals and birds around the farm and from that moment the television remained switched off as she dedicated her days to laying trails of food around the house, luring all manner of creatures into crude box traps, which she would then present to her abominable guest every Tuesday afternoon. Once she even managed to snag a feral cat and the monster had certainly enjoyed that meal, stripping the fur and meat from the cat's bones even as it scratched futilely at the eyeless face. It was a friendship of sorts, a twisted, nightmarish companionship, and for the first time in years, Margo was happy. The arrangement also seemed to benefit the creature. A ruddiness began to stain its skin, imbuing the beast with a healthy pallor, and Margo noticed downy patches of fur spreading out from its shoulder blades, spreading down its limbs like moss on sodden roots. True, it was a one-sided affair; Margo gave and the beast received with little indication of thanks or reciprocation, but still she found herself willing away the six days between each encounter, preparing ever more elaborate buffets for her new companion. She even began to confide in it, spilling out her fears and sorrows as the creature chewed down on voles, rabbits and chickadees.

Sadly, the cellar creature was not the only monster in her life and Margo had become acutely aware of her health deteriorating faster than her mood was improving. Roger spent more time out of the house, perhaps reluctant to witness the slow murder of his wife as he tampered further with her medication, his only connection with her being his regular Saturday morning drop-off of microwave meals and laundry. He ate and socialized in town and, judging by the cheap stench on his pants, was actively seeking her replacement. He had begun to notice a change in his captive wife, a change that irritated him to no end, and when he found some yard detritus scattered around his beloved bearskin his percolating rage erupted. He had accused her of trying to leave without permission, threatened to remove the wheels from her chair, and finally settled for nailing ten-inch beams across the base of the front and back doors in an aggressively petty display. Despite the tenaciousness of the smaller mammals, this barrier limited the food supply that could be lured into the house and Margo's monster was far from pleased. When the creature refused to show one hazy September afternoon, regardless of the squeaking bundle hanging above its lair, Margo was distraught. It was then that the dark thoughts that she had been suppressing for the past year ascended in place of her demonic companion.

The hardest part of Margo's plan was ensuring that Roger did not go into work on a Tuesday, and then had a reason to open the cellar door at 4:53 in the afternoon. Thankfully, the afternoons spent watching *Columbo* re-runs had not been a complete waste of time, and she was slightly taken aback by her own deviousness. Step one involved spiking Roger's whisky collection with syrup of ipecac taken from her own collection of medications. Small doses at first on the weekend preceding Roger's final days, enough to make him feel queasy. Then a stronger dose on Monday, ensuring that his pre-bed whisky shot resulted in a night of stomach cramps and vomiting. It had worked perfectly, and the following morning Margo had felt her own stomach tighten when she heard him call in sick on his cell phone.

The second part of the plan had begun a month earlier. Prior to tossing his slacks into the washing machine, Margo had carefully picked at the seam of his left inner leg with a needle, causing an imperceptible tear. For the following three weekends she continued to sabotage his pants, subtly making the rip longer and longer, until her husband finally noticed. Margo had to feign extreme weakness for the next few days, finding excuses not to repair them until the morning when Roger called the office through gritted teeth and went back to bed to sleep off the pain in his ribcage.

Now it had all come to this moment. Margo had felt truly nauseated for the remainder of the day as she wrestled with the nature of her scheme and now, as the hour drew near, she contemplated aborting the plan. Fittingly, it was Roger who orchestrated his own demise. With mere minutes before the portal would materialize, her husband thundered down the stairs, obviously feeling much better and craving a night in *The Wolf Paw*. He cut a pathetic figure in his shirt and socks, but the violence in his voice was anything but feeble.
    "Where are my fucking pants?"
    Margo obviously didn't respond fast enough, and he gripped the sides of her wheelchair, shaking it violently as he sprayed her with spittle. "I want to be gone before six, you useless cow! Get them fixed!"
    "I, I need my kit," she responded quietly, "my needles..."
    "What?" he yelled as he strode into the kitchen, returning with a bottle, which he hastily reconsidered, slamming it down on the side table, "What did you say?" Margo glanced at the clock. 4:52. "I need my sewing kit, it's in the cellar."
    "Oh, for fuck's sake," Roger Nakogee picked up his pants that had been draped over the back of the couch and flung them into his wife's lap as he strode over to the ugly bearskin rug. "I should roll you down this fucking hole, be done with you once and for all." He lifted the rug, rolling up the skin and depositing it on the couch.
    Margo looked again at the clock; there were still twenty seconds before the other realm would be in place. As her husband bent to grab the iron ring, Margo blurted out in desperation.
    "Wait!"

Roger paused and looked at her through narrow eyes, "What now?"

It was 4:53. Margo lowered her eyes and shook her head, "Nothing, sorry."

"Fucking useless." Roger yanked upward on the handle and slammed the door over, peering into the darkness below. His brow furrowed when he saw the obsidian steps fading into the mist, but if he had a final exclamation to make then it would remain unheard for the creature was upon him before he could take another breath. Roger screamed and staggered back as the monster wrapped its wiry limbs around him, curved talons digging into his flesh as it brought its monstrous head forward and opened its jaw impossibly wide. The two of them crashed to the floor as Roger freed one arm and tried to force it between his face and the cavernous mouth, but to no avail. The monster clamped down, its thin fangs sinking into Roger's face, and yanked back ripping away a perfect circle of skin from his hairline to his lower lip as effectively as a cookie cutter in soft dough.

Margo watched her husband's face slide down the monster's gullet and shuddered, unsure if it was abject horror or unadulterated joy that was causing her tremors. Then the creature began to devour the rest of Roger, tearing through his sternum into the soft goods hidden beneath; its writhing tongue sucking noisily at the fluids escaping from him, barely missing a drop. With his midsection torn out Roger folded back on himself, his tattered eyes meeting Margo's, as the monster squeezed down on him until the back of his head nestled in the crook of his knees. Then it scuttled backward, dragging its meal quickly into the hole as a golden glow throbbed once from below, and then the cellar was dark again. Margo wheeled over and looked down at the wooden steps. She closed the door and spread the bearskin over the remaining flecks of gore that peppered the edges of the cellar entrance. In the kitchen, her timer pinged. It was time for her pills.

The creature did not return the following Tuesday, nor the week after that. Her microwave meals had dwindled to the point where she was eating just one a day and her medication was almost exhausted, not that it was doing her any good. She felt weaker than ever and resigned to the fact that she needed to leave. Somehow she would have to mount the barriers, wheel herself down the gravel drive to the freeway and flag down a FedEx truck. At least she knew it would be on time. It was now the third Tuesday after Roger's death. His cell phone had stopped ringing after two weeks and only one visitor had banged on the front door, a large young woman, bursting at the seams, who had waited for barely a minute before stamping back to the main road, watched all the time by Margo from behind the net curtains. The front room had become a mess of crumbs and rotten fruit and Margo had a decent collection of mice, squirrels and birds crammed into a clear tote, ready to be served should her monster arrive. She had decided to wait one last time. If it didn't show this afternoon, then she would leave Cranberry Farm at 10:34 tomorrow morning.

As the afternoon drew to a close, she finished the last of her hideous frozen meals and turned off the television that had been keeping her company all day. Then she sat, watching the clock, listening to the tortured squeaks and chirps coming from the plastic box next to the cellar door. The second hand on the clock teased her, seeming to slow down as she watched it, until finally the minute hand clicked forward to rest between the ten and eleven. 4:53. Immediately Margo heard a faint noise, the soft clicking of claws on stone steps, and her heart began to beat faster as a heady anticipation washed over her. She placed her hands on her wheels ready to roll forward, to feed her monster and plead for a last embrace, but froze when the new sounds came.

Five thumps on the door, each one louder than the last.

Michael Thomas Knight
The Gates of Lament

Sheriff Dalton was the first on the scene at the Elwood house. Walter Elwood was clearly nervous, stumbling over his words and occasionally mumbling to himself between answering questions. The Sheriff felt bad for coming down on the old man this way, but he had to get to the bottom of this and quick. There hadn't been a serious crime in Clear Brooke Township in over 30 years. Early this afternoon a hit and run splattered that young Kitner boy all over East Main Street. The townspeople were looking to Sheriff Dalton for answers and the answers seemed to point to old man Elwood.

They were standing in the side yard of Walter's house near the slanted cellar doors that led to the old man's basement. Walter stood between the Sheriff and the doors, clearly in a protective stance against entry to his basement. Walter's neighbor, Ginger-Lynn appeared in the yard, along with several other neighbors from the block. Despite being tipped off by a call from the middle-aged housewife, he did not like that her and the others were gathering at Elwood's place.

"Yawl' can run along now," Dalton said with a dismissive wave of his hand. "There's nothing for yawl' to see here."

"We ain't goin' nowhere, Sheriff. I called you 'bout this; if I didn't you'd still be playing' tiddly-winks at the station with your two deputies. We're citizens of this town and deserve to know what's going on."

It amazed Sheriff Dalton that he had once been attracted to Ginger but now couldn't even stand to hear her voice. She would blab away about herself and launch her opinions like mud-pies about everything under the sun. She never realized that no one cared what she was doing next week or how she *told off* Meg at the dinner, and how she got the best deal on her car, house, groceries, and vacation stay. Everything with Ginger was I, I, I... and it was quite irritating.

Deputy Corey Blackwell finally arrived and Sheriff Dalton sighed in relief.

"Corey, keep these people back so I can question Mr. Elwood in peace."

Dalton turned his attention to Walter. Before he could resume his questioning he heard Ginger barking at his Deputy.

"Get your hands off of me, Corey Blackwell," she griped,

intentionally loud so everyone would notice.

Dalton rolled his eyes but didn't turn to look. Walter looked over the Sheriff's shoulder then turned to look at him.

"She doesn't like me all that much. One time her children were running through my garden and when I complained, she gave me the finger and told me I should move if I don't like it."

"Don't take it personal Walt; she's like that to everyone."

"I've lived in this town since I was a child; sixty years now."

"Yeah, Walt, can we get back to why I'm here."

"Oh yes, pardon me Sheriff, the mind tends to wander at my age."

"So today little Timothy Kitner was killed by a hit and run. Witnesses said it was a 1968 Ford, pick-up, red."

Sheriff Dalton looked over to the red pick-up truck parked on Walter's property. Walter wrought his hands over one another. He offered no explanation. Dalton tucked his thumbs in his belt and let his hands hang loosely, confident that he had Mr. Elwood on the ropes.

"A witness overheard you telling Meg Powers that you had fixed the mishap and put the perpetrator in his place... your cellar."

"That witness was Ginger, no doubt." Walter lowered his voice to a whisper. "I believe I have explained the tension between me and my neighbor."

"Yes you did. If she is telling a fib then you would have no objection to me and my deputy checking your basement. "

Sheriff smiled at Walter. Walter smiled back.

"And what do you think you'll find down there, Sheriff?

"I know your nephew has had trouble with the law. Had a couple DWI's to boot," Sheriff Dalton replied.

"So, you think I'm hiding my nephew, James, in the cellar?" Walter laughed.

"Well, if I am wrong, I will certainly apologize but, it is my due diligence to ask you to let us search your cellar," the Sheriff said.

"I hardly think that will be necessary, Sheriff. Unless you have a warrant, you best be on your way. Go help get some kitten down out of a tree, or whatever it is you do around this town every day."

Smiles disappeared from the faces of both men.

"I am investigating a homicide Mr. Elwood, I can go where ever I damn please."

"You will not be investigating on my property without a warrant. Your invitation to my property is rescinded, you are now trespassing. Shall I call the State police?"

"Now, now, there's no need for that..."

"You take it to the sidewalk, Sheriff Dalton, or I'll sue your little police force for so much, you'll be lucky if you can get a job crossing children at the street corner."

Sheriff Dalton was taken back by the sharpness in Walter Elwood's eyes and the grit of his teeth. He backed down. He had no choice. He had been in some trouble with internal affairs a few years back in regards to overstepping his boundaries as an officer. There was a letter in his file that would stay sealed, as long as there were no more complaints against him. How the quiet Walter Elwood knew about this seemed impossible. The Sheriff tipped his hat to Walter and walked to the sidewalk where a considerable crowd had gathered. A rumble of voices rose as the townsfolk attacked the Sheriff with questions.

A black Mercedes pulled up to the curb. Mayor Jenkins stepped out, his rotund belly preceding him. He smoothed out his suit shirt, pulled his jacket closed and ran his hand over his receding hairline, pushing his graying locks away from his pudgy face. His assistant, Steve Harbs, stepped from the passenger side and joined him on the sidewalk. The townsfolk gave them a wide berth as he made his way to the Sheriff.

"Sheriff Dalton, Deputy Blackwood." Mayor Jenkins nodded to each in succession.

"What seems to be the problem?" he asked.

"Old Walt won't let us investigate on his property without a warrant. Ain't that right Walt," Sheriff Dalton yelled, nodding his head in Walter's direction.

Walter waved.

"I think I can remedy that," the Mayor said.

He turned to his assistant.

"Steve, isn't there some jurisdiction that my position has over such circumstances?"

"Yes. I believe that in urgent circumstances, your officiating position can constitute you in a judgeship role, and allow you to create and sign such a document," Steve replied.

"Would you consider tampering or destruction of evidence an urgent circumstance?"

"Yes, sir, I would."

"Well, get some paper and write it up. I'll sign it," Mayor Jenkins said.

Sheriff Dalton felt emasculated. It was bad enough that nothing ever happened in town for him to prove his capabilities, but now that something had happened, the town was looking to him for leadership. He had to back down from old man Elwood, and then Mayor Jenkins had to ride in and save the day. The townsfolk were now asking Jenkins questions instead of him. Perhaps the whole town felt that he was only good for rescuing kittens from trees. Although the main thing was to find the culprit responsible for killing young Tim Kitner, Sheriff Dalton couldn't help feeling a twinge of jealousy. This public display would clinch a re-election for the mayor. Sheriff Dalton could see the pleasure in the man's face at how the events unfolded.

The Mayor's assistant handed Jenkins a clipboard with a hand written warrant scribbled on a white sheet of paper. Mayor Jenkins read it out loud:

"Warrant for the search of premises. I, Oswald Jenkins, acting in accordance with the power invested in my by the town of Clear Brooke Township, hereby assign Sheriff Dalton and his deputies the right to search the premises of Walter Elwood at 16 Clover Lane, Clear Brooke Township, regarding the investigation into the hit and run death of Timothy Kitner. I do further attest to.....blah, blah, blah...everything looks in order. Where do I sign?"

"Right here, Mr. Jenkins," Steve said, and pointed to a line with the 'X' in front of it.

Mayor Jenkins signed his name with a flourish. Sheriff Dalton knew this was all political showmanship. Mayor Jenkins knew damn well where to sign the paper.

"Looks like a need a third party witness signature..."

Ginger burst through the crowd.

"I'll sign it Mayor Jenkins. It's about time we got some justice here," she said, more to the crowd than the Mayor.

She scribbled her signature and Mayor Jenkins handed the document to the Sheriff. Ginger gave Sheriff Dalton a smug smile.

Dalton walked over the lawn to where Walter Elwood was standing, followed by Mayor Jenkins and the rest of the gathered crowd. They spread out into a semi-circle around Walter Elwood and the cellar doors. They left a ten foot space, a stage, for Sheriff Dalton and Walter.

"Well, Mr. Elwood. It looks like we have a warrant after all, a legal document for the search of your premises. We would like to start with your cellar."

He showed the signed document to Elwood. He motioned to move past him.

"Wait," Walter yelled. "Please, what you're expecting to find is not what you will find down there."

"And exactly what will I find?" the Sheriff asked.

Walter hesitated. He scratched his head and sucked air through his teeth. Finally he said: "Evil, Pure evil."

Sheriff Dalton lifted his hat and wiped the sweat from his forehead with the palm of his hand.

"Evil?" Dalton repeated in a condescending manner. "Yes, evil. Haven't you wondered why this town never has any crime?"

"I thought it was my good Sheriff-*ing*," Dalton said, turning to the crowd. They all chuckled.

"Do you know what the name of this town was before? Devil's Hill. It was a cursed place. In the early 1950's, a man came to town and gave my daddy a cane... a staff, if you will, and told him he could protect the town from evil with it. My daddy told me he forced all the evils that came to town into our cellar using that staff."

Walter paused scanning the faces of the townsfolk. They were all listening intently.

"When my daddy died, he passed the staff on to me. I didn't believe it at first but then things started happening. Bad things. So, I started using the staff to protect the town. That was thirty years ago."

"This is nonsense, Mr. Elwood," Sheriff Dalton stated. He turned to Mayor Jenkins.

"Have you ever heard anything like that?" Sheriff Dalton asked. Jenkins shook his head.

"No, that's ridiculous," he said, but his eyes darted away from the Sheriff quickly. Too quickly.

"What? You got something to say?" the Sheriff asked.

At first Mayor Jenkins said nothing but then he relented.

"No, nothing important, I guess. There was some old tale about this town being protected by the staff of Moses, but that's ridiculous."

Walter Elwood stepped to the side.

"You mean a staff like this?" He asked.

A few in the crowd gasped. The green, paint-peeled cellar doors were being held shut by a straight wooden cane.

Sheriff Dalton snickered through the side of his mouth. He did not believe this tall tale, but old man Walt had just put on an impressive show. What gave Sheriff Dalton pause for concern however, was the facial expression of Mayor Jenkins. His eyes bulged from his fat, sweaty face and his brows were raised in astonishment.

"Come on, this is ludicrous," he said to the Mayor.

Suddenly a voice boomed over the scene.

"I never heard something so pathetic in all my life."

It was Ginger 'loud mouth' with her usual grandstanding.

"Our weasel police force is nervous about some old tall-tale that children used to tell in school. Grow a backbone, Sheriff Dalton, unless you want me to come over there and open the door for'ya."

She took a step forward and Dalton turned on her.

"Back it up, you self-absorbed, attention hound. I am sick of hearing your acid tongued opinions! You're a selfish child and need to be put in your place," he growled.

Ginger's mouth gaped open and her eyes brimmed with tears. The Sheriff turned from her to look for his deputy.

"Corey, Corey?"

"I'm right here Sheriff."

"Go get the shotgun from my car."

Ginger's face flushed with anger and she charged Sheriff Dalton, grabbing his shirt sleeve to turn him around. Dalton turned back to her like an angry bull.

"Get your hands off of me or I will arrest you right now for obstruction of justice."

Dalton removed the cuffs from his belt and held them up for her to see. They glistened in the bright sunlight. She swallowed hard and let go of his shirt. She backed away from him not taking her eyes off the cuffs. Sheriff Dalton turned to the townsfolk.

"I want you all to back up ten feet, right now! I don't know who is in this cellar but when I open the door I want to make sure no one gets hurt."

Everyone began to back up. Part of him wanted to tell the crowd to disperse but a bigger part of him wanted them to stay. He was finally in control and wanted them all to see it. Cory came through the pack with a shotgun.

"Corey, cover me while I open this door and get this done."

Walter Elwood stepped in between the Sheriff and the door.

"I can't let you do that, Sheriff."

With lightning speed, Sheriff Dalton grabbed Walter by the wrist and threw him to the ground, placing his knee firmly into the old man's back. The crowd gasped. Dalton pulled the cuffs from his belt and snapped them violently around the old man's wrists. When he turned Walter over, tears were streaming down the old man's face. Sheriff Dalton felt immediate remorse and tightness clenched his throat.

"Damn it Walt, why'd ya' go and make me have to do that," he said.

He looked at Deputy Corey for moral support but, Corey stared back at him dumbfounded.

"Don't you understand, Sheriff?" Walter Elwood said, "All the darkness that should have befallen this town for the last 30 years will be released if you open that cellar door. All the bad things that should have happened in this town will be free to happen at once."

Sheriff Dalton helped Walter to his feet. He escorted him aside to Mayor Jenkins. Jenkins and Steve held Walter, one on each arm.

"I'm sorry Walt. I know that is what you believe, but we're in the Twenty-first Century and as Sheriff, I deal in facts, not superstitions."

Sheriff Dalton returned to the cellar doors. He grabbed hold of the wooden staff.

"Corey, get right in front of these doors. Anyone comes out without their hands up, you blast them, you got it?"

"Yes, sir."

Dalton looked down at the cane. He paused to think; something felt wrong. If someone were hiding down there, why would the wooden staff be on the outside of the doors? The Sheriff disregarded his thoughts; he had learned through life, it was best not to second guess his actions. He leaned down to the slanted doors.

"Okay, this is Sheriff Dalton of the Clear Brooke Township Police Department. Whoever is down there, we are going to open the door. I want you to come out with your hands on top of your head. We don't want anyone to get hurt. If you make any fast movements it will be perceived as a threat and we will shoot. Do you understand?"

Sheriff Dalton waited for a response but none came.

Corey positioned himself at the door. The Sheriff started pulling the staff from the door handles. He got a third of the way and stopped. He turned and looked at the townsfolk. They all seemed to be holding their breath. Something else felt wrong. Then he realized all the birds had stopped chirping. It was so quiet he could hear the hum of the highway miles away. The scattered white clouds had stopped moving across the sky and hung there in limbo. It was as if time had stood still. He had reservations about removing the staff but, he had come this far, he couldn't stop now. He pulled the staff the rest of the way out.

The cellar doors flung opened violently, sending Sheriff Dalton tumbling backwards and launching the staff into the air. It disappeared into the tall grass of the wooded area behind Walter's house. Corey jerked the shotgun to attention aiming it squarely at the open space. Initially, nothing happened. Dust and smoke made peering into the cellar impossible. Sheriff Dalton stood and drew his pistol positioning himself a few feet to the right of his Deputy.

A deep moan came from within the cellar, an inhuman sound that vibrated the ground. A wave of putrid liquid splashed from the darkness and onto the grass in front of the doors. The grass immediately browned and died. The browning spread out in a concentric circle across the lawn. Storm clouds rolled into the sky blackening the sun. The air temperature dropped twenty degrees. Sheriff Dalton lifted his feet as the grass died under his boots and he turned to watch it spread. Ginger wrapped her arms around herself as goose bumps rose on her bare arms. Dalton looked over to the wide-eyed mayor who in turn shrugged his shoulders. Flowers in the beds alongside the house withered and curled over, turning black.

Deputy Corey stiffened as if chilled by the cold air. His face turned blue then gray. His skin began to peel and flake.

"What's happening?" Dalton yelled.

Walter Elwood looked to the Sheriff with a grim expression.

"Several years ago, Corey would've been shot by the jealous boyfriend of some hussy from Oakdale he'd been screwing around with. This boyfriend was nasty and had no regard for human life. He was evil. He has been dead for some time, but now you released his spirit... and his intention," Walter explained.

Corey's body continued to disintegrate. His arms, still aiming the shotgun, broke off and fell to the floor. The rest of his body crumpled upon itself. Several townsfolk gasped and backed away from the scene. Todd Pickering turned and ran. The crowd thinned as several people walking backward, reached the sidewalk. They quietly turned and walked away.

Walter Elwood whispered, "Now do you understand?"

Another low moan emanated from the cellar. Everyone backed up a step, not sure what to expect. A vile odor seeped out from the dark cellar and spread outward. Sheriff Dalton covered his nose and several others turned their heads. It reeked of death and decay mixed with human feces. Steve Harbs relinquished his hold on old Walter and turned to the side. He vomited in the dying lawn.

Steve wiped traces of vomit from his bottom lip with the back of his hand. He didn't turn back to look at the cellar door. Instead, his mind went back in time to a distant memory when his mother was dying of cancer in the bedroom of their home.

She could no longer control her bowels. She had stopped eating but continued to soil her clothes; it was the chemo, it was digested blood, and it was her own decay that passed from her. She needed to be changed and cleaned; she could no longer do it for herself. However, Steve could not bring himself to do it. He walked into the room as she slept. The room stank. If she could just hold off until Monday, the nurse aid would be back. He had tip-toed out of the room, one hand over his nose and mouth. She heard him and called, "Steven?" He closed the door and stood there silently.

"Steven, please help me."

He couldn't do it anymore, he couldn't take it.

"Steven? Please?" she called.

He stood there, outside the door to her bedroom, crying, shaking uncontrollably. She called him over and over, until she ran out of energy. He snuck quietly down the stairs and out the front door.

The oak tree at the back of Walter's property withered and died. Several large limbs snapped and broke off, crashing to the ground with a thud.

Three dark shadow figures rose from the doorway. They morphed into skeletal figures in suits, black eyeless skulls grinning at the town's people who watched with shock and disbelief. The apparitions were only three-quarters visual but everyone could see the stride of their legs. The crowd parted, desperate to avoid contact with these ghastly apparitions. They continued past the gathered townspeople, chasing down those that had left.

"Sheriff, close the goddamn doors."

It was Bobby Tindall, the local mailman who had gathered at the scene with the rest of the crowd. The Sheriff moved forward and grabbed one of the doors. He began to push it until it could not be pushed any further.

"Come help me!" The Sheriff hollered.

Bobby moved forward to assist the Sheriff. A mist rose from the cellar and took the shape of a transparent hooded figure. It reached back and then swung at the Sheriff. Dalton's head jerked to the side as his face was struck, instantly turning beat red. The misty shape dissipated into air. Bobby Tindall picked up the shotgun from the pile of Corey's ashes and aimed it into the cellar. He shot the gun into the dark depths. Blood sprayed out of the cellar in a quick blast, covering his face. A deep sinister laugh followed then another, higher pitched chuckle. The blood that sprayed out was alive with worms and Bobby screamed as they ate their way into his face. As Bobby smacked and clawed at his face, an unseen force hit Sheriff Dalton knocking him away from the doorway.

When Bobby was eight-years-old he loved to eat pistachio nuts. One night he and his father were watching a game on TV, Red Sox against the Cubs. The Cubs were ahead the whole game but the Sox had a late eighth-inning rally to tie the score. Bobby could barely break his gaze from the television set to snack on his pistachios. He split the shells and devoured them at a steady pace. He tasted something rancid. He had swallowed it and shelled the next nut, popping it into his mouth. This one also had a sour taste. He spit it out into his palm to inspect. A half chewed worm was wriggling in the mushy mess in his hand. He yelped and threw it to the floor. His father, nodding off in the recliner barely noticed. Then he felt something squirming on his bottom lip. He pulled it off with his fingers and saw it was the other half of the worm. He tried to remain cool. He opened another pistachio and saw another worm wiggling in the shell. He realized that quite a few of the pistachios had that bitter taste and he had eaten several worms. He freaked out, screaming and crying. He threw-up on the rug and in his mind saw worms, hundreds of worms. It took his parents hours to calm him down. He never ate pistachios ever again and had birthed an extreme repulsion for worms.

Now, thirty years later, he stood upon the dead grass in old man Elwood's side yard with worms eating the flesh on his face.

Ginger screamed.

"Something touched me," she said.

The hair on the back of her head rose as if being grabbed in someone's fist. An invisible force yanked at her blouse, ripping it and almost fully exposing her left breast. She clutched the ripped blouse holding it closed.

"Oh, no!" Walter said.

"What, what is it?" Ginger snapped.

"You always liked to attract attention to yourself. Several years ago you attracted the attention of a bad seed. In life he was a rapist. A real sadistic sort that liked to inflict pain," Walter said.

There was an invisible tug at her shorts that brought them halfway down her thigh on one side. Ginger pulled them up with one hand. She began to cry.

"What do I do?" She asked Walter.

"Run!" Walter said.

She ran, screaming as something touched her in wrong places. She swatted empty air, unsuccessfully trying to bat it away.

"Someone go help her!" Sheriff Dalton yelled. Reluctantly, Sean Dixon turned and ran after Ginger.

Bobby Tindall screamed even louder and fell to the ground. The worms grew as his skin was being eaten away from his face. He could feel them boring into his flesh and muscle, separating his skin from bone and wiggling in behind his eyes. Excruciating pain raged in his head. Blindly, he felt around the ground and came upon the shotgun. He turned it upon himself and pulled the trigger, blowing his face and the top of his skull into the air.

Several of the folks screamed at the sight and sound of the gunshot. All became silent and still. The smell of feces lingered. Off in the distance they heard Ginger screaming. It was a horrible sound to hear in the otherwise quiet neighborhood. Then they began to hear other screams from various distances and directions as if the town was under attack.

"Sheriff Dalton? Walter whispered. "You need to go find the staff but, before you do - please throw keys to Mayor Jenkins so he can release me from these cuffs."

The Sheriff nodded. He unclasped the keys from his belt and threw them to the mayor. They landed in the grass in front of him. Sheriff Dalton made a slow retreat from the cellar doors. When he reached the red pick-up truck he turned and ran into the brush behind Walter Elwood's home, searching for the staff.

A moment later a disembodied voice came from the cellar. It sounded inhuman and garbled, like a warped record played backward. It was incomprehensible to everyone but Steve Harbs. He straightened up and walked to the cellar doors. He stepped over Tindall's dead body and gazed into the opaque depths of the basement. The garbled demon voice spoke from the cellar again. Steve's eyebrows rose and his forehead crinkled,

"Mother?" he said.

Mayor Jenkins had just picked up the keys from the grass when he heard Steve call to his mother. He stopped and watched the scene, frozen in place. Steve took another step toward the cellar door.

Steve heard his mother's voice.

"Steven, please don't leave me here alone ... again," the voice said to him.

Steve's bottom lip protruded and silent tears fell from his eyes. His shaking hand reached out toward the cellar.

"Steven!" Mayor Jenkins hollered, "Get away from that door."

Steve turned to Mayor Jenkins, a terrible grimace on his face.

"My Mother...," Steve said.

"That is not your mother," Mayor Jenkins replied.

"Mayor Jenkins, please unlock the cuffs," Walter Elwood said. Mayor Jenkins ignored him. He reached back absently to hand Walter the keys and they dropped in the grass.

The demon voice spoke to Steve again:

"Steven, please. I need you my son. Please help me," Steven's mother's voice pleaded.

Steve turned his attention back to the cellar.

"I'm sorry Lou, but she needs me. She needs me more than you do," Steven said, gazing into the cellar.

Tears welled up in the Mayor's eyes.

"Steve, please don't do this," Mayor Jenkins said in a soft voice, uncharacteristic of the Mayor's usual boisterous mannerisms.

Walter then realized the nature of their relationship. He knew Mayor Jenkins would not be of any help as long as Steve Harbs was in danger. Walter looked to the handful of townsfolk still gathered, three men and one woman.

"Can somebody please, get the keys and unlock these cuffs before another bad thing happens?" he asked.

Nobody moved. They were frozen in place by shock. They all feared that they'll be the next victim to the evil that had been released from Walter's basement.

With no one moving to help, Walter got on his knees and reached backwards to try and feel the keys in the grass.

Steve Harbs reached out both arms waiting for an embrace. A figure sprang from the dark cellar, trailing black ribbons of smoke. It had the head of a pig, exposed skeletal ribs, legs of a chicken and hairy arms with hooves instead of hands. Its eyes glowed vibrant green which reflected off of Steve's face. It had black leathery wings like a bat that stretched into the air, exposing another set of arms with sharp talons. One of those talon adorned claws rushed forward, piercing Steve's gut. Steve slumped forward, his arms falling to rest on the demon's shoulders. The beast yanked its talons from the hole in Steve's abdomen, pulling a string of small intestines in its clutches. Steve coughed up blood that dribbled down his chin.

"STEVEN!" Mayor Jenkins screamed, sounding both terrified and full of pain.

The demon flapped its wings once and rushed backward into the dark cellar. Mayor Jenkins ran to the mouth of the cellar and fell to his knees. He cried, staring into the black pit but seeing nothing but his own broken heart and empty future.

Walter grasped the keys with his pinky and struggled to stand. He ran to Annie Wilson who stood motionless, mesmerized by the scene unfolding before her. He brought his face up to hers so she could see him only.

"Ann, I am holding keys in my hand. Can you take them and unlock the cuffs around my wrists?"

Ann attempted to look past him, moving her head to the side in order to regain view of the cellar door.

"Ann," he called more forcefully. "I need you to unlock the cuffs. Hold out your hand."

She looked at Walter, finally seeing him, then extended her hand. Walter twisted his body around and carefully dropped the key in her palm. At first it seemed like she was not going to respond, but then he heard the keys jangle and felt her twist the cuffs into position. He heard the tumbler click and his right hand became free. He unlocked the other hand himself.

"Ann, you need to leave here immediately. Do you understand? Turn around and walk away slowly. Go pick up your children at day-care and leave this town with them."

Ann shook her head *yes*, as tears welled up in her eyes. She turned and began to walk. Walter turned to the three men standing in the side yard.

"I am going to need your help. We need to get Mayor Jenkins away from the house and then close those cellar doors. Can I count on you?"

The three men nodded weakly.

"Sheriff?" Walter called.

"I'm tryin' Walt! Damn it all to hell, I'm tryin'!"

"Sheriff, don't think about it. Just picture yourself holding it. It will…"

Sheriff Dalton cut him off, "Here it is. I found it Walt! I found it."

A terrible quake shook the earth just as Sheriff Dalton started running. He fell to the ground between two old cars and the staff bounced away from him and under a '72 Pontiac Lemans. Walter put his hands out to steady himself and one of the men kneeled down to keep his balance. Several car alarms erupted in wails, triggered by the trembling. A streetlight lost its housing and a glass gel crashed to the pavement.

"What was that?" one of the men asked.

"The master of this evil," Walter answered.

Walter looked to the Sheriff and saw him reaching under the car for the staff.

"Do you men know any prayers?" he asked.

They nodded and one said, "Yes."

"Then you should say them now," Walter said.

He headed toward Mayor Jenkins but turned his head back to add:

"Out loud!"

The three men blundered into prayer, two saying the "Our Father" and one saying the "Hail Mary." Walter put his arm around Mayor Jenkins and the guy with the ponytail helped Jenkins to his feet. They walked away from the door, the mayor in the middle with his arms draped over each man's shoulders. A plume of black smoke rose into the air behind them. Mayor Jenkins stopped. Walter was about to urge him to continue when the Mayor was yanked from between them. A tentacle wrapped around Mayor Jenkins's leg, dragged him back to the doors.

The beast rose out of the cellar stretching into the air. The head of a giant white worm towered twenty feet above them. It had no eyes. A gaping mouth filled with infinite rows of teeth drooled clear slime. Its underside was adorned with long cilia-like tentacles swinging and whipping chaotically. The tentacle holding Mayor Jenkins lifted him into the air. Walter grabbed his arm with his left hand attempting to keep Jenkins from being hauled away.

"Walter!" Sheriff Dalton hollered, and threw the staff.

Walter reached out his right hand to catch it when a whipping tentacle struck him in the chest, hurling him to the ground. When Walter let go, the Mayor went bouncing upward. The giant worm bit off the mayor's head. The worm's white translucent flesh was sprayed with red blood.

The staff lay only feet from Walter, but he made no attempt to retrieve it. Sheriff Dalton ran to his side and knelt down. Two of the other men ran away but one of them was caught around the neck by a tentacle.

Sheriff Dalton could see something was terribly wrong with Walter.

"Dalton, you have to assume the responsibility of the staff," Walter said with difficulty.

"I can't. You're the one that has to do it," Sheriff Dalton replied.

"I can't feel anything past my shoulder blades. If I survive, at the very least I am crippled."

"But I don't know what to do."

"Just hold it straight up to the sky. It knows what to do; just hold it tight."

Sheriff Dalton reached over him and grabbed the staff. It didn't feel like anything special. He looked into Walter's eyes.

"Send that damn thing back to hell!" Walter said, with conviction.

Sheriff Dalton stood. The beast held Mayor Jenkins's headless body in a tentacle. In another it held the upper torso of a man, intestines unfurled, hanging from the half body and strung over to the mouth of the worm. Dalton raised the staff into the air. Immediately he saw cloud to cloud lightning light up the sky in numerous places. Dalton felt his body tingle and the air took on an odd metallic scent. Three arcs of electric raced through the sky and met at the tip of the staff. Dalton could feel the power surge and he had to grip the staff with both hands to steady it. The electric, concentrated and focused, shot out of the tip of the staff in a straight beam and into the beast. It instantly began moving backward, being pushed into the cellar. Its multitude of tentacles whipped violently, seeking footing. Several grabbed onto parts of the house and others tried to borrow into the dead grass but were quickly pulled from their refuge as the beast was forced back. It tried to whip its tentacles at Dalton but he was somehow protected.

One tentacle managed to rope Walter's leg and pulled him along as the beast retreated. Dalton saw this and immediately moved to save the old man. As soon as the staff angled away from the sky, the beast began pulling itself from the cellar again, moving a good five feet forward. Dalton straightened the staff and the beast was driven back. Dalton had no choice but to keep both hands on the staff. He could do nothing but watch as the beast retreated into the cellar, pulling Walter along with it.

The head of the worm submerged into the cellar and all that remained were dozens of whipping tentacles. It had dropped the headless Mayor and the half body of the other man, but it would not let go of old Walt. Dalton took several steps forward and the tentacles retreated into the cellar, with Walter in tow. The electric currents broke contact and the beam of blue light winked out.

Sheriff Dalton looked around. The only person left on the scene was the man with a ponytail. Dalton remembered his name, Ralph, and that he worked at the Sunoco station up the block.

"Ralph, can you come with me into the cellar to look around?" Dalton asked.

"I... I don't know," he stammered. "I can't see. I think I'm blind."

"I'm sorry. Just wait there, I will drive you to the hospital. I just have to check the cellar first."

Dalton walked to the edge of the cellar and looked in. Dust swirled around in the darkness. He took a tentative step down. Satisfied that there was no danger he continued down the steps. The cellar looked normal from the inside. He walked around waving the dust away from his face. He turned to leave and tripped on something. He looked down and saw Walter's watch. It was half submerged into the solid concrete. Dalton couldn't pull it out. he thought he heard faint screams from a distant place. When he tried to focus on the sound, it disappeared.

Outside, he closed the cellar doors and put the staff through the handles sealing the cellar. He prayed he would have the courage and power to do what had been entrusted to him. Helping Ralph to the police cruiser, he saw a cat in a tree. It had probably run up there seeking refuge from the melee. Sheriff Dalton thought about helping it down but decided against it. When he started the car, the cat climbed down by itself.

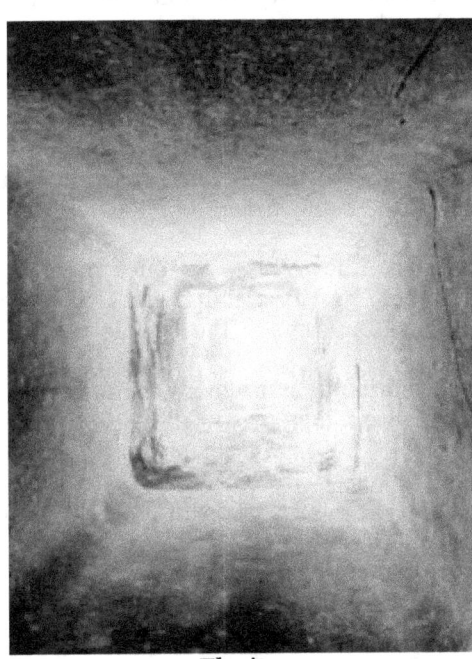

Elusion

Dona Fox
Forevermore

I slid my tarot cards into the red satin bag, hid it under my pillow, and stomped down the stairs. My new hope chest waited patiently in the darkness of the van.

"Come on, Jenny, come outside." Dad let the front door slam as he ran out to meet the delivery man.

I peeked out through the dusty living room window.

A fat red-faced delivery man and my tall skinny dad were having a vigorous discussion that involved hand gestures and arm waving – probably more exercise than the delivery man was used to getting in a month.

Palms up, negating any further interaction with the contents of his vehicle, the delivery man backed farther and farther away from the van. He pointed at the left front tire and shook his head, then he pointed at the left rear tire and shook his head. Finally, he folded his arms across his stomach and planted his feet in the center of the lawn next door, my uncle's lawn.

Dad was uncharacteristically out of patience, he closed his eyes to gather himself. Then Uncle Ron came out of his house on his way to work. Dad and Uncle Ron carried the large bubble wrapped box inside as the bright orange delivery truck sped away.

"Thanks, Ron. The idiot refused to touch my delivery. Said it jinxed him or something." Dad chuckled. "Good thing he didn't expect a tip." Then Dad ripped the bubble wrap off the hope chest. "Wow."

The three of us stared in amazement at the wooden chest as it reflected the living room light.

"What exactly is it?" I broke the silence.

"I had a carpenter make this chest for you. I was at an antique auction in one of the Victorians down near the waterfront and the cellar door caught my eye. It was clearly unique, special, but rough. There was something about it, it had a personality."

"The old carpenter was looking at it, too. We struck a deal. He agreed to make this chest for you and not to bid against me if I would let him have the remainder of the wood. I never imagined it would be this beautiful. I thought you could put some of your mother's things in it. Things to remember her by . . . and . . . whatever."

His glance slid toward the dining room. There were three

packing boxes stacked on the table. Some of Mom's things he must have just brought out from the spare room. He hadn't taken anything to storage yet, or even moved any of her things to the attic.

Dad and I exchanged looks but we weren't good at talking to each other, especially about mom, not yet, maybe not ever.

"It's called a hope chest. It's an old fashioned idea. Girls used to fill them up with pillow cases and dish towels, they embroidered flowers and stuff on the dish towels for when they started their own homes."

I laughed. "Dad, that's silly, only you would know that, Mr. Archeologist. But it is beautiful. Thank you." I stretched up to kiss his ear and instead, startled by sudden horrid noises near the wooden chest, I screeched in his ear.

My black cat, Bleach, was growling and hissing at the wooden chest, her back arched, hair standing on end, eyes round and wide, as she backed from the room.

"Wow, sorry, Dad. Bleach doesn't seem to like it, but I think it's gorgeous. Is there a key?" I fingered the intricate antique lock.

"Maybe it's inside or taped to the bottom?"

"No, nothing inside, or taped to the bottom – or in the bubble wrap." I shook the bubble wrap.

"The carpenter is a real old-timer, he doesn't even have a phone but, it's on the way, so I'll stop and see if the he has the key or maybe it's still at the old house, if anybody is still there. I've still got a couple of hours. I'll give you a call, either way." Dad was flying out with his students for a weekend dig in some old mine in California.

"Remember, if you need anything, Uncle Ron's right next door."

I was sitting on the couch reading my new book of spells. After I was sure Dad was out of town I was going to try a spell that might get Dewey Linder to return my follow on Twitter – and maybe even respond to one of my Tweets. I was hoping to buy his latest movie soon. I had already gone to see it five times.

I had the right herbs and the right colors of candles. I had been buying this stuff gradually so Dad wouldn't get suspicious. Now I was engrossed, trying to memorize the words, the spell would be more effective that way, instead of reading it. Bleach cried to me from the living room door but wouldn't come into the room.

I wadded up a piece of paper and absentmindedly tossed it down the hall. Bleach ran after it and brought it back circling the long way around the couch to avoid the wooden chest. I threw the paper ball a few times until Bleach was getting kitten-wild then, without thinking, I threw the wad of paper into the wooden chest.

Bleach started to run for the wad of paper but stopped short as if there were an invisible line around the chest. Then she backed carefully out of the room.

"Bleach, come back, baby, come here, I'll just throw it down the hall, come back . . . Ouch!" I had reached into the chest for the ball of paper and the lid of the chest slammed shut on my hand. "Dammit!" Reflexively, I threw open the lid, jumped up and kicked the chest. "Damn you to hell big ugly hard as a rock stupid hope chest!"

"Oh, shit. There's a mark in the stupid thing." I ran cold water over my hand for a minute then looked under the kitchen sink for furniture polish and a soft cloth to take the mark of my sneaker off the wood.

I rubbed the furniture polish on the wood and the mark came off easily. Then I polished the entire chest, admiring the wood as I polished. Although the wood was almost black, the variations in color of the grain and the patterns in the grain were brought out by the stain the carpenter had used.

"Ouch. Again! Damn." Now I had a splinter under my fingernail. I went upstairs and got my tweezers and tried to pull it out carefully, all in one piece, but it broke off. I dug at it a bit and squeezed it a bit, then cut my fingernail as short as I could, but I just couldn't get it all so I poured rubbing alcohol over it hoping at least it wouldn't get infected.

Bleach hopped up onto the bed beside me and I scooped her into my arms, the cat started purring, and we both went to sleep.

I dreamed that I tried to get out the front door but it wouldn't open, then I tried to break a window but it wouldn't break. I dreamed that I passed out and woke up in the hope chest staring at the ceiling, then I passed out again and woke up in the hope chest but the lid was shut and I couldn't get the lid open and the house was on fire. I could smell the smoke.

Then, in my dream, I was in a cellar. I saw bodies in the corner and heads in vices on a workbench, blowing steam from their noses. The heads were screaming soundlessly. "Find us. Jenny. Find us." Then the heads were crying. Giant tears were pouring from their eyes, putting out the fire. "It's too late, Jenny. It's too late for us."

I woke up on my bed. The telephone was ringing downstairs. The house was dark and my hand was throbbing. I reached over and turned on the bedside lamp.

The splinter was already festering. Green, smelly pus had leaked onto the blankets. Bleach was gone and the hope chest was beside the bed.

I got out of bed on the other side. I went into the bathroom and splashed my face with water, then I drank glass after glass of cold water, trying to get rid of the dryness in my mouth.

How did the hope chest get upstairs? Was it really upstairs? I peeked into my bedroom. Couldn't see it. I tiptoed into the bedroom until I could see the floor on the other side of the bed. The hope chest wasn't there, but there were marks in the carpet as if something had been slid across the room from the bedside and out the door.

I was going to call Uncle Ron anyway, but my phone was downstairs. The bedroom door wouldn't open. I was able to turn the knob. But there was something against the door. I pushed and pushed and got it open just far enough to slide through. The door had been blocked by the chest.

The lid was shut and Bleach was howling inside. I opened the lid and Bleach flew out leaving a trail of blood on the carpet.

I ran down the stairs and grabbed my phone and dialed Uncle Ron's phone number.

"Hi, Jenny, how's my girl?"

I was so relieved I started sobbing and couldn't talk, couldn't explain everything that was happening, "I had a nightmare and Bleach got shut in the hope chest."

"Jenny, Jenny, calm down. Tell you what. As soon as I have a break from work I'll come over and drop off some dinner for you and that movie you've been waiting to see, okay? Hang in there, kiddo, you can tell me everything then. We'll fix it all, then. Got to go for now. Love you." And Uncle Ron was gone. But he would be here in a couple of hours and Dad would be calling soon.

I turned on the television. Anime, I would watch anime. I sat on the couch and tried to get lost in the story. And tried to pretend I didn't notice the hope chest was right there next to the couch.

Then I realized, it was late, now Dad wouldn't be calling me until he was settled in for the night at the motel in California. He was out of town now for sure, and Uncle Ron wasn't coming for a while, it was time to do my magic spell.

I turned off the television, laid out the candles, the herbs and the book. I closed all the blinds and lit the candles in order – white, pink, red, black, white, pink, red, black. Then I said the words of the spell while throwing the herbs on each candle in order.

My hands were shaking. A draft blew through the room before I had a Chance to say Dewey's name, which may have been significant. The draft blew herbs into the hope chest and blew the candles out.

I heard Bleach's paws thumping up the stairs then I felt warm, strong hands on my arms. "Be quiet, Jenny. Stay calm. It's alright. I won't hurt you." For some reason I believed the young man's voice.

"Are you Dewey?"

"Don't ever ask me that again. No, I'm not Dewey. Let's just say I'm your friend, forevermore. Call me Chance. You called me up with your spell."

"Really? I did? Chance."

"You did. Jenny." His hands circled my neck, softly, then a bit harder, before twisting my hair in his hand and pulling back my head. I felt his hot breath and his tongue tickling my ears then he was at my neck in a fever, it was a delicious feeling I had only felt before in dreams. Finally, his breath and his lips swept across my face, finding my mouth . . .

The telephone rang. Guiltily I answered it. "Yes?" There was silence on the line. "Hello? Hello? Who is this?" Silence.

I hung up the phone and reached out into the darkness. "Are you still here?" There was no response. I turned on the living room light. I was alone with the hope chest. Bleach's eyes were twin beacons at the top of the stairs.

I sat on the couch and pulled Mom's afghan over from the arm and held it close to me. I turned the television back on and pressed the mute button so I could hear any sounds from outside, or inside.

I was in a daze and unaware of how much time passed until I was startled by the face of the delivery man from that afternoon staring at me from the television, I turned on the sound.

" . . . had worked for Delta Delivery for only five months at the time of the collision." I stood and walked toward the television set. This was unreal. Someone I had just seen that morning. Then I saw the other car.

"No. No. No. No." It was Uncle Ron's red convertible – they had made the license plate fuzzy so it could not be read but there was the ruby red dream catcher I had given him for luck when he bought the car, hanging from the rearview mirror.

"The name of the driver of the other car involved in this fatal collision has not been released pending notification of his family."

I had to talk to Dad. The University would know how to get in contact with him. I went to his desk and grabbed the rolodex. It was open to the number for his department head, Professor Lind. Her home number was listed too. I had met Professor Lind several times, I dialed without hesitation.

The line was busy, in frustration I tried the Professor's office number, that line was busy, too. I would try the Professor's home again in half an hour.

I went back to the couch. Back to the news. In astonishment, I watched as they carried students out of a mine shaft cave-in, in Northern California. Again - names withheld pending notification of next of kin.

Frantically, I dialed and re-dialed Professor Lind's number until, finally, Professor Lind answered.

"Professor Lind, this is Jenny. Is my father okay?"

"Jenny? Oh, Jenny. Well, as far as I know. He didn't go on the dig today. He didn't show up. We had to send another teacher at the last minute. I'm sorry, I've got my hands full, I have to go." The line went dead.

I put the phone down on the couch, turned off the television and stared at the hope chest; the hope chest, in the living room, where my father and my Uncle Ron had set it down when they brought it into the house, the beautiful wood gleaming under the living room lights. The ornate lock gleaming wickedly.

Maybe my father was still at the salvaged house or the carpenter's, I was going to have to find him.

The lights went out. I could feel Chance's presence again. "Jenny." He pulled my hair playfully. "Jenny." My t-shirt lifted gently.

"Jenny!" He screamed my name as he threw me against the wall, then pushed himself against me, pinning me by my wrists and covering my mouth with his. It wasn't exciting anymore, I was trapped, helpless, and he was hurting me.

The phone rang. The lights came on. No one was in the room.

I answered the phone. "Burn it. Burn the hope chest. Now, Jenny." It was Mom. The line went dead.

Dad had a small hatchet on the back porch for making kindling for the fireplace. I hoped that would be strong enough. I hoped I would be strong enough. I ran and got the hatchet.

Like a madwoman, I started chopping at the chest. The lights in the room began flickering, turning completely off then shining like the sun at noon. I could hear Chance cursing me and Mom praying for me to be strong.

It was like a battle between good and evil, Mom and Chance waging a war while I just kept chopping, little tiny bites with the kindling hatchet but I wasn't going to stop until this thing was small enough to burn.

I threw the little chunks of wood into the fire place, stopping only to get newspapers from the recycling bin to put under it to ensure a good start.

Finally, exhausted and sweating, I grabbed the matches from my little magic set-up and lit the newspapers. Black smoke and laughter filled the room. I grabbed the fireplace poker and opened the chimney vent.

Flames licked at the air - orange, red and black tongues. The crackling sounded like words. "Put your hand in the fire, Jenny. It feels so good. Lick your fingers and try it. It's hot like you wouldn't believe. Come on, Jenny. Put your face in, let me put my tongue in your mouth again, huh? Mmmm, Baby, come here."

I couldn't stop staring into the fire. I was beginning to want it. It was Chance's voice and he had made me feel good once before. Before he turned so savage. I took a step toward the flames. What would they feel like on my . . .

"Leave, now, Jenny. Go. Find your, Dad. He needs you." Mom broke the spell.

I went into my father's study and pulled open the center drawer. The receipts from the house salvage company and from the wood worker were right on top. I knew those addresses, they weren't far.

Maybe Dad was still there. I would go to the salvage house the cellar door came from first. I slid out the back door hoping no one would see me on the dark streets.

When I got to the house I stood behind a tree across the street and watched. A light was on in the house. There were half a dozen people moving back and forth in front of the light. There was also a bit of light coming from a cellar window. But not enough to detect movement.

I waited. Gradually people in hoodies with their faces hidden left, alone and in couples, hugging what looked like brown paper packages wrapped with string to their bodies, precious cargo.

Finally, I could see only one shadow upstairs, sitting at a table with a flickering candle and a bottle of wine. I crossed the street and crept across the lawn.

I crawled up to the cellar window. Then I put my head as close to the window as I could and tried to peer in. I saw my dad, laying on the floor in the corner of the cellar, under a single bare bulb, as I watched, his eyes opened.

My head was yanked back, a smoky hand clamped over my

nose and mouth. I was partially lifted from the ground and dragged away. Then I was thrown down a dark stairwell, all through this I smelled smoke and heard the sound of ragged coughing.

I was tied up and, by the light of the single bare bulb hanging from the ceiling. I could see I was lying on the cellar floor next to Dad. Chance sat on a chair in front of us with a half-empty bottle of wine in one hand and a full one at his feet.

As my eyes adjusted to the light, I saw that the floor was covered - in some places at least two foot deep - with blood, and hides, and guts, and there were large, dark piles in the corners. A workbench along the far wall was stacked with dozens of horses' heads.

As my stomach turned, I tried to sit up. "What the hell?"

Chance gave a rueful laugh then was overcome with a fit of coughing. "People like their horse meat." His voice didn't sound anything like the voice of my would-be lover, rather, it was strained and harsh.

"But it's illegal here." He paused to cough and drink more wine. "And there was so much blood in the cellar door. Wood soaks up blood like crazy. That's why they made the old meat-cellar doors and thresholds out of wood – to soak the blood up and keep it out of the house. And in this case, it would have been evidence, even so, we got rid of it too soon, there was one more shipment." His laughter was cut off by a fit of coughing.

Chance finished the rest of the bottle of wine. "No worries, more wine where that came from. I think you almost killed me, Jenny. These are some bad burns."

He closed his eyes then had another fit of coughing. Thin grey ribbons of smoke continued to curl off his body. "I'm still burning in your fireplace, you know." He looked down at his hands, his fingers still glowed orange, but his fingertips were becoming ashes.

I smiled, glad that he would be gone soon, that I had done it.

Chance leaned forward. "Don't you want to know what the old man did with the rest of the wood from the cellar door?"

My body tensed. "What did the old man do with the rest of the wood?"

Tiny rivulets of smoke circling his head, like a victor's wreath, Chance smiled. "He made a cradle."

Greg McWhorter
Sempiternal Denouement

"They say 'You can't take it with you' and I say phooey to that! No one will ever get my gold. The man who tries . . . dies. You can't beat the dead."

Old man Gower had been heard to say that in public many times during his last few years. Now that he was laid to rest, there was a lot of speculation concerning his vast wealth. Where did he get his money? Where was it now? Were there any heirs to inherit it? These questions were posed by people on the street. The local Louisiana newspapers held to just the brief facts.

The paper ran a short obituary on the late Emil Curtis Gower. It basically stated that he inherited wealth from his family that had settled in the region during the mid-1800s. The family mansion was built on thousands of acres of good land beyond some swamp areas, which made it difficult to get to at times. As far as anyone could remember, the Gower family had never used the land as a plantation and instead let the natural flora grow wild around the rambling Southern mansion with its great columns that encircled the ground floor of a three-story structure. The obituary offered little information on how they acquired their wealth except for a brief mention of past family members being at Sutter's Mill in California during the big Gold Rush. The Gower family also never used banks and was reported to have their own walk-in vault in which they kept their gold and money.

The last item in the obituary was that as far as anyone knew, Emil Gower was the last of his family and there were no heirs. After the obituary, a sidebar stated Gower that was laid to rest somewhere on his property by an elderly mortician that had been given exact instructions regarding the burial, which included the fact that no one except the mortician could witness the burial. The mortician completed his work in secrecy and left to return to his home. On his way, he suffered a heart attack and died without disclosing where he buried the body. This fact caused lively discussion and some speculation of evil afoot.

It was not long before men tried to break-in to the mansion and lay claim to some of the Gower wealth. A group of drunk young men were the first to try to get to the mansion, but found that the swampy landscape and all the thick growth around the mansion, made it too difficult and they gave up. The following morning some of the youths came down with 'swamp fever' and were near death for a few days before pulling through. Rumors started to circulate that the area around the mansion held some contagion and possibly the swamp leading to the grand house was haunted as well.

The more destitute, and thus desperate, men of the nearby town would not be deterred from what they perceived as childish nonsense. A group of rowdies formed and went out to the mansion with several wagons. They smashed open the front doors and went inside to discover that the mansion was in terrible order. Copious amounts of garbage and vague detritus had been strewn about.

"What is you all doin' here?"

The men turned and saw a thin old black man coming down the grand staircase. He was dressed in a dirty and stained butler's uniform.

"You has no business here! Get out!" rasped the elderly, but fit, butler.

One of the men promptly ran up to meet the butler on the stairs and hit him over the head with a lead pipe. The butler crumpled to the floor like a dropped coat and laid there without moving.

"Don't worry about him," shouted the leader of the mob, "He's still alive. Search the house! Let's find us some treasure!"

The men searched everywhere, but all they found was litter and heavily abused furniture. Since they had the carts, they loaded up as much of the furniture as they could.

"No one will recognize us at the next town over. We'll sell the lot there and split the money."

On the way, both wagons, loaded with furniture and men, disappeared within the murky swamp never to be seen again.

The beaten butler had stumbled into town and told the sheriff about the robbery and described the men. It was quickly figured who the men were that were now missing. More rumors started to circulate and the townsfolk, who were used to the supernatural like the voodoo that persisted amongst the blacks, decided that whatever wealth was left in the house was not worth the risk of life. Some even speculated that the butler, Sampson, may have been working his own voodoo around Gower's place.

Spying the butler leaving town through a dirty window, the barman at the Gilded Lily was heard by his customers as he said; "I don't trust that Sampson feller. He's got some bad mojo about him. The sheriffs lettin' him stay on at the house until everything is settled."

A few days passed and thoughts of Gower's wealth were almost gone from the townsfolk. One particularly ruthless man, Dave "Black" Barth was drunk one night in the bar when he stated; "No ghosts or voodoo zombies are tougher than me. If there is a treasure on that property . . . I'll find it!"

That same night, smelling of tequila, he rode out on his horse and picked his way through the swamp toward the house. When he got to the Gower place, he remembered the butler's tale that men had already searched the house without finding anything. As he looked at the large house in the midnight moonlight he got a glimpse of something creating a reflection of the moon from behind some bushes. He tied up his horse at a nearby tree that was on the edge of the property and quietly made his way across the small clearing around the house and headed straight for the bushes, hoping not to be seen. He made it to the bushes and looked behind them and saw a darkened window low to the ground. He realized that there was a cellar and figured that would be a great place to search for stashed treasures.

Dave found a rock about the size of his fist and wrapped it in his handkerchief and then hit the window as lightly and as quietly as possible. The third time he hit it, the window cracked and he was able to get the glass shards to fall out with just a slight tinkling sound. Before long, he was able to get behind the bushes and swing his legs into the tiny window ledge. The window was barely big enough for him to get his body in, but he managed to fall quietly onto the stone floor of the basement. He did not waste any time. He took out his fancy lighter that he had won in a crap game and proceeded to look around the abysmal darkness of the basement with the flickering light.

He found many boxes of archaic instruments, furnishings, and clothes, but nothing too valuable. He was just about to chalk up his adventuring to pure folly, but then behind a large crate and some rolls of wallpaper he noticed a giant doorway. He pulled the items away from the wall and exposed two giant wooden doors with extremely intricate iron work on them. He stood back and looked the massive doors. They resembled the doors he saw in a bank vault once. His pulse raced as he got excited and tried to pull open the doors. They would not budge. He tried with all his might and still he could not get them to budge. He stopped pulling and examined the doors carefully. He saw that there was a large padlock connecting the two doors. He did a quick search of the cellar, but could find no tools, or piece of metal strong enough to try and snap the lock off. He then figured to Hell with the noise as he drew out his revolver. He would shoot the old butler if it meant having great riches. He took aim at the padlock and fired. The bullet ricocheted off the luck, and in a stroke of pure bad luck, the bullet hit Dave "Black" Barth straight in the chest.

The roosters were crowing and the sun was peeking through the bayou as Dave's horse galloped into town with Dave hung over it's back like a flesh saddle. Someone found Dave and the horse and led them to the doctor's office. Stretched out on the doctor's table and gasping his last, Dave wheezed out a message.

"I found the . . . treasure . . . large doors . . . uhhh . . . I fired . . . Doors fired back . . ." and with that Barth was no more. His final words quickly spread around the town and more speculation ensued. Words like cursed, bewitched, voodoo, evil, spirits, ghosts, zombies, were all heard on the street that morning as the town awoke to, and shared, the news of Barth's passing.

"Six men have now disappeared or died trying to get at the Gower wealth Sheriff. What are you going to do about it?"

"I reckon I better ride out to the manse and see what is going on. Maybe Sampson can tell me what he makes of Bart's statement."

That afternoon, as the flies buzzed around his head and the heat felt like a weight dragging him down, the Sheriff made his way toward the house. He had not been out there in years. He was almost there when his horse suddenly became spooked and reared and the Sheriff was thrown off the horse's back. He landed head first onto a large rock and died instantly. The horse eventually returned to town sans rider. The Sheriff's body was found and recovered. The townspeople seemed to decide that that was an end to the search for the Gower riches. There were no further attempts from them.

Sampson had bided his time, waiting for a break in the influx of fortune seekers. He was thrilled that they had been thwarted in ways that created fear of the house and lands.

The butler thought out loud; "I wasted over thirty years taking care of Gower. That man owes me sumthin' and I aims to have it. I got to have sumthin' to live on now that I is old."

Sampson knew where a few valuable possessions were kept; silverware, old clocks, old coins, and such, but he never could get it out of the old man just where the real wealth was kept. He knew that the property had some secret panels, but he could never find one. Now that Dave Barth had uncovered the doors in the cellar, he had somewhere new to look. He could not believe that he had missed those during his own searches.

Sampson faced the large iron doors, with there intricate detail, and wondered what he would find inside. He pulled the doors, but they would not budge. He noticed the padlock was wedged firmly in place, but it had a dent in it. He decided to run upstairs and try and find some small tools to maybe pick the lock with. He found a few things and returned to the doors. He took an old sewing needle and worked it into the padlock. Somehow, maybe because of the damage caused by the bullet, he was able to get the padlock sprung open and it fell to the stone cellar floor.

Sampson wasted no time in trying again to pull the doors, but this attempt also failed. He finally decided to remove the hinge pins from the sides of the doors. He took a long screwdriver and a hammer and proceeded to pop out all of the hinge pins. Once he completed this, he tried to pull the doors again to no avail. Upstairs he had also found an old pry bar in the kitchen. He gripped it and tried to pry the doors off their hinges, but still nothing budged. Sweat covered and exhausted from exertion, he decided to relax a bit and again thought out loud; "Damn doors! I'll get ya' open yet! I just need to go into town and get a lil' help."

People in the town were afraid to deal with Sampson due to all of the rumors and deaths that had occurred and they had the view that he was tainted with the same evil that enshrouded the mansion. Even so, he was able to purchase a donkey from some stables. Leading his purchase carefully through the swamp, he made it back quickly and before much longer, he was in the cellar with the donkey, facing the doors. He attached ropes to the donkey and wrapped them around the door handles.

"C'mon on pull lil' donkey!" he said as took a whip to the animal.

The donkey pulled against the ropes, but at first nothing happened. Sampson started whipping the donkey furiously to pull harder. After a few minutes, he could hear the doors creaking and finally they both jumped out of their hinges and fell to the floor with a mighty crash.

"Thas' got it!"

Once the dust settled, Sampson saw that the doors covered a bricked up wall. He started to laugh at his own folly.

"Ha! What a fool I is. I done wasted all my time and sweat fer nuthin'. Damn Gower has the final joke on me after all. Man was always pullin' mean pranks on me."

He walked over and raced his hands over the wall and decided that those massive doors could not simply be covering a brick wall. His master had liked a joke at his expense, but this was old brick and must have been done before he became employed by the master. Sampson never recalled any construction ever going on at the mansion for as long as he had been there. He went and got a hammer and pick and started working on the wall. He was old and the work was tough. He was sweating heavily in the humid stale air. He worked for hours until he had broken through enough brick to tell that there was space beyond. He worked longer until he made a hole big enough to climb into. He lit an old kerosene lamp and lifted himself into the gaping hole, past the broken brickwork.

He was in a narrow passage that sloped downward and had steps. With the lamp in hand, he started down the rock steps and the air got cooler and felt damper with each step. There appeared to be a lot of moss, or mold, growing on the walls so he avoided touching them. He only went down one short flight before a room opened up. Stepping into the room, he realized that it was nothing more than a large rock cavern. He figured that this must be the foundation of the house and the reason why it never gradually sank like some of the other swamp homes. He looked around and realized that this was the family crypt. There were stone coffins strewn about almost carelessly. Most were closed, but a few looked like they had been knocked over years ago, spilling their contents onto the floor. He could see old dusty bones littering some spots of the floor.

As his eyes adjusted to the darkness that was only pierced by the soft glow from the lamp, he was able to walk around and read the inscriptions. He found his dead master's coffin in the middle of the cavern crypt. It was closed. He knew that any wealth might be in the coffin with the body. He carefully laid the lantern down nearby and managed to push off the massive stone lid. It fell with a heavy thud and Sampson came face to face with the corpse of Old Man Gower.

"Oh . . . Damn . . ." he whispered as his face contorted into a look of disgust tinged with fear.

He saw a hideous death's head grin upon the face even though flesh was still on it. It looked to Sampson as if his master was laughing at him from beyond the grave. He remembered the dead mortician had some secret way to get the body down here and was angry that he had been kept out of that secret. Infuriated, Sampson grabbed the body and threw it out of the coffin. There was no real reason to do this, but it satisfied a wish that he also held to someday treat Gower like this.

"I always wanted to do sumthin' like that to you old man. You was always bossin' and naggin' at me. When yous was younger ya' even switched me a few times. I still have the marks on my back. And all those mean tricks you used to play on me . . . now the Devil hisself will be playin' em on you! Ha! You don't deserve no eternal rest in a fine coffin. No sir. The cold, hard dirt floor is good enough for ya'."

Sampson felt better and thought about leaving the crypt now that he had his revenge. He picked up the lantern and something shiny caught his vision. Inside of the now empty stone coffin was a round object, about two feet across, made out of what appeared to be pure gold! He peered inside and touched it and knew right away that it was gold. This must be the fabled gold hoard the family had always kept secret. He remembered that Gower and boasted that the entire family had always depended on their gold. Now this gold could be his. The 'giant cold coin,' as he came to think of it, had two smaller rings of gold attached to it. He knew what to do.

After a few minutes of getting the donkey into position in the stairwell with a rope attached between it and the 'giant gold coin,' he was ready.

"Now, beast! Pull!" he screamed at it as he flicked his whip and ran to watch as the gold started to budge. It barely moved so Sampson whipped the donkey harder and faster until the gold finally popped out of the coffin and with it water started to gush out of the place that the gold had been. Sampson ran to look at the gold plug and saw that it was massive. It was shaped like a giant bath plug and it must have weighed a couple hundred pounds.

"I is rich! I can buy this whole land now! I can buy sumthin' even better! I can live like a king!"

Sampson was so intent on examining the gold that he did not notice that the floor was now about a foot deep in water. The coffin hole continued to pour the surrounding swamp into the cavern and Sampson finally started to realize that he should take his treasure and leave as the water got to a depth of about three feet. He realized that he could not pick up the gold so he was going to whip the donkey to pull it out, but he could not find the whip. He had tossed it aside and it was lost to him now. He made his way over to the donkey and tried to push it up the narrow flight of steps, but he could not get it to budge. The water was now rising faster and faster. He started to panic and hit the donkey repeatedly, as hard as he could, until the donkey kicked him backwards into the putrid waters of the crypt. The actions of the donkey caused a small cave in at the stairs and the animal died as he became lodged under the falling mass of stones and earth.

By the time Sampson regained his breath, the water level had risen to almost five feet. He kicked his legs around until he found on of the coffins to stand on, but this only gave him a short reprieve. As the water level rose to the top and Sampson desperately sought air pockets in the rock ceiling, the body of his former master floated by within two inches from his face. Sampson could still see a little as the glass lamp had floated up with the water. He could clearly see the head, with its evil grin. It seemed to be watching Sampson and gloating in its final triumph as the Louisiana swamp consumed everything in the crypt. Sampson's last thought before dying was remembering what his master had always said . . . "No one will ever get my gold. The man who tries . . . dies. You can't beat the dead."

David Eccles
The Esoteric Espial

We really should learn to pay more attention to what our parents tell us. By that I mean we should actually listen to what it is they have to say; hear the message behind the words; take it on board and act on it, 'cause at the end of it all, everything they ever say or do is for our own benefit. They only want their children to grow up safe and become well-adjusted adults, free from the pain and the sorrow they suffered due to their own selfish stupidity and unwillingness to follow the advice and guidance their own parents offered.

I know I sure wished I'd listened to my dad. I might have been spared from the awful dreams I've been having lately. I'll even admit they've gotten so bad lately I've woken up only to find out I've actually pissed the bed! It hasn't got to the point yet where I've woken up and found myself covered in shit, but I think it's only a matter of time, unless I figure out some way to end my nightmares.

I wish my dad hadn't asked for my help in tidying up the cellar and getting rid of all that old, unwanted stuff. When I say he asked for my help, what I really mean is that he expected me to do it all by myself, because he left me down there in the murky gloom, with a shitty light bulb that when lit, made the room look darker! To his credit though, he did warn me not to fuck around with or touch anything; he said I was simply to bag everything and leave it outside for some guys with a wagon to collect, which I did. Well, I say I did, but you know boys and their toys! I just couldn't help but play with some of the cool shit that I unearthed, and I did actually unearth something!

I didn't know where to start, at first; it was daunting enough just looking at the amount of stuff my dad had hoarded over the years. There were heavy hessian sacks piled up on top of even heavier iron-banded wooden chests, plus leaning stacks of long, wooden handled spear-like weapons, the tips of which appeared to be made of a black, glassy substance. And sharp! Fuck me! I nearly took my thumb off just testing the edge of one spear that had three parallel spikes! Tines, I think they're called. I put that fucker to one side; it was something I wanted to keep for myself.

Making the decision to take out all of the lighter items first, I hauled each of the sacks up the stairs, through the kitchen and outside, where I left them in a huge mound by the side of the trashcan. Dripping with sweat and covered in a layer of dust and dirt by the time I had dumped the last of them, my calf muscles and my thighs screamed in protest, begging for me to stop and rest a while.

I stopped for a moment, caught my breath and then pressed on with the task, gritting my teeth as I dragged each one of the heavy wooden chests up the stairs, aided by a harness I fashioned out of some leather straps and a length of rope that I found lying around. It definitely made life easier, though the leather straps still cut deep into my shoulders.

Before long, all that remained for me to do was take out a few dozen leather-bound ledgers that looked like they had been here since the beginning of time. Dust-covered, mildewed and blanketed in spider webs, they reeked like nothing I had ever smelled before, and I gagged as I randomly picked one and flipped it open to view its contents. All it contained was peoples' names, and I immediately recognized the author. The handwriting was my father's. I set it down, and chose another. More names. I snapped the book shut, sneezing at the cloud I had created. Dust motes floated in the stale air, made visible and somehow rather beautiful by the dim light radiating from the light bulb overhead.

Coughing, I picked up the books, a dozen or so at a time and carried them outside, depositing them with the rest of the trash. After the thirteenth trip, I was done, and all that remained for me to do was to grab a broom and sweep the place clean. I half-filled a bucket with water from the kitchen faucet and returned to the cellar where I set about throwing handfuls of water on the ground to help keep the dust down as I swept. In one particular spot where the books had been stacked, the water seemed to soak into the ground and disappear, and just for a moment I thought I could hear the faint sounds of people screaming beneath my feet. I paused, listened. There it was again!

I got down on my knees, clawed at the ground and moved the dirt and dust away with my bare hands before remembering that I had a broom to hand. I swept frantically, only slowing down as I began to recognize what it was that I had discovered: a man-sized door recessed into the floor of the cellar.

Covered in an illuminated, long-forgotten arcane script that could easily have been mistaken for graffiti, it appeared to be made of a densely-grained hardwood the color of blood, and was banded in broad belts of iron held in place with nails forged from the same black, glassy substance as the spearheads. There appeared to be no locking mechanism built into the door, and no handle to facilitate its opening. The screaming behind the door grew ever louder, and I knew that I needed to know what was on the other side of it.

Snatching up the trident I had left propped up in the corner of the cellar, I jammed the tines into the minute crack between the door and door frame, hyperventilating slightly as I prepared to exert all my strength and try to lever the door open. Pulling down as hard as I could, and using my whole body weight to assist me, I felt the door give slightly, and redoubled my efforts. Its hidden hinges freed up with a deep, groaning sound, there was an ear-splitting roar as an equalization of atmospheric pressure took place, and I found that I could lift the door to a perpendicular position with my fingers. Dropping to the floor from my exertions, I lay gasping for a few moments, and then rolled onto my side to investigate the noises I had heard.

I lowered my head into the gloom, and as my eyes grew accustomed to the darkness, images that could only have been spawned in a nightmare began to form before my eyes, and those terrible screams grew to a pitch so intense I feared that my eardrums would burst. I knew immediately that I was witness to a scene that was not of this world.

The foreground was a barren, fine-grained sandy desert, and yet a raging torrent of unimaginable height crashed down in the background, swallowing up strange, diverse creatures by the dozen; beings with skin of an insanely unnatural hue, stretched tight by the cruel sun under which they battled.

Two warring factions hurled a spherical weapon at each other over a partition of some kind, and although, while appearing to be of the same species the larger and more horrendously bloated of the two sets of combatants seemed to have a huge strength advantage, their more lithe and much smaller adversaries had an advantage with regard to speed and agility.

The smaller faction, however, seemed to be experiencing a rather painful form of torture whereby strips of cloth of extreme tightness had been bound around them at strategically determined parts of their body, for they clawed at the strips to prevent them from digging into their soft, giving flesh.

Their screams seemed to penetrate deep into my brain, and that, combined with the display of violence and the sheer ugliness of their deformed bodies forced me to turn away and to slam shut the cellar door and close forever the terrible portal between our two worlds.

In blind terror, I rushed up the stairs and out of the house, and to this day I have remained silent as to the horrors I was exposed to.

Some things are just better left unsaid, don't you think?

We couldn't have picked a better day, thought Kelly. Breathless, but elated at winning that last point, the four girls were in line to beat the guys for the first time, and it would be a sweet victory indeed!

"Okay, guys. Are you ready? Last point! You're going down!"

The hoots of derision from the four guys on the opposite side of the net were drowned out by the huge crowd that had gathered to watch this spectacular display of beach volleyball. They roared with approval at Kelly's bravado, and she turned and smiled at them, the perfect whiteness of her teeth in contrast to the burnished bronze of her skin. She wanted to finish the game in style, and Kelly paused for a moment before serving, taking the time to brush the sand from her body and retrieve her bikini bottoms which had somehow worked their way into the crack of her ass.

Readying herself for what she hoped would be the final serve of the match she shivered suddenly as an ice-cold blast assaulted her skin. Goosebumps rose on her forearms, and her nipples hardened. Kelly had the sudden feeling that she was being watched, but she shrugged inwardly and dismissed it as nervousness at the thought of winning. Of course she was being watched! She and her three friends were about to serve the guys a huge slice of humble pie.

Kelly launched the volleyball over the net, and a huge triumphal scream erupted from the crowd as the guys' return, hit rather clumsily, touched first the net and then the sand, sealing the win.

Matt Cowan
Numen

"By the way, John, the bathroom speaks at night," Amanda said, opening a box marked KITCHEN.

John glanced over from hanging a picture in the adjacent room. "How unique, surprised they didn't charge extra for it."

Amanda placed a toaster on the counter. "Definitely don't tell him then. We can't afford any more and won't find anyplace cheaper."

"We're living in the cellar of a rent--controlled apartment complex, can't get much cheaper than that," John muttered, inspecting his work. He'd bought the painting of a man and woman's hands clasped together highlighting their wedding rings while still employed at Baxter Finance. Things were good then.

Amanda hugged him from behind, kissing his cheek. Despair was consuming him again. He'd been that way since losing his job, blaming himself for their having to sell the big house to pay off the debts he'd racked up. She'd tried to warn him they were living beyond their means, but he was certain he'd get a promotion big enough to cover everything. "It's not so bad," she whispered in his ear. "Once we get everything situated, it'll be cozy."

"I suppose it'll have to," he said returning the kiss. "So what does it say?"

Amanda gave him a confused look. "What?"

"The bathroom, you said it talks. What does it say?"

Amanda laughed. "I heard it last night when I got up around 2 o'clock. It sounded like muttering in the walls, saying, 'Where do the mares dwell?' or 'There's the nightmare well'... something like that."

John shook his head. "Sounds like you were either half asleep remembering a dream, or you heard someone talking in the room above us. If that's the case, we should be careful ourselves, no telling who might be listening."

"I guess that must've been it."

John took her by the hand. "Now, what say we take a break from unpacking and grab a burger from that joint down the street?"

Amanda winced. "How about I fix us some macaroni and cheese instead? We can eat it on the picnic table outside."

John's smile faded. "We aren't so poor we can't afford a couple of burgers, you know."

Amanda raised her hands in a calming gesture. "I know, but we need to ration how often we do that. Our budget's going to be tight for a while. For today just let me fix us something here?"

The muscle in his jaw throbbed the way it did whenever he got angry. "Fine," he said before retreating to their bedroom.

The next day John left early for a job interview at a bank around the corner. He wasn't thrilled about it. The pay was a fraction of what he made before, but Amanda convinced him to give it a shot. The unemployment benefits wouldn't last forever. She got up soon afterwards to continue unpacking. Opening the linen closet in the bathroom, a sheet of paper floated down from the top shelf to rest at her feet. She picked it up, examining the rough, charcoal sketch of a tall man on a vast throne, his face nothing but a leering smile. A crown of long, curved bones jutted from his head. She wadded it up and tossed it into the trash.

By midafternoon Amanda felt she'd made enough progress to warrant a break. The bare cement hallway outside her apartment was dark, illuminated by dim, flickering tube lights. Approaching the dust--covered vending machine alcove, she glanced at the door closest to hers. Its pasty, tan metallic surface was marred by swelled paint bubbles that bled liquid rust, giving it a sickly organic appearance. When she'd first seen it, its deplorable condition nearly put her off taking the place, but the landlord said it was an old utility room mostly used for storage these days, and he planned to replace it soon.

Amanda dropped two quarters into the machine, retrieving the generic soda that clunked out before returning to her room. Settling in before her desk, she began working on an article she hoped to sell to the local paper about an upcoming art exhibit.

John had little to say when he returned home. The bank took his resume and said they'd let him know in a few days. Amanda tried to cheer him up by suggesting they go for a stroll around the block, but he wasn't interested. Instead he sank into his recliner and watched TV the rest of the day. At dinner her attempts to start a conversation received mumbled replies. He went to bed early, claiming the move had worn him out. If he didn't find a job soon, she feared depression would overwhelm him.

Amanda woke in the middle of the night roused by a scratching from the bathroom. She thought about waking John, but he was sleeping so peacefully she didn't want to disturb him. Sliding out of bed into her slippers, she shuffled to the bathroom closing the door before turning on the lights. A stench like unwashed, sweaty bodies permeated the small room. Pinching her nose, she listened for several seconds. All was silent. After a fruitless search, she was about to return to bed when she heard the garbled voice again saying something she couldn't understand. The only words she could make out were, *"sleep", "reason" and "produces"*.

"Hello?" Amanda said, quieter than she meant. "Whoever's talking, can you hear me?"

There was no response at first, but after a minute the scratching returned. It came from above her head near the ceiling. Amanda envisioned long, sharp claws digging their way through to her. She fled back to the bedroom.

The next morning John got his tools and promised to investigate. He'd heard nothing, but Amanda insisted he check it out. If it was a rat, they'd make the landlord get an exterminator. Amanda took the car they shared to get groceries while John worked. Exiting the apartment, she heard something moving behind the utility door. She ignored it as she raced up the dingy stairwell to the ground level of the Gallant House Apartment Complex and on to her car.

Amanda returned to find John in his recliner watching TV, his clothes speckled with white dust. "So, did you find anything?"

"I did," he said getting up to help with the groceries. "Let's set these down so I can show you how I solved the mystery of the blathering bathroom."

Drywall dust covered the sink and toilet below a new cavity in the wall.

"Stand on the ladder and take a look," he said, pulling it before the opening.

Amanda did as he asked. Mildewed air flowed from a tarnished, brass scroll--worked grate just beyond the drywall. Looking through it, she saw into a dark room filled with vague shapes. "This must be inside that room with the repulsive door. What do you think made those sounds... or the voices?"

"I don't know, but if it's a rat, I don't see it getting through that grate to reach us. As to the voices, maybe you heard a maintenance man getting supplies or something," John suggested with a shrug. "The vent must have been part of the buildings old ventilation system. I guess they've updated since then."

Amanda shook her head. "I don't think they use that room anymore, and the maintenance men avoid this level like the plague."

Before John could reply the kitchen phone rang. Amanda continued to peer into the blackened room while he left to answer it. She thought most of the shapes must be furniture, a couch, a large chair, an overturned desk with legs jutted up like a beetle stuck on its back. To one side something skittered away from the patch of light cast from the new hole in the wall. Its flailing movements seemed erratic, but it moved so fast she wasn't convinced she'd seen it.

John's excited voice drew her to the kitchen. Still on the phone, his smile was brighter than it'd been in weeks. "No, I completely understand. I can be there by 8:00 if you like?" He listened, chuckled, then spoke again. "Excellent, I'll see you then."

"Who was that?"

"Guy from an investment firm. They must've found my resume online. He wants to meet for diner tonight to talk about a job."

"That's fantastic!" Amanda said pulling him into an embrace. "Have you heard of them before?"

"No, I think they're new. I'll find out more tonight," he said pulling away towards the bedroom. "I need to get ready."

After showering and changing clothes, he gave Amanda a kiss on his way out. Once he'd gone, Amanda took the vacuum into the bathroom to clean up the drywall dust. She snapped it off, silencing it, when the voice began speaking again. Clip--clopping footsteps echoed from the hole in the wall. Pulling up the ladder, she peered through the vent. Everything looked the same. She thought something shifted in the shadowed recesses of the chamber but couldn't be certain. She tried to recall what she thought the voice said. "When opportunity knocks, the ambitious must pass through its door."

As the night ticked away, Amanda struggled to occupy herself, cleaning the apartment, watching TV, reading, but she couldn't focus on anything. Eventually she went to the computer to work on her article. She had trouble staying on task at first but soon fell into a groove. The artist whose work was being shown was a surrealistic painter named Artero Lima. His pieces were perpetually bleak, a tortured soul like so many artists tended to be. Flicking through an online gallery dedicated to him, she paused at a piece titled *Numen*, recognizing the garish, smiling man on the throne with a crown of giant bones on his head. The styles between it and the paper she found in the bathroom were vastly different, making her wonder if the sketch was a weak attempt to imitate Artero, or if they had perhaps been inspired by a common source. Tabbing over, she looked up *Numen*, focusing on the top search result for the latin word: "The presiding divinity or spirit of a place".

Shifting gears, Amanda began researching Lima's artistic influences. She came across a 1797 etching done by Francisco Goya. It showed the artist himself, head slumped on a table, assailed by a horde of bats and owls. It was entitled *The Sleep of Reason Produces Monsters*. Hadn't the voice from the vent the other day said something similar? Could someone in the other room have been mentioning the etching?

This drove her to research the history of The Gallant House. It catered to young, creative minds due to its proximity to the local art college and its affordable rent. Several prominent painters, sculptors and poets had stayed there. The few who spoke about it said they forged their bleakest but most inventive creations within its dingy walls, one going so far as to claim The Gallant House was 'home to a brilliant, sadistic muse'.

Moving on to news sites she found an article about a pair of coed art students, who'd gone missing. They'd been renting the apartment she and John now shared when it happened. The case remained open with no motive or suspect.

The sound of footsteps descending the hallway stairs led Amanda away from her computer. She had to tell John what she'd discovered. She needed him to help her make sense of it all. The footsteps continued on past her door. Peering out the peephole, she saw someone entering the utility room, a maintenance man perhaps. Maybe he would let her inside to look around, put her mind at ease. She entered the hall in time to see the utility room door creak shut.

Reluctantly, Amanda approached the pale, disfigured door. An animalistic stench wafted off it, reminding her of a dead mole they found in the pool at their old house a few years ago. She closed her eyes and gave it a single knock before snatching back her hand. The door was cold and beaded with moisture. It felt like the flesh of a drowned corpse. "Hello?" she called, voice shaking. "If someone's in there, I need to speak with you."

When she got no reply, Amanda steeled herself and rapped on the door again. It gave like a sponge, excreting a yellowed fluid onto her hand. A wave of nausea overwhelmed her. She turned and fled back to her apartment, vomiting into the toilet seconds afterward. Once purged of her dinner, Amanda knelt in the silent room trying to compose herself.

A quiet chuckle echoed from the vent. Amanda tensed as the voice spoke, clearly this time. "The court of the Dead Prince welcomes a new member this night," it said, sounding amused.

Amanda ran from the bathroom, slamming the door behind her as she snatched up her phone to dial John's cell. His voicemail answered. She repeated the attempt, leaving messages begging him to call her back. When she calmed down, she resolved to find out who had spoken now that she knew someone was in the room. Taking a flashlight from the pantry, she climbed the ladder and peered inside.

The stygian darkness absorbed most of the light, but some of the furniture became more visible. A rotting, plaid couch lay to the right, foam stuffing erupting from torn fabric. The upturned desk was dented and stained with red paint. Beyond it, half concealed by shadows, rested a large, obsidian chair. Something moved about the room, receding from view whenever she tried to catch it in her flashlight's anemic beam. Voices sounded from a corner. She stepped higher on the ladder, shifting her light toward it. Something large scampered across the beam, allowing her a brief glimpse. It moved upright on more than two legs, its flesh was white with a line of yellowed pustules along its core. Appendages thrashed above it, seeking purchase against the wall as it pirouetted out of view.

Amanda screamed, falling from the ladder at the sight of the abomination. Without stopping to assess any damage, she snatched her phone in shaking hands to dial John again.

It rang several times before he answered. "What is it Amanda?" he whispered sharply. "I'm at the interview." The anger in his voice surprised her.

"John, I'm sorry, but something's happening. There's some sort of... creature or something in that utility room. I need you here!" the words tumbled from her mouth.

"Do you understand what this means for us? This is the opportunity we've been waiting for! Everything depends on me getting this job, and you chose now to freak out about monsters of all things! Are you kidding me?"

"What? No, it's--"

The receiver captured another man's voice. "John, we are very interested in you," he said. "Your other employer may have been foolish enough to let you go, but I assure you... once you pass through our door, you'll never leave. What do you say? Will you answer this knock of opportunity?"

Amanda recognized the voice. "John! That's him! That's who I've been hearing!"

"I'm too busy for this nonsense. I'll deal with you later."

"No John, you don't understand. This must be a trick. I--" the line went dead before she could finish.

"Your turn's coming, my dear," the voice came again from the wall. It sounded closer this time, like the speaker stood directly opposite her bathroom wall.

Amanda's mind churned with all that had happened since moving in. Something inhuman resided in the dank utility closet in the cellar of The Gallant House, and if she didn't act soon, she feared it would claim her husband. She ran up the ladder in time to see something recede. Thrusting her dying flashlight into the cavity illuminated a figure moving toward the obsidian chair, she now recognized was a throne. It wasn't alone. Someone else stepped into view to regard Amanda.

"John?" Amanda gasped.

He looked confused. "What are you doing here?" he asked, as though in a haze.

A bulky, misshapen figure scuttled out from the shadows behind John.

"Get out of there, John!" Amanda screamed.

He looked perplexed, not noticing the bulky form shuffling toward him. "What are you talking about?"

"John! It's behind you! Look out!" she screamed, but it was too late.

A hideous creature moved into the halo of her flashlight. The unholy abomination was a mish-mashed collection of arms and legs topped by a pair of gibbering heads facing opposite each other. Its movements were uncoordinated causing it to turn several times as each head struggled to look at John.

The realization of what the creature was sickened Amanda; two human beings connected back to back to form a single torso, half of it male, the other female. Its eyes were glazed white like a corpse. Both faces stretched their mouths to bare teeth filed into spikes. They emitted an agonized moan in unison. John's eyes widened as the thing grabbed him with flailing arms. Sickening cracks and gurgles sounded as it pulled him from view. Amanda's light caught someone stepping off the throne before the batteries gave out. He was bloodless, wearing a crown of bones. His unnaturally wide mouth smiled at her with dry, split lips.

She ran from the apartment into the hall. The utility room door stood open. Beyond it the male side of the four--armed amalgamation struggled to reach behind itself to grab John who was held tight by the female side. The dead girl's head buried sharp fangs into John's neck, spewing forth blood in torrents.

The figure on the throne strode past the carnage. "Amanda," its commanding tone called from the doorway. "Come. Your husband needs you now more than ever."

She hesitated as the male side of the beast spun its snarling counterpart away to take its place in the feeding frenzy on John's limp body.

"Fear not," the crowned man said. "He will live again. I will immortalize him... and you as well. I will turn you and your husband into a new masterpiece. You will be together forever. Is that not what you've always wanted?" He asked, full--lipped mouth stretched into a wide grin.

"It was," she whispered through a sob as she turned and raced up the stairwell, exiting The Gallant House apartments forever.

M. J. Sydney
Ellensburg Blue

I imagine the town locals invisible and non-existent as they pass me on Saint Bernard Street, staring at me, giving me that look. Heads shake in disbelief, or maybe pity. To some, I am not even here. They look on and I am the invisible one. They think I don't see them, but I do. I hear their silent whispers of disdain, muttered amongst themselves as I walk by. I can't blame them. Even the real estate agent thought I was pulling a prank when I told him I wanted to purchase the old Waters' property.

I never had someone laugh at me for five minutes straight before. He laughed so hard he choked on his own breath. I think it was my silence and lack of joining in on the charade that replaced his cackling with a horrified look of astonishment. His voice trembled for the next hour and half as he recounted every rumor and story that had surfaced since 1997. His eyes sunk deeper with the signing of the papers but the deal was done. *That property is plagued with evil* he told me.

A hoax. It's all a hoax. I slip in through the open door of Tony's Hardware and easily find everything I'm looking for – small family run shops always have everything right there on the shelf where you'd expect. Not like walking into McLendon's or Home Depot. I talked to Tony yesterday and he agreed to deliver all the lumber, bricks, shingles and paint so that just leaves a few basics – nails, hammer, staple gun, screws, screw drivers, putty, plaster, window sealant, paintbrushes, broom, mop, shovel, four boxes of trash bags.

The man behind the counter, arms folded across his chest, watches me, skeptically, as I pull the yellow notepad from my back pocket and make some notes. His voice doesn't make a sound but his eyes speak loud and clear. *Don't even think about running out that door*, they say, contemplating who I am and if I have the money to pay for all this.

"You must be Walter Melbrook. I wasn't expectin' to see you here today." I recognize the stern voice from behind the counter.

"I told you yesterday when we spoke on the phone I'd be here. And I'm here."

"Just we don't get many people around here showing interest in the old Waters' place. With all the rumors and such. Hard to believe some out-of-towner just up and bought the place, ya know?"

"Well believe it. I did. And it's in bad shape. Doesn't look like anyone's been in that house since Waters himself left."

"Damn good reasons for that too, mister. You sure you know what you've gotten into? No one here'd blame you if you changed your mind and ran the other way."

"It'll be a nice place once I'm done with it. Here, I've added a few more things to the list. How soon can you have them out there?" Tony's arms loosen up and he almost cracks a smile as I tear the top sheet off the notepad and hand it to him. I can't tell if he's amused by the situation or thinks he successfully scared me off.

"Same as I told you yesterday. I'll deliver everything by tomorrow afternoon if you're still here. You sure you're still gonna be here? "

"I'm sure," I nod, slapping thirty-five fifty dollar bills on the counter, the hint of sarcasm in my voice surprises us both.

Tony's head tilts, eyes squinting down at the pile of Grant's on the counter. In less than a blink, he raises both eyebrows, darting eyes pierce through my skull and his mouth twists into a sour lemon pucker.

"That's quite a load of cash to be carryin' around," I barely hear his voice. *Where'd you get that? You rob a bank? Selling drugs? You kill someone?* His eyes speak louder than his voice.

"I don't like banks." More sarcasm. Not that I want to give Tony any more reason to be weary of my intentions in this town, but I'm damn tired of everyone questioning me. Let me go about my business and leave me alone. That's why I moved out here.

I can't help but notice the slight trembling in his hands as he places the bills securely in the register, coming back with two one dollar bills, three quarters, a nickel and four pennies. I slide the change into my back pocket with the note pad, tell him thank you and I'll see him tomorrow. As I open the door, the sound of cowbells clank against the handle, followed by Tony's voice from behind the counter.

"One more thing," he starts, pausing long enough to make sure I hear him. "You'll have to unload this stuff yourself. I won't be subjecting myself to no Goatman's curse or moon-shining ghosts."

Back at the house, I open the third box of trash bags, having gone through the other two boxes. With so much work to be done, there's no sense in waiting until tomorrow for Tony to bring the rest of my supplies. Rotten food, broken dishes, mildew-stained books, torn clothing, moth-eaten blankets, something that appears to have once been a rat or maybe a squirrel. There's nothing worth keeping. The broken floorboards, termite-infested wood, rat-gnawed furniture and most everything else, I heap into a pile out back. It's tempting to set fire to the whole mess now rather than wait on Tony for the bricks, but the need for sleep wins.

The old army tent from the shack out back serves me well. Despite the condition of the house and obvious neglect of the property, the little shack is in great shape aside from the musty smell that comes from having everything locked up for so many years. Sleep doesn't come easy– the glaring looks from the townspeople permanently imprinted on my eyelids. The lullaby of their whispering voices finally sings me to sleep, but I couldn't tell you what time. The next thing I hear is the screaming of a car horn telling me Tony arrived just as promised – although he's earlier than I expected.

I pull on my overalls and work boots, wishing I had remembered to buy a coffee pot while I was in town yesterday.

"This is as far as I go, mister," Tony calls to me from the bottom of the long driveway, engine still running. Through the partially rolled-down window of the old truck, his eyes dart around in every direction. It' an amusing sight to wake up to – he looks as if he's expecting something to jump out and drag him underground. Tony kept that look on his face for most of the day, sitting there in silence while I soak myself in sweat unloading the truck, carrying bricks and lumber up what felt like a mile long driveway by midday.

"You about done here? I want to get outta here before dark and I gotta piss something fierce."

Get off your ass and help you lazy bastard. I nodded, unloading the last of the bricks, laying them out at the end of the driveway. Tony was losing his patience and I didn't want to say something I might regret later in case I needed him again. I thanked him and he told me to call him if I needed anything else brought out to the house. I doubt he meant it but I thanked him all the same.

I spent the next week fixing leaks in the roof, replacing rotted out floorboards in the bedroom and burning rat-infested mattresses, along with everything else in the heap out back. The night air is still warm and I don't mind sleeping with the fire pit smoldering through the night, but I miss the firmness of a mattress lined with cool sheets and covered with warm blankets. With the bedroom finished, I spend the next week completely gutting out the kitchen, ripping out the leftover remnants of carpet throughout the house and wishing it were Wednesday already so I can sleep in a warm bed and eat something other than freeze-dried rubber.

The moving truck arrives early in the afternoon and I'm already covered in paint. Again, I'm forced to unload the truck myself. The deliverymen aren't even from this town but said they heard enough rumors to know better than to even think about setting foot up here. As I'm moving furniture and unloading boxes, I realize the two men sitting in the truck are intent on freaking each other out with the stories they've heard about the property.

I've come to the conclusion that the people around here are all crazy, no matter where they come from. Tales of the Goatman and moon-shining and dead animals coming back to life – nothing but ridiculous superstition. Hoaxes. How can anyone believe such nonsense? No doubt, a strangeness has come to haunt this town over the last fifty years. It's the townspeople themselves that have gone mad, not some mysterious hole that never existed.

A few minutes before midnight, I sprawl out in bed for the first time in two weeks. Sleep isn't coming as I intended. My mind has other plans. As I lay here staring into the darkness on the ceiling, my body relaxes and soaks in the coolness of the sheets while my mind focuses on Mel Waters and The Hole.

I can hear Art Bell talking to Mel Waters on the Coast to Coast AM Radio back in 1997, but that's not what keeps me awake. The realtor and Tony both offered to let me listen to the transcripts but I told them I had no interest in a fifty year old talk show. It's the words of the locals and the visions forming and floating overhead that keep me awake.

"That hole has magical powers, you know."

"That old German gun they found in the dirt by the hole don't even make a sound."

"They say if you set the gun next to a radio, it replays ancient broadcasts."

Magical powers, right. And a 1943 Roosevelt dime – they didn't even make those until 1946. I smiled at the thought of the old woman claiming the gun and dimes were the result of an alternate reality in which the Nazis won the war and created the dimes in Berlin.

Less amusing are the visions forming in the shadows on the ceiling – the hunter's dead dog, the Goatman, moon-shining, mine shafts, lava tubes, civil war slaves, roadblocks and Waters with his IV scars, surgical tape residue and missing molars. *And what about the Ellensburg Blue Agate, does it even exist anymore?*

My feet involuntarily slide off the side of the bed as I glance at my watch, illuminated by the glow of the near full moon creeping in through the window. *3:00 am. Looks like I'm not sleeping tonight.*

Downstairs, my eyes fixate on the gallons of paint lined up against the wall while I wait for the coffee to brew. I grab a brush and hunch over a beige-colored bucket of paint, one hand gripped on the handle. A flash of light jerks me upright and I spin towards the kitchen window. The bucket hits the cabinet and bounces to the floor.

"What the hell?" I barely notice the beige river flowing across the kitchen floor, mesmerized by the strange black light shining, seemingly, straight up from the ground. I must have grabbed the baseball bat I keep next to the kitchen door in case critters ever try to come inside. I don't remember picking it up but there it is in my hand as I walk out the door barefoot.

As I walk through the field towards the other side of the property, I'm sure a slug squishes between my toes, or maybe it's a snake. I pay no attention to it as I move towards the black light, holding the bat steadily above my right shoulder. There it is. The light shines up from underneath a nine-foot wide metal lid, like a manhole cover – but not. Is that even a light?

My mind replays the stories of the old well on the property where locals threw garbage, abandoned vehicles, deceased pets and livestock, old tires, run-down appliances and damned if I know what else. No one ever mentioned anything about a light coming up out of it. I hadn't made it this far out on the property before tonight, but I suspect this is the well the locals used as a public dumping ground.

That's one hell of a large well. I creep closer to get a better look at the cover, but my legs are weighted to the ground. Can such a light even exist? It's black, almost like a void – a light of nothingness. Yet, there it is coming up through the ground and around the rim of the metal plate. And it's quiet. Too quiet. A complete absence of sound. As I move closer, the light shines brighter and darker. I can't look away, nor do I want to.

Squatting down close to the ground, right hand numb from gripping the bat, I reach my good arm out towards the rim of the metal plate. I sense something following me, watching me. My head whips around and I look over my left shoulder. Nothing there. I reach out farther. Warm air encircled in ice touches my fingertips as they brush against the metal.

The sound of breathing – no, not breathing, panting – and the steam of hot breath running down the back of my leg hit me. The black light vanishes, replaced by a red glow coming from behind me. Cranking my head around to the right, from my crouched position, my eyes lock on snarling teeth. Blood red eyes meet mine, glaring back at me. Our eyes locked together, seemingly forever.

With snarling teeth pressed against my leg and blurry vision, I try to refocus and break free from the hypnotizing red eyes. The bat swings itself at the snarling teeth as I jolt up and run towards the house, all in one motion. I'm not sure I'm running in the right direction and I don't care. I just run. The slug squishes through my feet. I must be going the right way. The kitchen door. Did I leave it open? My feet slide across the beige kitchen floor as I fall on my ass and stumble to my knees. The door slams shut and deadbolts, rattling the cabinets, as I push the stove against the door, slip in the paint again and slide down the side of the stove.

What the hell was that?

I'm sitting in a damn puddle of paint. Brought back to reality, I jump up to look for my bat. Damn, I must have dropped it. Where, I don't know. I look through the kitchen window, gazing out over the field. I dismiss the thought of boarding up the windows. The locals already think I'm crazy for buying this place. The black light is gone. No snarling teeth or red glow. Crickets chirp in the distance and a light breeze passes by. Nothing unusual here. Must have imagined the whole damned thing. Sleep deprivation. Right, that's all it is.

The aroma of freshly brewed coffee fills the kitchen. It's tempting but I dump it down the drain in favor of the homemade blackberry brandy my sister gave me last year. I've been saving it for a special occasion and this is as special as they get.

Despite the night's events, I awake with the sun. The empty bottle of brandy sleeps on my pillow. I need answers and if anyone can tell me what the hell is going on, it'll be Tony. He knows everything about this town's history and must have memorized every story and rumor ever told about this place. He's also the only person around here willing to carry on a conversation with me or even directly look at me. I decide to head over to the hardware store as soon as I find my bat. I can't imagine there'll be anything out there during the daylight, if there was anything out there at all, but I grab the knife off the kitchen counter just in case.

Everything appears just as it should be – there's no sign of anything happening out here last night. The grass in the field is undisturbed, no shining black light, the birds are happily chirping away. If it wasn't for the stove in front of the kitchen door, the spilled paint and missing bat, I would have thought I imagined the whole thing. Maybe I did. The bat isn't anywhere in the field – and neither is the manhole-covered well. Giving up the search, I head back to the house and notice the door to the shack is wide open.

Funny, I thought I locked that. It was no simple task locking up the shack, which required wrapping a large-link chain through the handle, around the side bar twice and back through the handle before clasping both ends together with the padlock. The chain dangled freely from the door handle with the open padlock hooked onto the last link.

With the padlock in my right hand, I use the left to wrap the chain. First through the handle, twice around the side bar and ... a sharp, shooting pain stabs through the center my left hand. The padlock hit the ground with a "clink", landing on something other than grass. The skin in the center of my palm caught between the links, pinching hard enough to leave a nasty blood blister. I free my hand and reach for the padlock. Dull, scratched up metal stares back up at me, not from the padlock, but from my bat.

How? No. I don't want to know. With the lock in place, I grab the bat and head over to Tony's Hardware. Tony looks shocked to see me there. Was it the bat? The fact I was still here? The shop is empty this morning so I waste no time asking Tony to tell me everything he knows. He looks away, fiddling with something under the counter.

"Go talk to the crazy old witch lady on Fruitland Avenue."

"I'd rather talk to you. Seems to me you know everything about this town and..."

"Leave me out of it."

"Can you at least tell me where I ..."

"You'll know when you see it. I ain't got nothin' else to say." Tony held the front door open. "Best be on your way now."

Tony shook his head and closed the door behind me. The deadbolt slides into place. I stand there for a moment, ready to knock, wanting him to talk to me, or at least tell me who this witch person is and where she lives. Instead, I head down Fruitland Avenue.

Tony was right. The house is unmistakable. Skulls in various shapes and species, presumably all replicas, litter the lawn, which is more of an herb and weed garden than a lawn. Large oak trees cast shadows on the house. Wind chimes line the gutters and statues with piercing eyes keep guard. A few cats scurry under the front porch as I open the screen door and knock.

"Go away!" A scratchy voice from inside the house.

"My name is Walter Melbrook. I'd like to ..."

"I know who you are. Go away!"

"Please, I'd just like to ask you a few questions."

"I can't help you. Now go or be cursed!"

"Look, something happened out there last night. A black light came out of the well and something tried to attack me. When I went out this morning, it was gone."

Silence from inside the house. The doorknob turns slowly and the hinges creak as the door opens, just enough that I can see her beady eyes peeking through, staring at me through the screen. The women standing before me isn't that old, but her hair has more rat nests than a horde of swamp rats and her dress is made of torn rags tied together. She isn't ugly but I can see why Tony called her the crazy witch. She says nothing but I have her attention. I recount every detail I can remember from last night, even slipping through the paint. I stop talking and I'm not sure she even heard me. Her eyes dig deep into mine as if she's trying to pierce my heart, or maybe my soul, with her eyes.

"The Ellensburg Blue Agate is cursed."

"Cursed?"

"Shh..." A long bony finger presses against her lips and her eyes tell me if I open my mouth again, she'll shut the door. I give her a warm smile as if to apologize and she continues.

"You see in the blackness what no one else sees. The powers of the stone are strong but the curse is stronger. It feeds and grows. Its light calls you from the void. The stone has chosen you. Beware the beasts of the underground. They feed on the E-blue, their deadly teeth made from broken shards. You must stop the beasts before their final feeding. After will be too late, for they will release all that lives down the bottomless hole."

I open my mouth to ask how in the hell I'm supposed to stop something that nearly turned me into its last meal. What comes out of my mouth is more of a hissing, guttural *hhhhhh* sound trapped in my throat. The woman stands there, ready to slam the door in my face if I finish the word. Aware of the bat in my hand, I grip it tighter, suck in a deep breath and let her continue in silence.

"Go to the well when the light shines darkest. Remove the sphere and enter the void. Take with you a pickaxe. You must go alone. Find the mother agate and destroy it. Bring none to the surface." The door shut as if it never opened.

I take the long way back to the house, first stopping at Tony's Hardware to buy a pickaxe. The old lady sure sounded crazy, but I bought the pickaxe anyway. I didn't have one so why not? I may have a use for it someday. I wanted to talk to Tony but the kid standing behind the counter says he left due to a family emergency. The townspeople must really think I'm nuts now – walking down the street with an old baseball bat in one hand and a shiny new pickaxe in the other.

After scraping the beige paint off the kitchen floor, I busy myself painting the rest of the afternoon and into the evening, trying not to think about the conversation with the witch-lady. Nevertheless, by nightfall, I'm spending more time looking out the damn kitchen window than painting. An hour before sunrise, I crawl in bed. For the next three days and nights, I paint and wait at the kitchen window. No shining black light. No snarling teeth. Just the sound of crickets singing in the wind under the star-lit sky.

Tuesday, more painting – outside this time. And I don't bother waiting tonight. I'm not even sure I saw it before, but I doubt I'll see it again. I paint all the trim on Wednesday. Not much left to do after that. I'll get to the bathrooms and deck tomorrow. Upstairs, I crawl in bed, sliding my hand under the pillow, feeling for the pickaxe. It's still there and I fall asleep, fingertips rubbing the smooth wood handle.

An hour or two later, my whole body jerks awake and my eyes involuntarily open, staring up at the ceiling. It's quiet. No singing crickets. The wind is still. The moon and stars blackened by the night. I look around and see nothing. Grabbing the pickaxe, I feel my way to the door, down the stairs and into the kitchen. The black light glowing through the window is heavy and dark. *Its light calls you from the void.* No, get out of my head! *The stone has chosen you. Go to the well...*

I don't know why, but I'm compelled to go, grabbing the bat on the way out. The light is there, shining darker than before, which means the well is there. My knuckles cramp against the bat and pickaxe, one in each hand. I can't let go, not that I want to, and my grip tightens. Last night's dinner threatens to regurgitate and the tennis ball in my throat strangles me, ready to burst open. I feel the hot breath encircled in ice against my legs. I hear the snarling. I see red. My head is dizzy from spinning in circles.

There is nothing there, but I sense it. I feel it. I'm ready to swing at the beast from every direction. It won't catch me off guard again.

Remove the sphere... I bend down and reach out towards the manhole cover with the bat, my eyes unable to focus, waiting for snarling teeth to press against my leg. No snarling teeth. No glowing red eyes. Just quiet darkness, alone with the light. I force myself to move forward, lifting, pulling, pushing at the manhole cover. It doesn't budge. My hands tingle in the dark light, a warm sensation surrounded in ice moves through my veins. I know I should be scared but it's peaceful and calming like a warm, candlelit bath. The bat and pickaxe slide out of my hands and gently rest at my feet.

With my body fully immersed in the black light, I push all my weight against the edge of the manhole cover. With little effort, the sphere – more like a half-moon that rolled like a sphere – spins then rolls off to the side of the well. Looking down, I see nothing but darkness, emptiness, nothingness. *And enter the void.* I'd rather not, but I do.

I slide down on my ass, feet first into the hole. *Shit!* I spin around and reach for the edge. Dangling by my fingertips, I grab for anything within reach – the pickaxe. Kicking and swinging my feet, they hit nothing but air. If this thing has sides, they are nowhere near the ledge. It's too late to climb back up and my fingers slip, grabbing a handful of grass as I fall – no, float – down into the void.

I don't know how far I've fallen or how long I've been down here, staring into nothingness. I must be getting close. Blue agate lined walls appear, moving closer together as I glide further down the well. The stones glow with black light, surrounded by light blue and deep purple rays. A tingling numbness runs through my veins and every pore fills with an icy warmth. A perfect utopia.

My feet stop me from continuing on the downward journey. I'm standing in a beach made entirely of Ellensburg Blue Agate shrouds and powdered stone and I'm brought back to the reality of where I am. I turn on the balls of my feet, looking for a sense of which direction to go. *The mother stone is close. I can feel it.* Panting hot breath surrounded in a layer of ice puffs against the back of my legs. I twist my body around. There's nothing there.

The panting moves up my legs, down my arms, around my chest and face. I hear a pack of snarling teeth somewhere in the distance. The pickaxe swings and whirls around into nothingness. The panting and snarling move in closer. The hot breath consumes me. I'm surrounded by hundreds of pairs of glowing red eyes.

"Nooooo!!" The pickaxe swings wildly – left, right, up, down, diagonally, in spirals and zigzags.

Walter's voice trails off and the weapon falls in a pile of agate dust. The beasts eat their final meal, devouring Walter piece by piece, amputating the limbs first.

The beasts emerge from the well – cows, cats, dogs, chickens, rats, birds, horses, a llama, goatmen, moonshiners – snarling, showing off their E-blue agate teeth and glowing red eyes.

The phone rings at midnight.

"It's done, master. The beasts are free," a scratchy voice on the line proclaims.

"Very well, Maggie. Very well." Tony smiles as he hangs up the phone.

The crazy old witch lady balances the severed head in one hand and, with the other, pats her faithful companion on the head, blood dripping from its snarling, blue agate teeth.

David Perlmutter
Little Pony Ride

1.

If I had only known it from the start, I could have taken the right steps to prevent things from getting out of control. But, as usual, I got left out of the loop until it was too late. My friends put too much faith in me, always believing that, somehow, I, Midnight Glitter, have made some sort of pact with the equestrian gods that requires me to save their asses every time they screw up. I'll admit I'm a good sorceress, all right, but not *that* good. But they never *believe* me.

Anyhow.

When I got up that morning, they were all around me, at my front door. At first, I thought they just wanted to hang, since they *seemed* their normal selves. Floaterflip was hiding behind the nearest tree, Scarcity was checking the size of the rocks on her hooves, Moonshine had her cowboy hat on at its usual rakish tilt, Brainsblown Smash was up in the sky spreading her wings, and Cherry Tart was hopping around like her bladder was going to burst if she didn't piss right away. All in all, typical pony behavior for us typical pony girls here in Gymkhana.

It was only when I realized no one was actually talking that I felt the need to.

"All right," I demanded. "*What* is it?"

That brought a torrent of words across my ears that overwhelmed me.

"*HOLD* IT!" I shouted, which brought silence again.

"Let's deal with this thing one problem at a time, *okay*?" I continued. "I'm only *one filly, damn it*! Don't give me more than I can *handle* right now!"

That particular phrase would, unfortunately, simply be wishful thinking for the next little while.

I queried the group and soon, to my horror, discovered that each of them had been roughly turned out of their lawfully owned homes by a group of strange creatures calling themselves "Am-er-*icans*", or some such thing. Each of these invading groups had come, they claimed, from out of the doors of their cellars earlier that day, said that they now "fuckin' *owned*" my friends' properties, and drove them away with a variety of weapons I'd never heard of before.

"I couldn't do *anything about* it," Floaterflip moaned. "They *yelled* at me. What *defense* is there for *that*?"

"My spring collection is in *tatters*," Scarcity blustered. "They *ransacked* my supply of fabrics!"

"Dang busted varmints *stole* all my *apples!*" Moonshine grated. "Not to mention my *seeds*. How'm I gonna *feed* us all now?"

"Some asshole shot some little *pellets* at me!" said Brainblown. "Nearly took me out for *good*."

"They took my *mouth organ* and *threw it* in LAKE MUSTANG!" Cherry said rapidly, grasping my cheeks as she did. "How am I gonna *entertain* people *now*, huh? HOW?" Oddly, she seemed more emotionally distraught than the others, but she's usually like that, anyway.

I wrenched Cherry's hooves off from my face and whinnied for their attention again.

"Look, girls," I said. "There has to be some logical explanation for all this. We're threatened on all sides all the time in Gymkhana. Somehow or another, there are forces at work that don't *want* this bucolic, all-female horse utopia to exist peacefully!"

They gasped in horror.

"I'm sure that *this* is just one of those occasions," I said, reassuringly, "and it's only a matter of time before...."

"So you'll *talk* to them?" shouted Cherry.

"Well," I said, "I suppose...."

"I knew we could count on you, Midnight," said Brainblown, coming down from the sky. "You're the only one of us who's tough enough to fight them. Besides *me,* of course, but I don't want to *deal* with those ugly *bastards!*"

"Wait a minute!" I said. "I never said..."

"Yay, Midnight!" said Cherry Tart, as she embraced me in a constricting bear hug.

"Cherry, you IDIOT!" I gasped. "I need *air!*"

She released me and I fell on the ground.

"Sorry," she added, as an apologetic coda.

"All *right,* already!" I said, preparing to leave. "I'll *talk* to them, since none of *you* seem to be *pony enough* to do it YOURSELF! But don't expect me to...."

The last part of my speech was buried under their euphoric cheering. I brushed flecks of dirt out of my purple mane and stalked off.

2.

I discovered the interlopers on what had formerly been Moonshine's land. They were a strange group of creatures, walking only on two legs rather than four, who seemed only to have hair on the top of their heads and nowhere else. My first attempts to get their attention proved to be futile, so I had to get tough.

"HEY, *MOTHERFUCKERS!*" I shouted at the top of my voice.

That got their attention, for sure. Particularly that of the creature who seemed to be in charge of the group, who ordered all of the people under his charge to point their strange weapons at my head.

"I mean...." I said, nervously, "welcome to Gymkhana!"

"Shit on *that!*" said the group's leader. "You in *America,* now, *bitch!*"

"Am-er-*ica?*" I drawled phonetically. "Never *heard* of the place!"

"You little *fuck!*" the soldier said. He was about to have the unit fire on me, but an older being who appeared to be the soldier's superior ordered him and the other soldiers to "stand down". The soldier and the other being argued about "infringing" on each other's territory, but when the older creature threatened him with something called a "court martial", the soldier and his associates withdrew their weapons and left me alone with him.

"I'm Agent Strathairn, FBI," the older man said to me. "And *you* are...?"

"Midnight Glitter," I announced proudly. "2ND Degree Mage Of The Mystic Knights Of The Royal Equestrian House Of Gymkhana, And Personal Deputy Of Her Royal Highness Princess Celestina In The Conduct Of...."

"I only *wanted* your goddamn *name,*" interrupted Strathairn. "The rest of that means *nothing* to me!"

"Your *FBI, sir,*" I countered, "means *less* to we citizens of Gymkhana than the *droppings* from our collective ASSES! And it will mean even *less* if you do *not....*"

"You are *not* in a position to dictate terms to *us,*" Strathairn replied. "The United States Of America does not negotiate with TERRORISTS!"

"HOW *DARE* YOU!" I blazed. "We are *loyal* citizens of our realm, and we do not resort to..."

"We received word that Al-Qaeda has infiltrated this territory," Strathairn interrupted me, very firmly. "Until such time as we can neutralize this threat, this entire territory is effectively American soil, and you will subject yourselves to...."

"Are you *implying* that you have CONQUERED Gymkhana?" I blazed again. "Because we would *not* have *submitted* without a *fight!*"

"Please," Strathairn said, arrogantly. "That is such a nineteenth century concept! We simply wish to use your land for our purposes...."

"Does that include BANISHING MY FRIENDS from their HOMES?" I shot back.

He did not answer me.

"How did you figure out how to *come* here?" I continued. "Because if you figured out how to *come* here, you can *damn well....*"

"*America* can do *whatever* it *fucking* WANTS to protect itself!" he interrupted me. "And, if that means taking some pithy land from some bitchy FOALS who make trouble for us, *or* breeding you and your terrorist friends to the U.S. Army's stud horses to *shut you up,* then so *be* it!"

FOALS? *Breeding* us? Oh, no, he *didn't*!

"YOU SON OF A *BITCH!*" I screamed.

Before he could do anything, I leapt, teeth bared, at his throat. I wasn't big enough to land on it, but I bit him in one of his fingers, and hit him enough times with my hooves when he hit the ground that I might have killed him, for all I know. But his screams and my snarls and whinnies of rage got the attention of the other beings.

"Get that fucking UNICORN before she *kills* us all!" was the cry, and I was forced to flee for my life as they shot their weapons at me.

3.

With blood stains on my hooves, I ran, and I was able to make my escape to my house before they were able to wound me. The others were still there, waiting for me, when I arrived.

"INSIDE!" I ordered. "There's not a moment to lose!"

We entered the house, and bolted the front door with furniture so they couldn't get in. Or so we hoped.

"Spook!" I called for my lizard assistant bookkeeper. "SPOOK! Where *are* you, you damned...?"

"You're standing on my *tail*," he said.

"Oh," I said, embarrassed. "Sorry."

"No need," he said. "I know what happened."

"How?" I said.

"I saw the first bunch of those foreigners come out of Scarcity's cellar this morning," he said. "I tried to tell you, but...."

"But *what*?" I responded.

"You said you were...busy."

"I *was*. I was trying to..."

"You *knew* about it, you little *fool*?" Scarcity was outraged. "And you didn't *try* to..."

"What could *I* do?" said Spook. "You know I'm not...."

"Look, it doesn't *matter*!" I interrupted. "We have to stay together on this! Like *always*!"

They murmured agreement.

"Spook," I said, "is there any spell in the master spell book we can use against these Am-er-*icans*?"

"One," he said. "But it's pretty dangerous. It'd involve all of you, and it might *kill* you if it goes wrong..."

"We'll have to take that chance," I said. "You willing, girls?"

"If we gotta do it to get them varmints out of Gymkhana," said Moonshine, "I say *yeah*!"

Nobody disagreed with her.

4.

"**O**pen the door and get out of here, you fucking pieces of *horseshit!*"

The soldiers had, by this time, caught up with us, and this cry, accompanied by the sound of weapons being loaded and other actions of that kind, was clearly designed to insult us, and draw us out to attack them. We did, but not in the way they would have expected.

After the command, we exited, all of us wearing our magically powered tiaras and the sparkling robes Scarcity had designed for all of us as a token of her esteem many moons ago. Cherry set the tone for things by coming out at the head of the line, beating steadily on her conga drum- one of the few of her performing instruments that the invaders hadn't confiscated- chanting to the god Equus, while I- as the mage of the group- came out last, with my spell book cradled around one of my hooves. The others surrounded me, amid the laughter and gawking of the foreigners, I prepared to begin the chant the spell we needed for this occasion. The problem was, Cherry started overdoing it with the beating and the chanting, like she usually does with everything, to increased sniggering. The rest of us had to bark her name at her in order for her to quit it, and then I began.

"We, the free ponies of Gymkhana," I said, "have endured the taunts and threats of you invaders *long enough,* and we intend to counter you on terms which are our own- and *not* yours!"

"Now wait a *minute....,*" said an authoritative voice.

"SILENCE!" I commanded, and advanced threateningly, along with the other ponies. The invaders backed away from us, but only for a moment.

"You will *not* speak to the military and intelligence forces of the United States of America with such....," the voice answered me back, ignoring my command entirely. But I cut him off.

"FOOLS!" I snapped. "You know *not* what forces we have at our command, nor to what lengths we will go to remove you from our land!"

"Even *we* don't know!" said Cherry Tart, unhelpfully.

"Would you SHUT UP!!!???" Brainblown Smash said to her.

"We will not stand for you speaking to you with such an impudent intent...." said the voice.

"That goes for *you*, too, ya *FUCKS!*" said Brainblown. And she flapped her wings briefly, creating a gust of wind that blew them back, just as my words had. Only temporarily, again, though.

"I take it that you will not leave our realm at our command," I said.

"We will not," said the voice.

"And you will not return our property to us, as we requested?"

"We will not."

"*And* you have every intent of annexing our territory to your land, without our assent, simply because you believe that some so-called "terrorists" may be hiding in our midst?"

"We do have that intention."

"Then you will FACE OUR WRATH!"

The other ponies surrounded me, and we linked hooves. We also linked our internal magical energies that would gradually come to create the force and light we needed. We began by slowly chanting "depart" until we reached the climax, when we screamed "DEPART! DEPART! *DEPART!*", and flung our combined magical energies at the invaders....

5.

Well, Princess, I'll admit that it was a bit of a struggle for us to clean up all the blood, gore and melted metal that was left after we obliterated the Am-er-*icans*, but we got it done together like the pals we are. We also took careful steps to start filling our cellars and removing their contents, so that they can never try to bother us again. Yeesh! Autotune *himself* never gave us that much trouble, and he's never actually tried to *kill* us, like the Amer-*icans* did.

Anyhow, I have to go now, Princess. Cherry Tart says that she found a group of beer-drinking lunatics calling themselves Can-ade-*eans* in her attic, and she needs my help. Sigh! Here we go again....

Niall Parkinson

Lee Forsythe
Karni Mata

Sloane Mackenzie put her suitcases down at the entrance to the apartment building and rifled her pockets for the slip of paper with the entry code. Where had she put it?

She studied the building front as she rummaged, hoping it lent an air of nonchalance to her search. Beside the walkway red tulips swayed in the Washington D.C. sunshine. Four gargoyles, deftly executed years ago by an Italian stonemason moonlighting from his job on the nearby National Cathedral, frowned down on her, each holding in its mouth a long iron chain with a large lamp at the end.

After locating the slip in the outside zippered pocket of her small suitcase, she buzzed herself into the carpeted entryway, illuminated by a crystal chandelier reflected in a wall of mirrored tiles. At the back several steps rose to the doors of two elevators. As she reached them, a gray-haired Indian woman in a tangerine sari backed out of the elevator to her right, her aluminum walker banging against the door. The woman turned a fierce gaze upon her.

"You have the manners of a pig!" she shrieked. "Have you had an eyeful?" As she spoke, she machine-gunned bits of food out of her mouth. A pea, a sliver of chicken, and bits of rice landed at Sloane's feet and a pungent mix of curry, garlic, and foul breath blasted her in the face.

"A point well taken, Senator," Sloane deadpanned, swinging her luggage past the woman onto the elevator.

She pressed the sixth floor button and stopped. A young black woman in a nurse's uniform stood at the back of the car gently sobbing, her arms crossed before her, clutching her purse.

"Are you going up? " Sloane asked.

The woman nodded. "Four, please," she said softly.

"She's obviously completely off the beserkometer," Sloane said as the nurse exited on four.

"Obviously," the woman said over her shoulder. "I'm sorry. Just been a very long day."

Two weeks flew by with Sloane settling into her new place and a new job as a research assistant at the Census Bureau. One evening after work she discovered the trash chute at the end of the hall was blocked with overflowing garbage bags. Potato peels and coffee grounds had spilled onto her feet when she opened the chute door. She checked for her key before dragging her own trash bag onto the elevator and riding down to the basement for the first time.

After looking over the small, deserted laundry room, she turned down a long dim corridor around the corner from the elevators. A low unfinished ceiling with exposed pipes and wiring ran the length of the hallway, a naked 20-watt bulb at the midpoint providing the only light. A metal door at the far end opened and the Indian woman came out. The click-clack of her walker echoed down the corridor as she shuffled toward Sloane.

Sloane slipped back around the corner, hoping she hadn't been seen. "How they love dead skin," the old lady said to no one in particular.

Sloane retreated to the laundry room until she heard the elevator arrive and depart, and then proceeded back to what she believed must be the trash room. The sticky concrete floor and overpowering aroma of garbage confirmed her suspicion, although the room's only light was reflecting in from the hall. She flipped an old-fashioned bow-tie switch next to the door with no result.

When her eyes adjusted to the limited light, Sloane realized she was standing on the top landing of a small flight of stairs with black iron railings descending steeply to the floor of the trash room proper. She could make out the opening of the trash chute and, beneath it, a raised metal platform extending along the wall to below an incinerator door. Bags of trash lay here and there on the metal table, in front of the open door of the darkened incinerator, and on the floor. Sloane was squinting into the gloom, weighing whether to go down the steps, when she noticed pairs of red eyes glaring back at her. Amid scattered trash bags on the floor, huge rats huddled around saucers of what Sloane assumed was poison.

The rats were unmoved by her presence. Their defiant beady eyes seemed to say, "What the hell do you want?"

She shuddered, heaved her trash bag over the railing, and left.

The next Saturday in the afternoon Sloane answered a knock at her door to find the black woman, smiling warmly and holding a bottle of wine. Instead of her nurse's uniform, she wore jeans and a red t-shirt.

"Welcome to the neighborhood," she said. "I'm Eleanor Peterson. Here's a little house warming gift."

"Ooh, already chilled. Please come in," Sloane said. "It's great to finally meet you. I'm Sloane Mackenzie."

"Sorry about the other day with Mrs. Singh. She guards those elevators like Cerberus at the gates of hell. Cusses out anybody that comes along."

"Don't worry about it. Have a seat and tell me about this place. I was just about to have a little something to eat from Nick's down the street. Would you join me?"

"Sure. One of my favorite places. He and his wife are so nice."

Sloane took the wine into the kitchen and began arranging the food. Eleanor called after her, "Oh, I love what you've done with this dining area—all the light from those windows. My table's all crammed into the kitchen."

"Thanks, but the decorating's courtesy of the previous tenant, an old family friend," Sloane said. In a few moments she brought out the wine and two glasses, then a plate of cheese, pate', crackers, and grapes. "Here's to new neighbors!"

"And new friends. This cheese is delicious."

"It's Prima Donna from Belgium. Mmm, this wine is good too."

"Chateau de Plonk from the bargain bin."

"How long have you lived here?"

"Two years since I started at GU Hospital. Did your friend live here then?"

"No, she's not actually my friend. She subbed it to a string of relatives. To tell you the truth I don't even know who the last one was."

"I'm in the same boat. My oldest brother Reggie rented this place when he went to Howard and it's been handed down ever since. You can't beat the price for a neighborhood like this."

"I know. I never imagined I could afford a place in Northwest. But why's it so empty?"

"Rent stabilization. The owners probably want to force the last few old tenants out so they can institute a huge rent increase across the board. You can't blame them, considering the DC real estate market."

"I guess not. Speaking of owners, how do you contact them?"

"You don't. The number downstairs by the mailboxes is a recording. I had a small plumbing problem once. Never heard back from them. Fixed it myself eventually."

"I saw rats as big as cats down in the trash room. I think somebody laid out poison for them, but if not, the authorities need to know. And all the lights are burned out."

"Jeeze, you went down there. That basement creeps me out. Sometimes these deserted hallways remind me of The Overlook Hotel. Like I'm going to run into twin girls or a kid on a Big

Wheel. You could call the Health Department. I'm reluctant to give my name around here. Technically the lease prohibits the kind of sublet you and I have."

"Oh yeah, I remember now being warned about that. I could call anonymously. It's the Department of Public Works. I already looked up their number. Do you know the other tenants? I've seen only one other person here on my floor—an older lady who's always sporting either a gold or silver shoes and purse ensemble no matter what else she's got on."

"That's Jean Hagen or Ms. Precious Metals, as I call her. Some other tenants weren't exactly wrapped tight either. Miss Culp used to live at the end of my hall. Whenever I got off the elevator, she would crack her door and stare out at me. I'd wave, say hi. Nothing. Just kept staring with her eyes just above the safety chain until I went inside."

"I asked another woman, Delores Winslow, if she'd pick up my mail once while I was out of town and she said, 'I'd rather not get involved.' Do you believe it? Like I was asking her for a loan. Anyway she moved out in the middle of the night shortly after that. Place has been vacant ever since."

"What about Mrs. Singh?"

"Been here forever—long before Reggie even. Her son Ravi used to live with her. Reggie said they were very close. Supposedly Ravi was with the Agency—some kind of biological warfare expert. Anyway, one day he just abandoned her. Never seen around here again. Maybe that accounts for her mental state."

The next morning Sloane woke with a start, bright sunlight streaming into her bedroom, before she remembered it wasn't a workday. She sat on the edge of the bed, rubbing her face and remembering the great afternoon with Eleanor. It was going to be nice to have a friend in the building. They'd discussed doing laundry together—would today be too soon to call her? And she had to make her regular phone call to Indianapolis to catch up on family news and assure her mother that she hadn't been murdered in her sleep.

She made coffee and looked for her cell phone. What had she done with it? She remembered getting a call Saturday morning while shopping—hadn't she thrown it into the bag with her purchases as she was leaving the drugstore? It dawned on her that with the unexpected visitor and wine that last night she may have tossed the bag, assuming it was empty, with the rest of the week's detritus down the recently cleared trash chute directly into Rat Central Station.

Should she see if Eleanor would go with her or would that be tossing cold water on a possible friendship? What a flake! How could she have done it?

Easily. New job, new place, and too much wine—she wasn't much of a drinker. No sense beating herself up over nothing. She'd take a flashlight down to see if the rats had, in fact, been taken care of and come back up for help depending on the situation. She needed that phone and felt stupid for throwing it away. Besides it might serve to update her on the situation before calling the authorities.

Sloane aimed her flashlight down at the trash room floor at the sounds of foraging coming from the bags scattered there. Suddenly a rat ran up her leg. She screamed, dropped the flashlight, and tried with both hands on the outside of her jeans to force it back down to her ankle. She spun partially around and tumbled backward down the concrete steps.

Sloane regained consciousness on her back on the cold floor, overwhelmed by a damp, mangy stench. The rats were biting her face and fingers. A living tangle of brown fur and pink scaly tails undulated over the length of her body. She heard their high-pitched squeals, the echoing patter of countless feet scratching toward her, and something more—the ring of her cell phone.

Sloane struggled to her feet, dizzy and sick. She found her flashlight and, plowing through the rats and garbage, ripped open her trash bag and fished out the phone.

She thought she recognized Eleanor's voice. "Please help me," Sloane croaked. "I'm in the trash..." The phone beeped and went dead.

Something shiny caught her eye. She turned the flashlight's beam to where Miss Hagen's legs and upturned feet protruded from the incinerator. A hungry swarm of rats worried her body and made her gold shoes quiver and flash in the light.

Mrs. Singh's walker clattered down the hallway outside. A light came on in the room and Sloane saw that the walls were pockmarked with half-moon holes from floor to ceiling with a rat peering out of every one.

The door opened and above her on the landing a bare-footed Mrs. Singh appeared in flowing ceremonial robes of white and gold. She picked up a rat's drinking saucer from a recess on the wall and took a long slurp from it before spying Sloane.

Sloane stumbled back over to the base of the stairs. "Please," she said. "The rats ..."

"They are not rats, you meddling little toe-rag," Mrs. Singh thundered. "They are the messengers of God. And you—you are another offering for my kabbas."

Mrs. Singh pushed her walker aside, slid down the handrails on her forearms, and landed at the bottom with her gnarled hands around Sloane's throat.

"Let me go, you rat-worshipping old witch," Sloane said, although Mrs. Singh's choke-hold reduced her final words to a whisper.

Her mind reeled at the old woman's agility and strength. She felt herself blacking out and tried to pull away, but Mrs. Singh only leaned in closer, her gaping mouth revealing two pairs of curling yellow incisors gnashing together in excitement.

A thudding blow against the back of her skull loosened Mrs.Singh's grip and sent her pitching onto the floor. Eleanor stood above her on the steps with a large aluminum flashlight.

Although Mrs. Singh had been a doting benefactor to the mutant strain, with their sensitive noses and poor eyesight they somehow mistook the smell of her blood for that of her son, who had shocked, starved, and otherwise tortured them in the name of research.

The rats' squeals rose to a deafening pitch. With fur raised straight up on their backs they streamed from every crack and crevice, engulfing the defenseless woman under a tidal wave of rodent fury.

Eleanor helped Sloane up the steps ahead of the advancing horde. They slammed the metal door behind them and made their way to higher ground.

Justin Hunter
Geisha White

The emaciated, naked body of the woman lay face up on the earthen floor that surrounded the burning pit. Her eyes bulged out of their sockets. Her face, neck and chest were flecked with redness beneath the skin, speaking of broken blood vessels in her last struggles to breathe. Her body was stiff. Her joints were locked from the violence of her final conflict for life, which rigor mortis kept perfectly set. Gavin knew the look well.

He had burned hundreds of people bearing that same countenance in death. They died in terror and pain. Gavin picked her up by the shoulders and dragged her toward the pyre, grunting from the cumbersomeness and the dead weight of the human form. He heaved her body over the side of the pit. The woman dropped a meager two feet, landing in the inferno of the piled dead beneath her. Soon there would be no more room for bodies in this pit. The front loaders would come and cover the mass grave with dirt. Then they would dig another pit and Gavin would set to work again, eliminating the immense diseased biomass the sickness had left in its wake.

Gavin stepped back from the burning pit and wiped the sweat from his forehead. He pulled at the cheap rubber strap of the face mask he had been issued from the government response team in charge of the burning project. The face mask was nothing but cheap filtration paper which Gavin didn't think was able to keep out something as simple as ragweed, let alone the sickness. It didn't matter too much to Gavin anyway.

There was no apparent reason as to why some people hadn't been infected yet. The best scientists were supposedly meeting about the subject in some sort of secret international pandemic think-tank. Gavin didn't suspect that he was immune. He'd known too many people who thought they couldn't get the virus end up gasping their lives out like the rest. As far as Gavin knew, nobody knew why the sickness happened and what they could do to stop it.

He was alive and showed no signs of disease. That meant that he was able to participate in the government lead compulsory clean-up program. That meant Gavin had to burn bodies twelve hours a day, six days a week.

Gavin walked over to the body of a child. He kept his eyes closed as he picked up the rigid body of a young boy. He couldn't bear to see one so small die in such a horrible way. He tossed the body into the burning pit and swiped his arm across his forehead again. Instead of sweat, he removed tears. He retched once but couldn't vomit on an empty stomach. After his first day on the job he was smart enough to skip food until his shift was over. The air was filled with the smell of smoke, burning flesh and sickness.

It made Gavin think of his son, Chad, now dead from the flu. When Chad was very young he used to get strep throat pretty regularly. His pediatrician had called Chad a 'Carrier' of the virus. Whenever Gavin entered his sick son's room to bring him some water or a cold washcloth for his head, there was a particular rancid smell in the air. Chad's strep made his breath smell like a mixture of stomach acid, putrefied meat and curdled dairy. The burning bodies gave off that same smell. It filled the air and permeated Gavin's clothes and skin. No matter how much he washed, he could never totally get rid of the smell.

Gavin looked up from his work and gazed across the barren landscape. Hundreds of pits just like his dotted the open plain. The smoke gathered in the windless atmosphere, nearly blocking out the light, giving Gavin the feeling that he was trapped beneath the shroud of sickness and death. He lowered his gaze and went back to work. There were still six hours left to his shift.

Steve turned off the lone lamp that dimly illuminated the concrete stairs that led down to his basement tavern. His lone customer for the evening was already inside. The bar was the non-descript sort and seemed proud of the fact. There were no flashy neon signs, no banners advertising drink specials and definitely no valet parking. Most people wouldn't even know the place existed, and Steve liked it that way. He liked his customers quiet and at ease. He wasn't into any of that high-octane nightclub business. If you drank at his bar, you were either a regular or there by freak accident. Steve's was a shot and a beer tavern. If a customer ordered a beer, he got it. If he ordered a strawberry margarita, he got a beer.

Steve walked carefully down the now dark steps to his bar. He pulled open the heavy wooden door at the bottom. It swung soundlessly inward. He breathed in the familiar smell of stale cigarette smoke. He ignored the local business anti-smoking laws. Steve preferred the smell of cigarette smoke to the odor of cheap beer and urine, which is what he thought his bar would smell like if he stopped his customers from lighting up. He pulled the door shut behind in and locked it from the inside. He ran his hand over the notched and heavily lacquered wood. Everything street level and above had changed and conformed to the times. He loved and cared for his antique cellar bar door just as much as he did his richly stained mahogany bar. His customer, Jeff, was sitting by himself at the far end of the bar.

"Steve, we fucked up. It's as plain and simple as that," Jeff said. He was drinking a tumbler of straight Vodka. It was already his third drink of the evening and he was showing no signs of slowing his pace. He was looking to get dead drunk. The alcohol didn't seem to be doing anything about Jeff's loquaciousness.

Steve looked at the shine in Jeff's bloodshot eyes and the way he braced himself with his elbows on the table, like he expected to tip over at any moment. Normally Steve would have stopped serving this customer liquor and thrown him out of the bar, but Jeff had been coming there for weeks and Steve knew he could hold his spirits. Steve didn't have much to lose in letting the man drink himself blotto if he wanted too. Jeff was his only customer. Weeks ago, Steve had struck a deal with the government for ten thousand dollars a day to keep his bar open just for Jeff.

The government man, a large guy wearing all black, his eyes covered in sunglasses, gave him only a small bit of information. "He's a scientist who is in the process of looking for a cure to the pandemic," the man said. "He likes to blow off steam after working, and we need a place that's private and discreet. Give him what he wants."

"Sounds like he's an alcoholic," Steve said.

"Just give him whatever he wants," the man said. He handed over a black duffel bag filled with cash and left Jeff to look after the important scientist. Steve found out that Jeff didn't need much except an open bottle and an active listener.

"Who fucked up?" Steve said.

"We collectively fucked up," Jeff said. "I mean fucked up in the royal sense. You fucked up. I fucked up. The whole world fucked up. How could we be so safe on most things and so ridiculously negligent on something so important? "

"You might want to take it easy on that stuff," Steve said. He gestured to the half empty glass of Vodka in Jeff's hand. "You'll be of no use tomorrow."

"Who cares?" Jeff said. "It's over anyway. There's nothing we can do." Jeff emptied his glass of Vodka and suddenly bent forward in a wrenching coughing fit. Steve reached behind the counter and handed Jeff a clean bar towel. Jeff took the cloth and covered his mouth as he gagged and spit in the worn cotton towel. Jeff regained his composure and held the towel out for Steve to see. It was covered in small red droplets of blood. Jeff dropped the cloth to the floor and wiped his hand on the counter. He gestured for Steve to fill up his glass. Steve complied.

"You've got it?" Steve said.

"I guess I probably got a couple days left at most," Jeff said. "This may be the last day I'll even be able to sit up."

"You guys anywhere close to finding a cure?"

"There is no cure," Jeff said. "We've spent billions of dollars and spent decades of time trying to find a cure for AIDS and cancer. How are we doing on that? This disease wiped us out in six months, world-wide, ninety-five percent kill rate for the infected. We're fucked."

"I'm not sick," Steve said.

"Science has never accounted for luck," Jeff said. "Your time will come soon enough."

"Want to let me in on why I'm going to die?" Steve said. "Bartenders have short memories. Speaking to us is kind of like talking to a shrink, only cheaper."

Jeff looked at the bloody rag on the floor and felt his lungs gurgle and rasp from inside his chest. "Why not?" Jeff said. "Who are you going to tell? There aren't a lot of people left alive to tell anyway. Even if you did, there's not a whole lot that could come of it. It's over."

Steve grabbed the bottle of Vodka off the shelf and took another tumbler from behind the bar. He walked around the bar and sat next to Jeff. He poured Jeff's glass full and one for himself.

"Let's hear it," Steve said.

"You have to start with globalization," Jeff said. "Natural and cultural resources are being shared and homogenized among everyone on the planet. That, along with urbanization's effects on biodiversity in nature and the animal kingdom. Living in such a way, zoonotic diseases have increased. Animal pathogens mutate faster than we can track and they change into increasingly nastier strains of disease which humans are susceptible too."

"You've lost me," Steve said.

"I'm talking about animals making us sick," Jeff said.

Gavin's shift at the burning pit was over. He returned to his empty house. He opened his front door and walked inside, tossing his backpack on the floor next to the coatrack. He felt a cool breeze coming through the broken front windows of his home. Most of the windows of his home were broken. His home was a mess, destroyed by the riots and looting that happened when the pandemic started picking up steam and killed people by the millions. Gavin never bothered to clean it up. Living in a well-kept home didn't matter to him anymore.

Gavin's wife and son had died of the sickness before the looting. Gavin had been alone in his home when the mass of people had come. They came with bats and knives. They came with shovels and picks. The rioting wasn't about stealing, raping or any other vile human endeavor that takes over in a time of chaos. It was about destruction. It was about humanity's rage at being destroyed. If the sickness was going to be the end of everyone, they would leave nothing in their wake.

Gavin wasn't prepared for the onslaught. His only weapon, a twelve gage shotgun he had purchased from a sporting goods store for home defense, had been confiscated by the army two weeks before. The military declared martial law in a last ditch effort for control. Part of the martial law ordinance was searching and seizing registered and suspected ownership of firearms from the populace. Gavin remembered the armored van that went door to door in his neighborhood. He was greeted on his porch by three SWAT team members and shown what they called an "Across-population open search and seizure warrant." One of the SWAT team told him he would have to surrender his firearm immediately or face criminal charges. They had his shotgun listed in a database down to the serial number. He surrendered his weapon, in awe of the ferocity of the order and the assault rifles pointed at him. His name was taken off the list and the SWAT team moved on to the next house. Those that fought against the search were taken away in the van and never returned. The rumor was that their refusal to cooperate labeled them as terrorists. They were tried for treason and shot.

Gavin remembered when the first bricks were thrown through his window. He picked one of them up to defend himself from the rioters when he was sprayed in the face with a liquid that made his eyes feel like fire, and he felt his throat close as his esophagus ballooned from the poison. He fell to the floor. The rioters pummeled him with feet and fist. He blacked out.

Gavin awoke that night to a destroyed home, fractured ribs and a broken nose. He saw an empty can of wasp spray lying on the floor next to him. He thought that must have been what they sprayed in his face. He left everything as it lay and climbed up the stairs and fell asleep on his torn and rent mattress.

Gavin was always dead tired after a long day at the burning pits. He usually had just enough energy left to eat whatever government supplied food he had been given for his work, before he made his way to his bedroom and much needed sleep. Sleep wasn't in the cards for him tonight. He couldn't get the images of his dead wife and son out of his head. He remembered tucking his little boy in to sleep for the night. He would brush aside the child's unruly, curly brown hair and kiss him on the forehead. He would sing 'Jesus Loves Me' as many times as the boy wanted. When his son finally fell asleep, Gavin would gaze at him, grieving the years that had flown away so quickly, but at the same time, excited to see his little man getting bigger every day. Whenever he thought of his boy, he couldn't stop himself before the images of the sickness came. He saw his son coughing up gobs of blood and bits of his lungs while he struggled to breathe. Gavin was there for that last breath. He would never forget it. It seemed to hang in the air for an indeterminate amount of time as Gavin's psyche refused to believe that the world could continue after his son had passed. His wife had died much the same way. The sickness brought a quick death, but painful and without dignity.

Gavin didn't know why he hadn't yet caught the sickness. There were so few humans left now and those he spoke to all had the same question, "Why not us?" Even those who lasted so long without becoming sick were beginning to die. Gavin didn't expect anyone to be spared in the end. It was just a matter of time.

Gavin went into the bathroom to brush his teeth. He took his toothbrush out of the cabinet, stared at it for a moment, and then put it back. He took his wife's toothbrush instead and vigorously brushed his teeth with it. Then he took his son's toothbrush and brushed his teeth with that. He took his wife's lipstick and licked the end of it until his tongue was the color of a ripe raspberry. He felt an ache in his stomach. He was tired, grieving and alone. He didn't want to be alone anymore. He wanted to be with his wife and child. He walked back to his bedroom and got into bed. He turned to his wife's side of the bed and licked her pillow.

"Ever hear of 'Uguisu No Fun'?" Jeff asked. He and Steve had finished off the bottle of Vodka and were about a quarter of the way through another.

"No."

"I didn't know what it was either at first but the words did spark something in the back of my mind. I used to be into reading epic Japanese novels like "Musashi" and "Yoshikawa" and it turns out that 'Uguisu No Fun' is an ancient, Japanese facial product that Geishas used to whiten their skin and remove blemishes."

"I think we should be about done with this stuff," Steve gestured to the bottle. "You're starting to ramble."

"Just fucking listen. Bartenders are supposed to listen."

"Fine," Steve refilled his drink.

"Uguisu No Fun facials worked. It doesn't really matter why. What matters is what Uguisu No Fun translates to. Any guesses?"

"No."

"Nightingale excrement," Jeff said. "All these ladies were putting bird shit on their faces, mixed with a helping of oat bran, to clear up their acne and give them that ghost-like appearance that Japanese men seemed to dig."

"You're kidding me."

"Look it up. Putting bird shit on your face was the 'in' thing to do. You would think that nowadays with all our scientific advances on cosmetics that women might choose something that wasn't excreted from some animal's bowels to put on their faces, but you would be wrong."

"People are still doing it?"

"It's big fucking business," Jeff said. "Posh New York Spas were putting 'Geisha Facials' on their services list at $180 a pop."

"Let me guess," Steve said. "People were buying."

"Men and women were buying. Anyone with money to burn, from runway models to professional athletes, put bird shit on their faces."

"So what?"

"So fucking China, that's what," Jeff said.

"Geishas are Japanese."

"I'm not lumping my Asians together," Jeff said. "Name me one thing that makes money in this world that China doesn't have a piece of. The American spending power is nothing compared to that big, red country. If they called in our debts, our economy would be fucked. The Chinese learned about the increasing business of 'Geisha Facials' and wanted their piece of the pie."

"So the Chinese started manufacturing Nightingale poop cream?" Steve asked.

"Fuck that. Nightingale excrement isn't a money maker. China thinks big. You could put all the Nightingales on Ex-Lax and still not get anywhere near the amount of shit China needed. So those birds are out. Ducks are in."

"Ducks? The Chinese were making Duck poop cream?"

"You got it," Jeff said. "China has, and this is a very conservative estimate, over 700 million ducks. Hell, it's probably over a billion and that's a lot of shit. Duck shit by itself doesn't make money. China found a way to take all that waste and turn it into a fortune almost overnight. The marketplace was flooded with the product. Something that only a rich person could afford was now available to the common man. What cost New Yorkers' $180 for one treatment, a middle-class woman in the Midwest could now obtain for $29.99. We're not talking thirty bucks a throw either. That money would buy a whole tub of the stuff that the consumer could use nightly for a whole month."

"Nobody questioned the price differential?"

"Who would?" Jeff drained his tumbler of Vodka and poured another. "People don't care about the details as long as they think they're getting a good deal."

"What about truth-in-packaging?"

"They didn't even have to lie about that. They called the product, Niǎo shǐ miànbù, which means 'bird excrement facial.' They just didn't specify what type of bird the excrement was coming from."

"I don't believe it," Steve said.

"You don't fucking have too. It is what it is. People have been sacrificing their safety in the name of cheapness for as long as I can remember. Where would we be without China? We wouldn't have half of the possessions we do if it wasn't for that country. We even get most of our food from there now. It's cheaper to send mechanically separated chicken meat overseas by plane, let Chinese food processing plants turn them into chicken nuggets and fly them back over here then process the damn things ourselves. That country doesn't have half the food safeguards we have over here, and we don't have any idea what chemicals they're putting into our food. We just want to be able to buy thirty of the damn things for five bucks. We want cheap and we don't care about the longitudinal price of our actions."

"So people are putting duck crap on their faces," Steve said.

"By the millions. Worldwide."

"Which means?"

"Which means the biggest outbreak of avian influenza the world has ever seen," Jeff said. "China and other countries have had some problems with this before, but it's been contained. Most of the people who've gotten sick were actually living with these types of farm birds in their home. They had to basically exist in shit to become infected and the disease didn't easily spread from human to human. The only reported cases of human to human transmission being sick parents caring for small children. We're talking close contact."

Steve pushed his glass away from him. It fell over the back of the bar and shattered on the ground. Jeff didn't seem to notice.

"People focused on the H5N1 virus that was responsible for all the deaths thus far. They didn't give much thought to subtypes of the disease or mutations, which were very prevalent. The particular strain H27N15 was much more easily passed from human to human. People all over the world were dosing themselves in bird shit, giving themselves the flu, and kissing their children goodnight, cuddling with their husbands. You don't think that stuff washes completely off your face during your morning shower, do you? Daycare workers provided care for rooms full of babies and infected them all. They in turn infected their parents. Families infected other families. Whole businesses shut down because their entire workforce was too sick to show up. We're dealing with a worldwide pandemic and there's not a damn thing we can do about it."

"We're fucked?" Steve said.

"Proper fucked," Jeff said. He clapped a hand on Steve's shoulder, stood up and walked out of the bar.

Steve put his head down on the polished marble counter and passed out in a drunken stupor.

Gavin stood at the edge of the burning pits. The bodies piled high and burned hotter than the flames of hell themselves. For some reason, the disease wouldn't touch him. His lungs felt fine. His muscles were taut and limber from the months of lugging bodies and casting them into the fire. He couldn't get sick. No matter how hard he tried, he couldn't get sick.

Gavin took one last look across the open plains. He saw the trails of smoke from a hundred fires obliterate the sun in the sky. He spread his arms and jumped into the pit. The flames welcomed him. They welcomed him home.

K. Trap Jones
A Soul's Lullaby

I have done terrible things to people who did not deserve it. I have watched the life drain from my victims with no remorse and no pity, but still the doctors try to spare my life. They are offering me a second chance to life, of which I did not offer to those who met my knife. Strapped to the table, my muscles convulse, prompting the doctors to keep their distance. The wounds I received from the officers are life threatening to me and drain my energy along with any chance of freedom. I felt the needle puncture my vein and release the sedative to calm me, but I would receive no peace; no tranquility. Unable to stay awake, my vision fled me and followed my mind as I plummeted deep into the pits of insanity.

I tried desperately to grasp anything for leverage as my soul rose above my body. I pleaded with God to grant my return and he heard my prayers as the doctors revived my pulse. My vision was of my own as I stared up into their facial masks. I flat lined again as my soul rode the last breath out through my mouth, trying to grip the heads of the doctor's. They could not see me; they could not hear my screams of agony. They merely kept working on my body. I tried to keep my corpse within my sight as I elevated up to the ceiling. Fear gripped my thoughts as I watched the walls turn black; forming a horde of reapers. I felt myself crying, but there were no tears. The elongated arms of the reapers slithered through the air like a serpent. Even without flesh, I felt the pain of their bony, clawed fingers tearing my arms. Ripping into me, the reapers took turns trying to grasp the essence of my spine. My mind was destroyed; any rationale that was left was swallowed by their gaping mouths.

"Clear!" I heard from below.

Quickly, my soul reentered my body as my eyes opened, scouring the operation room for the reapers. I was frantic, but the white walls somewhat soothed me, even as I gagged on the tube that was shoved down my throat. I felt a cool wind chilling my open wounds from the gunshots and the clanking sound as the bullets were dropped into the metal bowls. I will never leave my body again; I wanted to stay inside and imagined my soul holding tight to the rib cage for support.

I would not savor the moment long, as I felt my mind slipping. The doctor's quickened their pace and the sound of my heartbeat was becoming sporadic. I was able to shed a few tears as my soul seeped through the lips once again. I became angry with my body for given up and not fighting to keep my soul within it. The flesh was weak and I showed my disgust by trying kick the stomach as I sifted through the air. It just laid there as the walls blackened around me. I wanted to go back into it and cause it harm. I envisioned my hands wrapped around the throat, squeezing every ounce of life that remained.

A quick rise from my chest pulled me back in, but I was no longer weak; I was no longer afraid. The doctor's held my head down as the restraints carved into my wrists. I wanted to be free so that I could teach my body a lesson in respect. My muscles trembled in fear at the thoughts my mind were portraying. One bullet to the head; one slash across the neck would suffice. Dwelling inside my body, I felt disgusted by its lack of help and inability to protect my soul. It abandoned me to fulfill its own self-preservation. It wanted the wounds to be healed, but did not fight to keep me intact. My mind became sadistic and created visions of my own demise. It felt like I was smiling even though my lips were quivering. My eyes were stained with resentment even though they cried hysterically. I knew exactly what the body was afraid of and I battled it with vengeance. Only the needle that entered the IV tube was able to calm the involuntary movements of the pathetic muscles.

Resting there like a slug, my body had given up. The machine was still registering a pulse, but I could feel none within my heart. The anger was subdued with sadness as I knew that the end was near. There's a certain beauty to death when it can be seen from a distance; after all of the turmoil has subsided. It's a reality check that brings about a sense of serenity even when fear of the unknown presents itself.

I was always told that there was a light waiting, but no such thing would be waiting for me. As my body lied there, the doctor's announced the time of death. I slipped through the lips for one last ride and looked down upon my body not with anger or resentment, but with respect. It was not my body that concocted the crimes; it was only following the orders of my mind. I looked at the flesh as being released from the devilish torment that my mind had inflicted upon it. There was no choice once my mind was made up. The bones and muscles could not battle the evil visions and for that, I did not try to claw my way back inside. Not again.

The walls seeped with blackness as a sheet covered my face. I watched patiently as four reapers pulled themselves from the darkness and stood before me. There was no more reason to fight; there was no more reason to deny the inevitable. I thought I was strong as I stood there with outreached arms, waiting to be clutched by death, but everything that constructed me as a man flew from me as I was pulled through the wall and out into the darkness of the night. Above the streets I was dragged through the air at a blistering speed. The wind watered my eyes and clutched my throat. Everything became a blur.

The velocity slowed as I was able to recognize the location; it was my street. Up the driveway and through the closed front door, I was dragged. The bolted cellar door provided no resistance as my soul was thrown hastily down the stairs into the blackness of the basement. I had no heartbeat; I had no breath, but still I was frightened. If I had nerves, they would've been rattled.

Twisting and churning through the shadows, I was not allowed to breach the edge of the darkness. The absence of light served as a prison cell, but my mind plagued me with the reality as the shadows began to shift. I was not alone; the four reapers were observing me and crept from the walls. I watched as each of them pulled back their tattered hoods, revealing the angered souls of my victims. Fear skewered me like a sharpened scythe.

My cellar was where I kept them and allowed the darkness to devour their essence until I stole their bodies from them. I kept each one as trophies for weeks before I ended their lives. I was fascinated with the endurance of the body and conducted many experiments to fulfill my research. Their bodies are still here; their families are still hoping to find them alive. The police had no idea who they were pulling over. One inch was the difference between the second officer dying and not me. He was dead in my sights until he stumbled. My bullet missed, but his didn't. My deceased body will lead them back to my house where they will find the others, but that will never help me now. I am too far gone as my soul spins in place, wondering which one will strike first.

Each of them grinned at my trembling soul, tormenting my death virgin mind. Their hallowed faces laughed until their pain was reflected within the howls. They converged upon me with vengeance in their demeanor as their arms tore into my soul, severing everything that I had left. Without flesh, I thought there would be no more pain; I was wrong. They went after the one thing that was still intact; my mind. Their claws gripped my thoughts and controlled my dreams. Everything else didn't matter as I became whatever they wanted me to be. I was theirs and they were eager to control me for eternity. Diverging upon my mind, they swallowed me wholly into the darkness.

I do not hate my body for dying, I envy it.

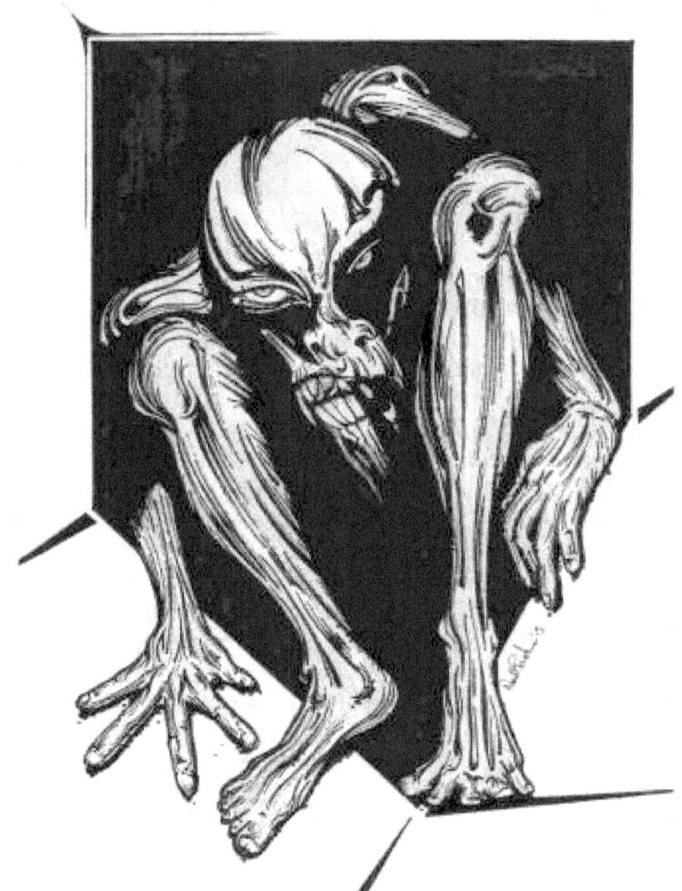

Niall Parkinson

Lori Safranek
Angels Behind Glass

My brothers and I had lived our entire lives in the woods surrounding our small Missouri town. Once the sun went down, the woods scared me, but I couldn't say no to a chance to join a search party with the men that night. I'd never live it down with the other boys and, anyway, I was determined to be in the search party that found the missing woman. I wanted to be hero.

So I had stuck my dusty, bare feet into my shoes and hooked the straps of my bib overalls before I slapped a beat-up cowboy hat on my head. I was ready for adventure, and in my pleasure at being included, I gave little thought to the poor woman we would be looking for.

John Steadman, George Clemmons and Ezra Teeters had come to our place to fetch Granddad and Pa when they heard a woman had went missing. Jessie Bickens had gone off her head again and we were going to try and find her before something bad happened to her and her baby.

Jessie was about four months pregnant; this would be her fifth baby. Every single time Jessie turned up pregnant, even the first time, she took off at nightfall and ran and ran throughout the dark Missouri night, while the town's men would hunt the dark Ozark woods, calling her name, praying she wasn't hurt.

We always found her by morning, tired out and dirty, her dress half off and her shoes long gone. One of the men would pick her up and carry her back to her husband. And five months later, another little Bickens would join the world, never seeming any worse the wear for his mom's fear-crazed run through the woods. Throughout the night, someone would catch a glimpse of her running along a ridge, her blond hair flowing behind her, her long strides eating up the miles in no time. Then, near morning usually, they would find her. She'd been found hiding behind an outhouse, and tucked into the corner of a chicken coop, setting all the chickens to squawking. She was even found inside the Baptist Church once, sound asleep.

I was already thinking "we," when in fact I'd never even been in the search party, let alone been in the one that found her. I was just turned 11 and Granddad said I was old enough to come along. He even let me carry his little rifle we used for squirrel hunting.

All the men were armed, not that we would shoot Mrs. Bickens. She was a lady and besides that, she was pregnant. Plus you just don't go shooting people who've gone a little crazy. If we did that, half of Carter County would be dead, to tell the truth. Not too many stayed crazy all the time, but there were a goodly number who would just go buck wild every once in a while and some we'd have to chase, some would just tire out and come home and some didn't ever come home, lost forever.

So the guns were more to protect us from anything out there in the dark, like a panther or a dad-gum copperhead. I hated snakes. They don't seem very dangerous, just lying in the warm sun, but if they get their fangs in you, you are in big trouble.

We had just starting marching off down the dirt road that ran north to south in front of our house. I heard a strange sound and instinctively grabbed for Granddad's hand. He chuckled, gave my hand a little squeeze, and then pushed it away before the other men could see his grandson acting like a scaredy-cat.

"Just an old whippoorwill, boy," Grandpa whispered. "Nothing to fear."

I nodded, my cowboy hat slipping too far forward and nearly sliding right off my head. I reached up and planted it more firmly. The bird called again, so Granddad shined his lantern that way and there it was, sitting like a rock on the side of the road. I stuck my tongue out at the bird for scaring me and almost revealing me as a coward to the other men.

The road was familiar, since we all walked it several times a day. It led to the spring, it led to the dairy farm, and it led to the artesian well, a local treasure. The best, coldest, purest water we'd any of us ever tasted. Folks would walk quite a ways to get some artesian water and tote it home. Also, some of the men like to shuffle down this road late at night and meet up by the creek for a quiet smoke.

As we walked, the men used their lanterns to scan the sides of the road, including ditches, which were fairly deep and could hold a hiding woman. Or a dead woman, which is what we of course were all dreading. One of these days, the poor lady was going to be running along these dark roads in the dark and come to great harm. So we checked everywhere.

Before we got to the dairy farm, Granddad said, "Fellers, we don't' want to miss the Jameson place. Turn here by this little bare spot in the grass."

The men stopped walking, except Granddad, who moved steadily forward. I tried to be as brave as him, but I'd heard some really scary things about the Jameson place. Haints and spooks and ghosts just plain took over the place after the Jamesons left town. Not even the toughest older kids would risk exploring the farm. And here Granddad was fixing to go down there to find a crazy woman.

"Hey, Homer," one of the men said. "Why'nt we just skip this place. She may be crazy, but surely she'd not go in that place."

Granddad, already in the yard, stopped and turned half way back toward the men.

"We're going to search here too."

He turned back around and I guess that was that. We all followed him on in. The house was falling down, half the roof caved in and an old dead tree had fallen in front of the front door last winter. No one bothered to come remove it, since we all had enough of our own chores to do and besides, no one lived there.

So the Jameson place was a mess, I swear. We passed their well as we entered the yard. Someone had come and boarded it over to keep kids from messing around and falling in the dang old thing. I noticed all the men walking far to the right of where Granddad strode, sure and straight as an arrow toward the front of the house. They were none of them eager to walk too close to the old cellar on the left side of the house.

Ozarks is tornado country and nothing scares us hillbillies more than a twister coming down from the sky, skipping around like a little school girl, hitting this house, missing that one, hitting five more. We saw dark skies when it was warm out, noticed a greenish tint to the clouds, and, worse yet, hail started to fall, we all hit the storm cellar. And you stayed there till it was safe.

Thinking back on it, I guess the Ozarks gave folks a lot to fear. The woods were thick with pine trees growing so close you could get lost 10 feet in. The only street lights were downtown, a little six block long strip that held the bank and grocery story. Past that, we had only the stars and the moon to guide us. The men had brought some kerosene lanterns, too, lighting up a circle around us, a circle of safety and it did make you feel better. Once you felt safe, then you tried to look past the circle of light and saw nothing but blackness. You were one kerosene lanterns reach from danger.

Haints were just about everywhere down in our neck of the woods. Old Indian haints, our ancestor's haints, just about anyone in the county who'd ever died unhappy, they turned into haints and lived in our woods. Ozarks are a beautiful blessing from God, but it is a dangerous, scary place for an 11-year-old boy.

As we all dawdled behind Granddad, he was nearly at the porch when the cellar door flew open. Every man with us jumped a foot, even Granddad. That cellar should be empty; no one should be smashing the door open.

And bang! That old cellar door slammed shut. What in the world? Was Mrs. Bickens hiding down in the cellar this time? If she was, she had surely lost her entire mind. That cellar was no place to be hiding in, especially in the dark.

And the door flew open again and every man there, including me, had their gun at their shoulder, finger quivering near the trigger. Everyone but Granddad. He was standing still, listening carefully, and shining his torch at the cellar door.

It was made of planks of rough wood, same as our own cellar door, with a rusty old metal handle hanging by maybe one nail. Knee-high grass made it hard to see the cellar, but we could see the edge of the door sticking up in the air.

Granddad casually started moving closer to the cellar.

"Jessie? This is Homer Wolfe," he called out in a voice just loud enough to carry to her ears, if she was indeed hidden in the cellar. "Jessie, come on out, there's a bunch of folks worried about you, and there's six of us men here to protect you, get you home safe to Jim."

The door slammed shut again. We all jumped at the loud bang of wood hitting wood and echoing in the empty cellar. We took a couple steps back, but Granddad was still calmly stepping closer.

"Jessie..." he started, then all hell broke loose. That old cellar door slammed open and shut BAM! BAM! BAM! like a hammer hitting a nail. How could Mrs. Beitner open and shut the door so fast? I couldn't even shut the door by myself, back then when I was eleven. It took me and my brother to lift the heavy door and let it drop closed again.

"Jessie, if you're in there, come on out," Granddad's voice stayed calm. "No sense in hiding, we just want to get you and your baby home safe and sound."

Did Granddad really think that little pregnant woman was slamming that door back and forth like that, having her a temper tantrum or something? He must because he was moving closer again. *Dang it, Granddad,* I thought, *get away from there afore the haints get you!*

But no, stubborn old man just walked right up to the cellar and reached down to open the door. He was a strong man, after working his whole life chopping wood at the sawmill, but he still strained as he lifted the door.

"Jessie?" he called. No answer came out, but we all heard a loud squeal, like a pig. Some of the men laughed.

"Oh, hell," John Steadman said. "We got a damn pig fell in there and scared the piss outta us."

He lowered his gun and wiped a hand over his face. "Whoo-ee, Homer, you had me scared, calling that woman's name while that door kept a flappin'."

Granddad looked at him with a shake of his head. "I can see inside here, John. Ain't no pig in here."

The men all quieted and edged forward. Granddad got impatient.

"Well, when you womenfolk are done mincing around, maybe you could send some men over here to help me," he growled.

The men looked at each other sheepishly, especially my Pa, and walked quickly to the cellar door. Granddad's lantern lit up the whole cellar. Nothing. No pregnant woman and no clumsy pig. Granddad stepped down the first stair leading down into the cellar.

"Whoa, there, Wolfe," George Clemmons called. "Could be snakes in there. We know the woman's not here, let's just move on, keep looking."

Granddad hadn't even paused. He was at the bottom of the stairs now and one or two of the men swore, but they all followed him. As far as cellars go, the Jameson's had done themselves well. It was plenty deep enough and I bet the whole family could spread out a bedroll down here and sleep if need be. They even had canned food on some shelves against the far wall.

Another ear-piercing squeal caught us all of guard, even Granddad who, in spite of himself, took a scrambling step backwards. We were all jammed against each other when a strong wind pushed itself past us, tugging at our clothes and blowing up dry earth in our faces. In the middle of it, we heard the cellar door slam shut. We were stuck in here! I was scared out of my mind at this point, didn't know where my Granddad or Pa was, and the wind had blown the lamps out.

Voices were raised as we all panicked. Granddad finally shouted, "Quiet!!" and the men at least stopped talking, still scrubbing dirt out of their eyes and coughing from the windstorm. The hiss of a match lighting and suddenly the lantern was shining again. We were all here, each and every man. And me, no longer wanting to be a man, but wishing I was back home with Ma and Grandma, waiting for the men to return.

Granddad said we should get the door open and three of the men squeezed up the stairs and pushed against the door. No winds fought them now, but the door still wouldn't open. No amount of pushing seemed to even budge the door until all at once it pounded open, hitting the ground outside hard. The men nearly fell back down the stairs, but now the door was open, they had calmed down and all made their way up to the surface. I hung back, waiting for my Granddad, who was poking around the shelves full of canned goods. My Pa said, "What you got there, Pa?"

"Don't rightly know," he said, blowing dust off a gallon Mason jar, and then using his thumb to clear a spot to see into the jar. He stared at the jar for a minute, and rubbed more dirt off. After getting a better look at what was in the jar, Granddad told Pa, "Get the boy out of here, son. Right now."

Pa took me by the shoulder and turned me toward the stairs, I tried to look back and see what Granddad had found, but Pa was having none of that, and got me up those stairs in no time. He told the men to keep me there while he went back down.

The men were quiet, still reeling a bit from the scare of that crazy door trapping us inside the cellar. They mostly just looked around, as if making sure something hadn't sneaked up behind us while the cellar door held us in a trap. After a few minutes my Pa came back up and said he was walking me home, and he'd be back.

"You men need to go down with my father and see something," he said. His voice quivered a bit, but I couldn't blame him. This was a hard night to be brave.

We walked on back to our house, where we lived with Granddad and Grandma. All of us, Pa, Ma, two more boys, and me all packed in our tiny house, but we fit. The women were standing outside the front door, waiting for us.

"Henry, where's Granddad?" my Ma called. "Did you find Mrs. Beitner?"

Pa shook his head. "No, we didn't find her, but I need the boy here to stay back to home. I'm heading back. And he didn't do anything wrong, so don't be a'chewing him out. It's just turning out to be . . . well, no place for a boy."

Just then we heard shouting and turned toward the road. One of the Giles boys was running full tilt down the road shouting, "We found her! She's ok! We found her."

Pa raised a hand to indicate that he'd heard the boy, so the kid spun around and headed full-tilt back to town.

"Oh, that's good news," Grandma said. "That poor woman."

Pa put his hand on my shoulder and gave it a quick squeeze. "You did good, son, now you stay here with the others. We'll be home soon."

I nodded and smiled at Pa, even though part of me wanted to head back to that cellar and see what had alarmed my Granddad. But part of me wanted to sit next to my ma out on the stoop and feel her warmth and not be worrying about haints.

Pa left and Ma and Grandma decided it was time for bed. I begged to be allowed to wait up for the men and by some miracle they agreed, only warning me to stick close to the house, no wandering off. I solemnly promised them I would not leave the yard and they went off to join my brothers in bed.

I plunked down on the front steps and took off my hat. It was ringed with sweat and my hair underneath it was soaked. Mosquitos buzzed me as usual. When the last light went off in the house, it left me sitting in that solid black of night that made me just a little jumpy. I tried to imagine what my Granddad had found in the cellar that was so bad he sent me home. Was it a dead critter? No way, I've been around dead critters all my life, killed a few myself.

I finally decided I would die if I didn't go find out what the men were doing down there by the creek. I settled my cowboy hat on my head again and stood up, determined to not be left out of this adventure. I walked a few steps across the yard through the pitch black and when my feet hit the dirt road, I turned south and remembered how dark that long walk had seemed earlier tonight, and that had been with lanterns. I would have to walk through the complete darkness by myself. I could encounter snakes, critters, mean dogs. Even haints.

Back then I didn't fear other people. Children ran free, never thinking another human could be a predator. We only feared the uncontrollable, like wild animals and ghosts. We thought people were guided by morals and the Good Lord. That's what I thought at the time, anyway.

Finally, I screwed up my courage and marched down the road, intent on finding the men and learning what had happened. The entire walk I was plagued with eerie sounds, rustling bushes and oddly shaped sticks that always, always looked like a danged snake. I felt a burning in my eyes and knew I was one scare away from tears. I was plumb crazy with fear when I heard my Granddad's deep voice nearby. My knees were weak with relief and I took off running.

I was about five feet away from the men when I remembered I wasn't supposed to be here. I was supposed to be waiting at home. So I slowed down and, with the lights from their lanterns now brightening the night, I hid behind a tree and listened.

"Do you think the Jamesons did that?" Ezra Teeters asked, his voice quivering. I could see the men were passing around a bottle and my Pa passed it to Ezra, who took a deep swallow.

"Naw, some of those jars look 10 years old or more, they're so filthy," Granddad said. "I'm no expert, but that's what I think, anyway."

"You'uns think we should call the sheriff?" George said, glancing nervously at Granddad.

My Pa shifted around a bit and reached out for the bottle. Taking a quick swig, he said, "Call the Sheriff? For what? Them babies are dead, been dead a long time. Sheriff can't find his ass with both hands, don't think he can figure something like this out."

Granddad grunted a sort of half-agreement and Ezra said, "Ain't that the truth."

Our Sheriff wasn't a real lawman. He wore a star on his jacket, which was corny as hell, and drove his old beat-down truck up and down the roads pretending to look for trouble. Mostly he bullied the kids and leered at the women. None of the men paid him no mind.

Granddad was taking a long drink out of the bottle now. He wiped his mouth with the back of his hand and sighed deeply.

"Fellers, I think we had best take care of this ourselves," he said. "This here's Satan at work. Only possible answer."

The men murmured their agreement.

"No human mind, no matter how sick, could conceive of what we found in that cellar," my Pa said. He spat on the ground. "The devil's been at work here."

In the silence, the bottle was passed around again and the men were thinking hard.

"Homer, have you ever heard of anything like this?" John asked. "You've been a preacher. You read the Bible more than anyone I know. Does God talk about something like this happening?"

"Land's sake, no," Granddad answered. "I almost wish it did. We might get some sense out of it.

I stood there trying to be quiet but I was dying to ask questions. What was so horrible about the jars? What was so bad it frightened my Granddad, a man of faith and braver than anyone I knew?

George Teeters suddenly spun around and stepped away from the group. He vomited for a few minutes, then spat and used his handkerchief to wipe his mouth.

"You all right, George?"

He nodded but in the lantern light I could see his hands were shaking and he seemed paler than anyone else.

"I ain't never going to forget that . . . that. . . .," he faltered. He looked up at my Granddad. "There were dead little babies in them jars, Homer. Babies! Whose babies are they?"

He dropped his head and covered his face with both hands. Shaking shoulders were the only sign that he was crying. The other men took out their handkerchiefs and wiped at tears.

Granddad's voice was cracked and weak when he answered. "Like I said, it's got to be the work of Satan, fellers. Ain't no human would do such a thing. No human so evil."

Tears were flowing down his weathered cheeks now, but he merely swiped at them with his fingertips. I clung to the tree I was hiding behind, sick to my stomach as I tried to understand what the men were saying. Someone had put dead babies in jars and hid them in the Jameson's cellar? For what? What the heck was the purpose of such a thing?

"There's only one answer," Granddad said. "We need to burn the cellar up. Don't no one else need to know about this."

The others nodded, except my Pa. He took a big swig from the bottle. "That's probably a bad idea, destroying the evidence. Maybe we could figure out who did it. Satan had to have some human help to get hold of those babies."

He looked around at the other men. "Don't you'uns want to know where them babies came from? Was it our wives? We've all suffered the loss of a child at birth or a miscarriage. Are these our children in there, stuffed into jars like garden vegetables? Our children?"

His voice was loud now and high-pitched. Ma had lost a baby last fall. It had been hard on her and she had cried and cried. Pa had sat on the porch, his arms around her, night after night, until at last she could think of something other than her poor dead child. But it was still not the same around home. Ma was still a'grieving.

Granddad put his hand on Pa's shoulder, then pulled him closer. Pa let his head fall on Granddad's shoulder just like I did sometimes and cried his heart out. The other men turned their heads, trying to give the father and son a little privacy. Finally,

Pa was cried out and he raised his head and said, "I'm sorry. I just about can't bear it."

Granddad finally spoke. "You see? All of you? We gotta just destroy that cellar and those jars and the . . . the things in it. All it will bring is pain for the rest to know. And maybe by burning and destroying it, Satan will leave this place. As much as he ever does leave a place."

The men nodded, each one of them thinking of wives or sisters or their own mothers, who might wonder if it was their baby in one of those jars. If they had to make the decision on their own, so be it. Standing in the blackness, with the faint glow of lantern light, the sight of those babies, faces smashed against the sides of the glass jars, Satan was the most likely answer.

"It's what makes her run, I figger," Ezra said.

"What makes who run?" Pa asked indignantly.

"It's what makes Jessie run ever time she's pregnant. She's seen this cellar or the devil's tried to get her babies before," he said. "So now she's a'feared and so she runs."

Granddad laid his hand over his heart. "Dear God. That poor woman."

He snatched up his lantern from where it sat on the ground and said. "Now. We do it now. And we swear amongst us to never speak of this again."

All the men nodded and followed Granddad on down the road. Grateful that I hadn't been caught and too sick at heart to follow the men, I raced through the night back to our house. I only stopped to catch my breath while I kicked off my shoes and threw my hat on the floor before climbing into bed.

Later Pa and Granddad came home, quiet, bringing the smell of burning wood with them. They undressed and climbed into their beds, their women waking up to ask what happened. Both men said "There was a little fire at Jameson's. It's okay now. Go back to sleep."

The next morning I snuck off and hightailed it down to Jameson's. The cellar door was gone, but smoke still rose from inside the cellar. Even the house had burned to the ground. It was all done and hopefully forgotten.

A year later, Jesse got pregnant again and, like always, took off a runnin' one night. We found her in the road in front of the old Jameson place just smilin' and singing a little lullaby to her unborn baby. She wasn't all beat up like usual, in fact her face shone like an angel's and her hair was neat and clean. Her dress was white, with little rosebuds embroidered on the collar. She was a beautiful image of motherhood at that moment and she smiled as the men approached her.

"Howdy, you'uns," she said. "I reckon I'm ready to head back home now. I done run enough."

I kept my promise; though no one was aware I made it, to not tell this story until now. Everyone else is dead of old age. I'm no spring chicken myself. But I seen a lot of babies born around town since then, a few of my own, and not one of those births failed to fill me with wonder and joy.

And it always filled me with pride in the men who raised me, to know they destroyed the evil that dwelled among us, even though it wasn't Satan alone. When the men burned the cellar, my Pa told me years later, a woman came running out of the decrepit Jameson house. Her hair was tangled and knotted with sticks and leaves and her dress was filthy, smeared with her own waste and what looked like blood. She held a butcher knife above her head and came screaming like a banshee.

"My babies! My babies!" she screeched. "They're mine! Leave them be."

Then her head jerked back and she fell into the high grass. My granddad still held his rifle at his shoulder but his eyes were squeezed tight.

"Dear God, forgive me for what I have done," he whispered. Pa carefully approached the woman but she was dead. One bullet, right through her eye. The men gathered her up and placed her body inside the house, then lit it on fire.

No one knows why she did what she did or where the rest of her family went. We don't know a lot about her. All we could figure was that for some reason, her sanity left her and Satan found a home in her, and a vessel to use to do his evil bidding.

One Sunday, soon after it happened, my Pa and Granddad went to the cemetery and put up a small wooden cross inscribed "For the Babies in Heaven." No one questioned them. It was a small thing to do, Pa said, to honor those poor babies.

The cross is gone now. I went to look at it last week, and it's just gone. It was there last year, when my Pa was buried. I am pretty sure it's just damned ornery kids pulled it out of the ground and ruined it. Then again, Satan might have taken it out of jealousy. He can have it, but I'll not build another for him to steal.

Suzy Saylor
A Halcyon Panacea

I guess it was more curiosity than anything that led me back to that house. I only remembered snippets of memories; I wasn't any older than a toddler the last time I was there. I walked up the beautiful tree lined drive, crunching the earth-toned leaves that skittered about in front of me. I hardly noticed the distance as the past flashed in bits through my mind. It was all so dark and sad, and I couldn't remember why. I mostly recalled the screaming and my brother pushing me into my closet and closing the door. I remembered when the state came and took us to our Aunt's house. From there, the memories feel warm, happy, real. There was no more screaming after that.

I clomped up the steps onto the massive wrap-around porch that sagged under the weight of age and decay. The light green paint only showed in splotches where it hadn't rotted away yet and there were cobwebs ensnaring a broken rocking chair. A porch swing hanged by one rusty chain, the other end falling apart into the rotting boards beneath. I took the key the lawyer had given me out of my pocket, examining it as if I expected it to look like the rest of the house so far-rotted and decaying. It was just a plain key, like any other. The locks had been replaced at some point because the tumbler was still somewhat shiny compared to the splintery wood of the old door it sat in. I did remember those doors. They always looked so big to me, but then again, I was only a small child the last time I saw them. Dark wood with a beautiful ornate carving of a tree centered in the middle of the doors, branches stretching strong and noble outwards towards the hinges, leaving windowpanes that could be peeked through in between the outstretched limbs. Now the tree just seemed to sag in the wood, as if beaten down by time. With an effort, I pushed open the warped wood door and stepped inside, back into a past I couldn't recall.

I didn't recognize anything within the house at all. It was a massive mess of cobwebs, broken furniture, dust, and spots of black mold and rot. I wandered through the downstairs, past the sweeping staircase that led up to the next floors. Despite the decay, it still managed to give the appearance of regality in dark wood, like something out of the Roaring Twenties. I peeked around the various rooms on the main floor, ending up in the kitchen. It looked as if it was once a great space, but was now just grey and bland. There was a door to one side that caught my eye. It had been nailed shut with multiple boards. Some of the boards looked old and rotted, but there were newer ones over top the rotten ones. Whoever replaced the locks must have replaced some of the boards as well, but why? It struck me as odd, but when I walked over to the door itself, something gave me an icy chill that sent goose bumps up my arms and culminated in a shiver that shot down my spine. I backed away from it, as if I expected something to burst out of it like a haunted house.

I walked back to the vast staircase and began my ascent to the next floor. There wasn't much there except some old bed frames in a few rooms, some dusty toys and dressers. I couldn't even recall which one was mine. They looked so strange and foreign; part of someone else's past. I continued down the hallway to the doorway at the very end. I knew that it led up to the attic, but I couldn't remember how I knew that. Could have been just common sense, it was a smaller door that didn't look like the other bedroom doors. It stood slightly cracked open, a mass of darkness beyond was all that I could see. I pulled it the rest of the way open and was amazed to see that the darkness was so deep within it that I couldn't even make out the steps. I grabbed my cell phone and lit up the screen to act as a flashlight, and slowly made my way up the steps, watching my feet the whole time.

I emerged into the attic, shocked at the amount of light that filled the room. It didn't touch the stairwell at all. I looked around me and didn't see what was wrong at first. It seemed like a typical attic, old and dusty, filled with old trunks and boxes, discarded toys and furniture. I walked over to a floor length mirror and brushed away a swath of thick dust and jumped back startled from what I saw in the reflection. Instead of my face staring back at me, I saw two little girls playing dress up with clothes that looked like they were from before WWII. They were giggling and posing like models. I snapped my head around to look behind me, and there was nothing there. I don't know why I expected to actually see them, there I knew I was alone in the house. I turned back around and still saw them playing in the mirror. I was still staring at the mirror, slack jawed, when all of a sudden the girls became extremely frightened and began panicking. I watched as they ran out of sight of the mirror's reflection, hiding behind or under something I couldn't see. Out of nowhere, a massive shape took up the entire mirror. I could hear the girls whimpering, and I swear I felt the floor beneath shake under the weight of heavy footfalls. There was a growl that thrummed through the air like distant thunder, threatening to come your way. The footfalls got louder and louder, and I heard the girls crying now. I leaned into the cleared part of the mirror, trying to see something and it suddenly exploded into millions of little daggers around me. I jumped and tried to cover my face reflexively, but I could feel the sting of shards as they pierced any exposed skin I had. Before I even had time to think about the pain, something grabbed me by the scalp and picked me up so that my feet were barely scraping the floor. A massive hand wrapped around my throat and I was suddenly staring into the face of a man the size of a giant, angry and red. I couldn't make out what he was screaming because a black fuzziness had begun to set in as I felt my windpipe begin to crush under his intense strength. I could still hear the girls crying from their hiding place, but everything was disappearing. A split second before the whole world shut off, I felt him throw my body to the floor and stomp away. I coughed and choked, my eyes rolling around trying to settle on which way was up. I rolled onto my side and saw the behemoth throw aside a small table that splintered against a nearby beam, next a trunk of clothing that scattered clothing everywhere. That must have been where the girls found their dress-up clothes. Then I saw them, the girls, small and terrified. I looked around and the landscape of the attic had changed dramatically. The wood floor beneath me was newer and there was hardly any dust covering anything. The girls shrieked as the ogre found them. I watched in horror as he grabbed them both by the hair, as he had me, and lifted them like dolls into the air. Before I realized what I was doing, I was mid-air grabbing them out of his hands. We tumbled to the floor, and slammed against the back of an old couch. I looked down, to see if they were hurt, but they were gone. Just gone. The man turned towards me, as if really noticing me for the first time and began to charge. I threw myself to the left and hurtled into the pitch-black stairwell, tumbling painfully all the way down.

I crashed through the door and into the wall on the other side of the hallway. I looked up, expecting to see his hulking shape bearing down on me, but there was nothing. It was silent. My head swam with the images of what I had seen. I rubbed my neck where it still ached from his grip. I slowly stood up and stumbled down the hall until I found what looked like the bathroom. It smelled like mold, and the tub was covered in a thick black substance. I went to go look in the mirror to see the damage I had sustained. There were bruises in the beginning stages of turning purple and little streaks of blood running down my forehead and cheeks. I heard a door slam behind me and I whipped around, expecting to see the giant from the attic. I didn't even see it happen, but the room had changed. There was some kind of hideous psychedelic wallpaper all around, mustard yellow tile on the floor and pea green toilet and sink. The only thing that looked familiar was the lion's foot bathtub, but what it contained was the most disturbing of all. Dark red water sloshed over the edge as a naked woman stood up from within. She was covered in numerous cuts, gashes, and skin that split open like a carved turkey. Blood ran in sheets down her bare body, pattering on the surface of the water and then onto the floor as she stepped out of the tub towards me. She held razorblades in each hand and made no sound. I didn't wait around to see if she would. I ran for the door, yanking it open with all my strength. I ran down the mammoth staircase and swung into the little cupboard that hid beneath them and slammed shut the door. I didn't realize that I even recalled the space was there until I sat coiled up in a ball inside, pulling desperately at the latch to hold the door closed.

As I sat shaking in the dark, I recalled my brother pushing me into the very same space and telling me not to make a sound, hold the door tight, wait for him to come get me. The memories started to flood back. I heard the screaming and thumping outside the closet, my brother's voice yelling, then crying. I opened my eyes in the darkness, wishing not to recall anything else and felt the salt from tears stinging the many little slices on my cheeks. It was then that I noticed the small scratching sound coming from somewhere in the dark of the small cubby. I peered into the blackness, trying in vain to see where the noise was coming from. There was nothing but darkness all around, but something scraped again along the wooden floor, louder and deeper. I could feel a presence pressing closer, a chemical smell filled my nostrils and made my already irritated throat slam closed. A low moan filled the cupboard and I scrambled to push open the door. I had accidentally let go of the handle and couldn't find it again. As I scrabbled and grabbed around for the handle, I hit a switch next to the doorjamb. I stared at the light bulb that flickered to life a short distance above my head for just a moment, puzzled that there was electricity still flowing to the house before seeing what was really making the sounds I'd heard in the dark. A creature was slowly pulling itself out of the wood of the stairs above the low end of the closet. I couldn't identify it as human in any aspect with the exception of its shape. Hypodermic needles reached out like fingers, scratching against the lumber as it wriggled itself slowly free, some kind of viscous liquid dripped out of the tips. Something my brain rationalized as a face made of what looked like all kinds of pills and little white rocks was emerging as well. An orifice that stood agape was the source of a sound, a lament that held the sentiment of both pleasure and despair at once. A powder poured out of the strange cavity and piled up in the cracks of the floorboards, leaving white lines behind in the strangest pattern. Arms emerged covered in puncture marks, weeping blood and pus in thin streams. I scrambled even harder to find the handle to the door, fearing to take my eyes off the abomination developing in front of me. It's chest pushed out from the wood, making it appear as if the wood itself were suddenly smoldering. Acrid smoke puffed in and out, like breaths forced from hell. I thought I was screaming but all that came out was a harsh squeak as I pounded back against the door. It finally gave way and I launched backwards into the hallway. I scuttled down the hall away from the stairs, my legs failing to give me leverage to stand. I slid into the kitchen and hid behind the corner, gasping and wheezing. I tried to slow the pounding of my heart in my ears so I could hear if that atrocity was coming after me. I ventured a small peek around the corner, tentatively edging just a sliver of my face past the wall. There was nothing there, absolutely nothing. The door to the cupboard under the stairs sat slightly ajar, but showed no signs of movement. There was no sound of grating metal on wood or smell of permeating chemicals, no acrid hallucinogenic smoke either. I took a moment to catch my breath and tried to wrap my mind around everything had just occurred. I had unconsciously curled into a ball, squeezing myself tighter and tighter, as if I could wring out the panic that flowed freely through every cell of my body. I just sat there shaking for what seemed like an eternity. My heart finally slowed and I began to regain some semblance of control over my thoughts again. I noticed a tickle on the back of my neck, like someone playing with your hair, but it spread in icy tendrils down my back and arms, and just as it clicked that I was leaning up against the previously boarded up door to the cellar it swung open and I tumbled backwards down a set of roughhewn steps. I came to rest on a dirt floor that was packed hard enough to leave me seeing stars when my head slammed into it. It was freezing cold and the air was thin. I sat up, peering into the gloom, debating on if I really wanted to see if there was something there or just shut my eyes and wish for home. Out of nowhere, a light flooded the room, blinding me. I flinched my eyes shut, trying to adjust to the sudden brightness. When I opened them again, a face filled my vision, mere inches away. I screamed as she laughed and said, "Is that any way to greet your mother?" My mother. The psychopath that forced the State to come and take my siblings and I away. My brother had committed suicide a few years ago because of the damage done by her. Since then, the house passed through 4 other siblings before reaching me, the youngest. The malevolent woman behind the pain of 6 children died over a decade ago. I didn't bother going to the funeral. I never really knew the woman except from the stories of my brothers and sisters and a few recurring nonsensical nightmares I'd had my whole life.

Her face was emaciated and decaying. Spots of bone showed through ragged holes where the flesh had either torn away or was eaten by something. Her clothes hung off her skeletal body, dirty and tattered. She looked like she just crawled out from her coffin. The spooks you see in a haunted house couldn't come close to the horror of seeing the real thing. What was left of her skin seemed to ooze and slide on her bones. There were definitely things crawling and wriggling underneath it in spots. A brownish-yellow slime dripped from under her dress, and slid down the bones of her legs where her skin had pulled away and sat bunched and sagging at her knees and ankles. My lunch made reappearance all over my lap. She continued to laugh as I wretched and tried to clamber backwards up the stairs. "Did you really think you could escape me your whole life? I am your destiny, you little bitch. I never wanted you to begin with. I survived my whole life, all the pain and torment just to be saddled with *children*," she spat the word out like it was poison. "Your stupid spineless father thought he could hold me that way, keep me quiet. I made him quiet instead." she laughed, a sound like gravel put into a blender. "What do you want with me now?" I wheezed, throat still hoarse and now burning from bile. "I want to finish what I started," she screamed, "I want you to understanding the meaning of suffering, of pain. You spoiled little shit, you don't know what agony is. I outlived my father a man who could crush you with his fist. He touched me one too many times and I proved his face wasn't stronger than a shotgun blast." An image of the man in the attic flashed in my mind. "I proved to the world that nothing could take me. Do you know how it feels to drag the cold metal of a blade across your skin? To feel the rush of warmth as blood flowed over your skin? It's remarkable. You should try it some time." She sneered at me, shoving her wrists in my face. The flesh still clung to her body there. It was marred and puckered, cris-crossed with scars. There were stich marks over some of the larger slices and puffed out where some had never fully closed.

The girl in the bathroom, it must have been my mother. What the hell was going on? "I don't understand. You DIED! You're dead! How are you here?" I yelled back at her, surprised at the intensity of my voice. She laughed again, that terrible cacophony of sound. "You fucking moron, nothing can hold me. Not even death. I survived more horrors than your tiny little brain could ever imagine. I did every drug known to man, I drank more alcohol than most distilleries contain, I poured out my veins, and yet I lived! You shits put me in the ground, and here I am! YOU did this!" She jutted out a bony finger towards me. "So, here's my thanks for that." Before I could react, she grabbed me by the throat and pulled me up to eye level, well, what would have been eye level had there not just been holes of ragged flesh and pus. I felt the sharp edges of bone cutting into my skin as she hissed, "I will give you all you deserve for ruining me, for ruining my life." With that she slammed me into the ground with a force that fiercely betrayed the appearance of her wasted body. She dropped a knee onto my neck, forcing the breath out of me and the slime from her shredded skin. It spilled over into my mouth and gagged me beyond the physical restraint of the body that now pressed its full weight down on my windpipe. "I'm going to take the breath that you never should have breathed in the first place. I never wanted you-ANY of you little rats," She screamed as she covered the rest of my face with her hands, "I should have died long ago, long before you ever came along. God wouldn't let me die, he kept me alive, tortured me with a life that never should have been lived. Consider this a gift, from your dear Mother." A split second before everything went dark, it all hit me.

I woke up in the cubby under the stairs, scrunched up against the plaster wall. The light was on, and the demon was still slowly emerging from the boards. I wasn't sure if I was real or just remembering the last moments of my life. I dug my nails into my hand and felt the sting of skin breaking open. It was real. I looked at the strange creature advancing on me by inches. I could easily get away from it, easily avoid it, but I let it crawl up to me on its needle hands and burnt glass pipe legs. It made a noise that sounded almost like a purr and speared me with all ten needles at once. I gasped reflexively, and all at once it poured itself into my mouth. Pills jammed down my throat and smoke filled my lungs. There was a moment of complete euphoria, and I briefly forgot all the pain I was in, but then it dissolved into shear agony. My stomach twisted and burned, trying to force back out its new contents. I could feel my body begin to convulse and flail about, but my brain seemed confused as to what was happening.

I felt a sudden stab in my chest that brought with it the weight of an elephant. The light began to fade in my sight, and somewhere distant I heard scream like twisting metal.

The harsh contrast of colors hit my eyes like a sledgehammer. The crazy wallpaper of the upstairs bathroom was enough to drive anyone mad. The bloody woman's steps sounding like the splat of meat being slapped on a butcher's block. She advanced quickly, but stood silently in front of me for a moment. I held out my arms, baring my wrists to her. There was a blur of motion, an intense pain, and then warmth that covered the length of my arms. I looked down and saw the blood pouring from deep slices that followed the main arteries in my wrists. It fell like rain to the ugly tile floor, and pooled quickly around my feet. The warm sensation I had felt soon retreated to a bone chilling cold that filled me from head to toe. My head swam and began to get fuzzy. The woman looked at me as I collapsed to the floor and whispered, "This debt was not yours to pay, yet you paid it anyway. Such an act carries quite a weight." I couldn't keep my vision steady or clear any longer, so I just closed my eyes. I heard that scream again, this time it seemed closer.

I heard a crash behind me and unclenched my eyes to try and see what was making the noise, though I had a pretty good idea what it was already. The giant man was crashing around the cluttered attic, tossing or smashing everything in his path. I stood up from behind the couch I was stooped behind. I saw the two girls from earlier standing directly in his path. I saw their expressions and while one wore terror, the other wore a mischievous smile. He grabbed the scared one, and hoisted her high above his head. She squirmed and screamed, begging him to stop, "Daddy no! Please Daddy, don't!" The other girl started giggling as she watched him take hold of the terrified twin, an evil, vile sort of laugh. "Hey you fat bastard! Put her down!" I heard myself screaming at him. He stopped mid-squeeze and turned to face me. I remembered his face from an old photograph, Grandfather. He dropped the little girl and stomped towards me. His face almost purple with rage, his breath stinking of bourbon. "Come and get me, I dare you." I taunted and prepared for the hit. He swung a massive fist at my face, hitting me square in the jaw. I heard popping sounds and felt the weight of bone not sitting right in my mouth. He grabbed me with both hands, and shook me so hard, I could feel my joints separating in places and slamming back together. "You! You are an abomination! The seed of some other man! I will put you under like I did your mother!" He growled at me. He dropped me to the floor and walked away for a moment. I saw the two girls across the attic, the one he had dropped lay in much the same position I was in, the other one now held a look of consternation, and fidgeted nervously in place. "Now you die, you crazy little bitch." I whispered to her. Her face dropped, and she opened her mouth to scream, the same scream I'd heard before, just as the monster swung the thick pedestal of a table down onto my chest. Pain surged through my body and I felt the air in my lungs explode outwards. I looked over to where the girls had been and saw the one vanish into wisps of nothing, scream disappearing with her. The other had pushed herself up and was looking at me with a strange combination of terror and pity. She stood up, grabbing a long piece of splintered wood that resembled a primeval spear. Her ribcage was shifted hard to one side, and her jaw very noticeably broken. Without warning, she ran full force towards her father as he was preparing for another downswing of the giant club. I winced in anticipation of the blow, but it never came. I looked up and saw the jagged end of the beam sticking through his chest. Blood and bits of tissue hung from the uneven point. He dropped to his knees and fell over, sending a massive shudder across the floor. I could feel the air getting harder and harder to suck in and closed my eyes waiting for it to end. I felt a little hand on my tender cheek, and I looked up to see the little girl kneeling in front of me. I could see the resemblance in her young features to those I remember of my mother much later in life. She couldn't speak, but I could see she was saying thank you. I smiled as best as I could, closed my eyes and let the dark overtake me.

As I watched the house being bulldozed, I thought about that strange day when I first returned to the home of my mother. I had discovered in the time since that she had been the product of a rape by a madman, and the victim of terrible abuse by her father. When he nearly killed her that day in attic, he caused a split in her. She became the psycho we later knew. It was her only way to survive. I understood it all when she had said to me that she should have died long before. That scar, that evil part of her, should have died rather than take over her physical body. It was so strong, so hateful; it remained behind in the place that created it, holding her spirit there long after it should have moved on. I released her by giving the other part of her a chance to end the cause of all her pain, her father.

I had awoken that day standing in front of those great big wooden doors, holding the key about to put it in the lock. I never went back inside. I sold the land to developer and only came back to watch when they tore it down. It was like a massive sigh of relief watching it go down. All the bits of my memory from childhood had filled in, and I remembered the suffering my mother had endured, and that she had inflicted upon us, her children as well. As hard as I tried, I couldn't forget what happened when I had returned to that house, the terrible things I saw. I couldn't decide which was worse; finally remembering it all or wishing I were still ignorant. I paid a debt of suffering and death for my mother, though she would never have done the same for me. I rid her of the pain that tormented her spirit, but no good deed ever goes unpunished. I can never rid my thoughts of her; the pain, the anger, and torment haunt me everyday. I see her decaying face in my dreams, feel her cold bony fingers on my neck, and hear her laugh in the silence of the night. I thought I would be rid of her memory if I released her, but all I did was let in past. The house may have been razed to the ground, but she built a castle in my head, one I could never escape from.

Patrick Lacey
Last Words

I didn't know it at the time but my father was signaling me with his eyes.

He lay in his hospice bed, coming in and out of consciousness every so often. He couldn't speak on account of the stroke and the tube shoved down the back of his throat but sometimes he would mumble. The nurse told me he wasn't quite aware, that he could hear and sense my sister and I, but that he couldn't make sense of the situation.

"It won't be long now," she said. "Our main priority is to comfort him as he moves on."

My sister cried, snot dripping from her nose. I handed her a handkerchief. She sobbed loudly into it but I didn't feel bad for her. She had visited him twice in the last five years and she lived two hundred miles closer. She couldn't watch him grow old, she'd said. Couldn't sit around and wait for him to die like our mother.

The nurse was getting ready to change my father's catheter and I was ready for another cup of coffee. I stood, ready to go into the kitchen, when my father opened his eyes and reached out. His liver-spotted hand pointed toward me.

"He's trying to say something!" my sister said.

I leaned in, putting my ear close to his mouth but there was only his heavy and uneven breathing, his last bits of life leaving in a hurry. I shook my head. "I don't think he's saying anything." I leaned back.

And that's when I saw it. His eyes were open as far as the lids would allow. They were ancient and tired and bloodshot and there was something in them, a message I couldn't quite decipher. I wanted him to speak into my mind, but the room remained quiet, save for the sobbing to my right and the hum of the machinery to my left.

I got the sense, without really knowing why, that he wanted something from me, some last errand as his dying wish.

"What is it, Dad?"

I was about to say I loved him and then he died. It wasn't long or dramatic. His arm simply fell against the bed's railing as if some invisible string had been severed. His eyes lingered for one last moment before shutting forever.

My sister's cries grew to a crescendo. The nurse comforted her with rehearsed lines. "He went peacefully. This is all part of grieving. It'll get better."

I stopped listening after a while.

A few hours after his death, my sister declared she would take care of everything, the funeral, the paperwork, the will—everything. That was fine by me. I'd been the strong one for too long.

I wandered into the kitchen for that cup of coffee I'd wanted so badly.

As I sipped I wondered if this was from the same tin he'd used last time I visited, before the stroke. It made my skin come alive. The cupboards were filled with soup and beans and other things that he'd purchased, that he'd planned on eating.

Grief is a funny thing. It affects us all differently. At least that's what I'd read in the books my wife bought me. While my sister was in avoidance and now denial, I'd already moved toward the acceptance stage. I knew he was dying and that was that. But now, drinking his coffee and standing in his kitchen, I wondered what the hell happened next.

I didn't cry, though. He didn't feel far away yet. And neither did his last words, though they hadn't been spoken out loud.

"What did you want?" I said to the empty table.

No one answered me.

My sister refused to stay in the house. "It's too soon," she said. "Maybe someday but not now. I've made reservations at the Waterfront Hotel."

"Of course," I said. "Might as well make a vacation out of it. Enjoy the hot tub."

"That's not what I mean."

"Good night, Sheila." I smiled and shut the door and the house seemed to pulse.

I saw holidays and parties and arguments and everything in between, the things that make up a family's lifetime. Most of all, though, I saw clues. Thousands of them. My father had been telling me something. I knew it like I knew he was dead. It was a certainty.

The last time I'd visited, I'd known it wouldn't be long. He'd had open-heart surgery twice. His bones were visible through his clothes. He was looking at his lifetime achievement plaque given to him by the high school on his last day of teaching.

"You ought to move it into the living room instead of the study," I said. "That's something to be proud of."

"Yes, I suppose so but it's been just fine in here all these years."

"Is something wrong?" He seemed distant.

"Wrong?" He shook his head like he was waking. "No, nothing's wrong. I'm awfully tired and achy but other than that I'm fine. It's funny, though. I never wanted to be a teacher in the first place. I never wanted any of it. I went to school because my parents made me but I would have been content travelling. The truth is I didn't care about anything. I just wanted to get by."

"Well you certainly did well for yourself without any ambition."

"I think that everyone is really two different people. There's the person you are to the world, and there's the person you are to yourself. In my experience, they're quite...incompatible."

I'd thought he was rambling but after his last stare I could see now he'd been getting at something, at some secret that was now eating away at me.

My wife and kids were on the plane now and I was thinking too much. I decided to clean the place up a bit, make it more presentable for when they arrived. I'd bought a half dozen plastic bins from the hardware store and I began gathering things in no particular order.

I filled the first bin and brought it into the basement. It was partially finished, with storage and the washer and dryer in the first room and tools and more junk in the second room. The finished section was full enough as it was so I opened the door and stepped into the unfinished portion.

The light bulb was an energy saver. It took much too long to power up and for a few moments I was left standing the half-darkness, telling myself I was alone in the house and there was no way my father was down there, tidying up or going through old photo albums.

Eventually the bulb became bright and I tossed the bin into the corner.

On my way out, my foot caught beneath the area rug and I lost my balance. I tried to break my fall but misjudged the distance. My head collided with the ground and the world turned bright white.

I felt my forehead. There was a small gash, the blood already coagulating, and the beginnings of an egg-sized bruise. It would look marvelous as I gave the eulogy that weekend.

I tried to stand up and regain my balance.

Something seemed off. I looked at the floor and tried to make sense of it. On my way down, I must have moved the rug over. Where there should have been floor, there was a trap door.

Its edges were crude and it didn't fit evenly into its space. I had been in the basement thousands of times. Surely, my parents would have mentioned it at some point. But I thought for a long time and I was sure they hadn't.

Just a crawl space, I thought. *Probably where he kept his spare half-ass light bulbs.* But it was the basement, not the attic, and every inch of my flesh told me there was something wrong about what I was looking at.

I checked my watch. My wife and kids were probably still states away. It would be another few hours until they arrived.

There are plenty of bins upstairs to be filled. Just go up there and clean. Get your mind off things.

I kneeled down and grabbed the latch and wondered if there had ever been a lock attached to the small chain. It was an odd thought. Why should my father want to lock a trap door, one that he'd never once spoke of?

There was still time, my mind told me. Still time to get away before everything changed. And that's exactly what it felt like. Things would not be the same if I opened it.

I opened it.

It creaked like a dying animal and dust erupted into the air. I covered my mouth and coughed and waved away the cloud of dirt.

When it cleared, I grabbed a flashlight from the other half of the basement and shined it down. At first it seemed like absolute blackness, but as my eyes adjusted, I saw that there was a floor down there, and other objects in the shadows.

There was a ladder that led down. I expected my mind to scream at me again but it was silent, as if I'd already done something that could not be reversed. I descended the ladder slowly, not wanting to fall and break my neck alone in this house that suddenly felt foreign.

At the bottom I stepped off and shined my flashlight, and I felt all of my sanity drift away.

It was an eternity before I accepted what I saw, although sometimes I still question some of it.

It was the stress and the grief. It was the lack of sleep.

Bones. Hundreds and hundreds of bones. Of all different shapes and sizes, some much too small to belong to an adult. Most of them were stacked into the corners of the room.

My senses seemed to catch up with me. The smell struck without warning. I brought my arm up and covered my nose. It was all-encompassing, a sticky sweet and rotten odor that cannot fully be explained without living it.

There were other things besides bones, contraptions of some sort. They looked archaic, something from the middle ages, from the age of public executions.

One of them was a rusty seat. There were clamps on the sides, meant to trap wrists. The closest clamp still housed a hand, most of the flesh rotted away, the bones peeking out as if begging to join the others.

On the far wall were countless small squares. I didn't want to know what they were. I didn't want to know any of this. But my legs moved on their own, bringing me closer, until I saw that they were photos, small Polaroids neatly arranged in rows.

I shined the beam toward one at random.

It was a close-up of a woman's face. She was dark-skinned, with blonde bangs and a ball gag shoved into her mouth. The others were worse, pleading eyes watching and begging.

I turned to the bones and then back to the pictures.

The room began to shake and I fell further down, into a black void that lasted forever.

"Peter?"

I came to, wincing and holding a hand to my forehead. It felt more swollen now and the back of my eyes were sore. I almost screamed when I remembered where I was.

"Peter?" The voice was louder this time and I swore there was someone else down there with me, someone trapped beneath the bones.

"Are you home?" It was my sister, calling from upstairs.

I looked around and panicked. Her voice grew closer. I climbed the ladder, almost slipping twice along the way, and closed the door. It slammed loudly.

"Peter, are you down there? We need to talk."

From the finished half, I heard the door creak open.

I grabbed the rug and slid it over the trap door, trying my best to make it seem straight.

I walked toward the stairs and realized I'd left the flashlight down there. It bothered me beyond words, thinking of its beam, still on, still shining toward the bones and the pictures.

I nearly walked into Sheila on my way out. "You're bleeding," she said.

"I took a bit of a fall on the way down. That's what I get for trying to do anything off two hours of sleep." I smiled. It hurt my head and it felt like the most insincere gesture I'd ever made. But a real smile was no longer possible.

"Listen," she said. "I'm sorry about earlier. I know it seems like I'm running away, and to be honest, maybe I am. Maybe I've always been running. But they're gone now, Peter. Both of them. It's just us now. And that's all I could think as he got older, and after Mom. One day it'll just be the two of us. I couldn't bear it."

"It's fine. Really."

"No, it's not fine at all. I'm going to cancel my reservations. I'd rather stay here with you. I'm tired of running."

"No!"

She flinched, backed away a step.

I fake-smiled again. "Sorry, I didn't mean to shout. What I mean is, I think it's good for you to get away, at least for a bit. The funeral is coming up and you're going to need your strength. This place isn't going anywhere. At least not until we sell it. So, please, go to the hotel. I mean it. Do whatever you need to."

She smiled and her eyes glossed over with tears. "I'm sorry I've been such a bitchy sister."

"Big sisters are supposed to be bitchy."

She hugged me then and I returned the embrace, pulling harder when I remembered how close we were to that other place.

"Now let's get you cleaned up," she said, leading me upstairs.

I made sure the basement door was closed tightly, checking twice for good measure.

"Are you okay?" my wife asked that night in the hotel room.

"I'm fine. Just tired."

"Liar." Megan turned toward me. Her body warmth was intoxicating and I wanted so badly to drift off into a sound sleep. But I knew what I'd find waiting for me when I closed my eyes for too long.

"I'm trying my best." I rubbed my tired eyes and accidently scratched my gash.

Megan brought a hand to it and the pain seemed to fade. She kissed me. "You don't have to be the hero. For once, it's okay to let it out. Don't be a rock like you were with your mother. You've got to promise me."

"Grief affects people differently."

"Yes, and if you bottle it up inside for a lifetime, it's going to come out at some point. It'll only get worse. Promise me."

I ran my hand through her hair. It was dark and I could barely see her but I didn't need to. "I promise."

"I'm holding you to it." She kissed me again, this time longer. "Peter, why are we in a hotel room? Why not stay at your father's house? It's where you grew up. It's home."

"I wanted to, Honey. Honestly."

Bones. Hundreds of bones. Scattered all around that dark room.

"But it's just too much right now. I just can't."

Every single face in every single photo. Dead. All of them.

"You're not going to do any good from running," Megan said.

Devices scattered in the dark. Meant for one thing and one thing only.

"I'm not running. Sheila was running. Not me."

Your father was a murderer.

"Okay." She rubbed the back of my neck and gave me a third and final kiss. "I believe you."

She rolled over and left me to my thoughts. I stared at the ceiling. Moonlight peeked from behind the curtains. In the conjoining room Sasha or Katie snored softly.

And a few miles away there was a place I wished to God I'd never discovered.

After I drifted off against my will, I dreamt of my father.

He was not old or dying. There were no bones.

He was young again and we were playing catch in the field down the street from the house. It must have been early spring. The air was warm but I could feel a cool breeze on my arms as I caught the ball, stumbling back a few feet, and throwing it back to my father. He caught it with no difficulty. It was a memory I'd forgotten, pleasant enough but nothing of major importance.

My father smiled. "You're getting pretty good at this. You should try out for the team next year."

I wanted to scream at him, to run away. I suddenly became aware that I was a prisoner, trapped in my younger body. I couldn't control any of my movements. I wondered, feeling sick in my dream stomach, if the trap door and the space beneath it existed at that moment, during that boring game of catch with my father.

I thanked him against my will and we kept on playing. I cursed my tired mind for showing me this. It should have been a nightmare, filled with things that would make me jump up in fear. But somehow this was worse, a nightmare in its own right.

It forced me to see the truth, that I loved my father and that he'd done terrible things.

And as far as I knew, I was the only one with this knowledge.

I begged my younger self to run away, to kick and stomp and wake up.

But it was useless. The game of catch went on for what seemed like years. When it was done, my father walked me home, a hand over my shoulder. We took our time, enjoying the weather.

I screamed inside of myself, my dream-voice becoming hoarse after a while. The younger me didn't seem to notice. He just walked on with his father and wound up at his childhood home, which seemed so safe at the time.

I woke early, before the sun was in the sky. I snuck out of the bed, freezing each time Megan murmured in her sleep. She turned over and faced me and I was sure she'd wake up and ask me where I was going at this hour.

Not that I would have an answer for her.

The air outside was frigid, nothing like the dream. My breath was fog and I wished I'd brought a jacket to the hotel. I laughed at the thought of giving Sheila such a hard time for spending the night out, when I'd gone and done the same thing. But I supposed we both had our reasons.

I drove in circles, trying to clear my head. The only place open in town was the gas station over on Maple Street. I pulled in and bought a coffee. It was stale and acidic but it warmed me up some.

On my way out, I looked at the pumps and something erupted inside me. I nearly ran to the hatchback, throwing open the back. The canister lay in the corner. It was empty now because I'd mowed the lawn just a couple weeks ago. I put my coffee on the roof and unscrewed the cap, filling the canister with gasoline from the pump.

Five minutes later I pulled up my father's driveway. It had never seemed so foreign as it did then, in the darkness, with every light turned off. There was still time to back out and go back to the hotel. My wife and kids were there, my life.

I shook my head. I wouldn't let this place exist for a moment longer.

I got out of the car and grabbed the canister from the back. I walked up the drive and opened the front door with shaky hands. In the darkness I swore I was not alone but when I turned on the living room light, there was no one there.

I imagined the place burning, turning to ash until there was nothing left of it. I'd begin pouring in the secret room. I'd wipe that awful place from existence.

Except that bones didn't burn all that well and neither did metal contraptions. And how would I explain myself? How would I tell the police that I wasn't after the insurance money?

It was useless. I could not burn my old home down and I could not tell anyone about what I'd found. I was trapped, like the faces from the photographs.

I sat down on the front steps and waited for the sun to come up.

Three days later I stepped up to the podium and cleared my throat. There were hundreds of eyes watching and waiting. For a moment they were bloodied and bruised and begging me to let them out before they became a pile of limbs.

I closed my eyes for a long time and I suppose most of my family and friends thought I was crying. I opened them back up and began.

"My father was a good man. He was a loving husband and a caring dad. He was a patient teacher and a determined coach. Most of all, he was my friend. Out of all the memories I have of him, one comes to mind. A simple game of catch on a warm spring day."

I went on, cursing myself inside, like I was in the dream all over again. I wanted to tell them the truth, but there was another part of me—the part I couldn't push away—that would not allow it. He screamed at me, told me to just forget it. What good could come from it? My father was dead and it was over now.

And what about the victims? I said to that other part in my mind.

It didn't answer. It didn't have to.

I hated that part of me.

"One of the last things my father told me was somewhat of a riddle, at least at the time. He said that everyone is really two different people. There's the person you are to the world, and there's the person you are to yourself. And they're not always compatible. I think I know what he meant now. I think we have to choose which of the two we are to become. And my father, well, he chose the right one. He chose the good one."

There was a standing ovation, as if I'd just given a valedictorian speech at my graduation. I couldn't bear to be up there a moment longer. I nodded to the crowd and stepped down.

"You did great," Megan said. "He would have been so proud."

I kissed her, hugged Sasha and Katie, and stepped outside to gather myself.

A few minutes later Sheila came out and put a hand on my shoulder. "Thank you for doing that. Lord knows I couldn't have. The way you spoke about him...you described him perfectly."

I was ready to tell her the truth. It's the closest I ever came, though there were plenty of times when Sheila and I were alone, plenty of moments when I thought I'd finally found the courage. But that other part of me always stopped the words, just as it did that day. "Say, Sheila. I wanted to talk to you about the house. I know now's not that great of a time."

"I'll call a broker first thing on Monday. I heard a couple of names tossed around inside."

"I don't think that's a good idea."

"Did you have someone else in mind?"

"What I mean is, I don't think we should sell the house at all."

It was almost a year before I went back. Megan insisted we get away for a weekend, just the two of us. Her mother had offered to take the kids and the weather was supposed to be beautiful. We could have dinner on the beach, drink wine on the porch, and maybe make love a few times while we were at it.

It sounded lovely, all things considered.

The urge didn't come on until the second night.

"Are you coming to bed?" Megan asked. By the tone of her voice, I knew she wasn't quite asking.

I smiled. "I'll be up in a little while. Just want to take a shower first."

"Don't be long."

I watched her walk up the stairs. I went into the bathroom and ran the water but I didn't undress and I didn't step in. Instead I walked slowly downstairs, into the basement, first the finished portion and then the unfinished half.

I tossed aside the carpet. The rational part of me was still shocked to see the trap door in the same spot. That part had hoped it had been a bad dream. But the other part knew damn well it was as real as could be.

I kneeled down and thought of my father's dying face, how his eyes had darted open that day. Over the months, I'd come to realize his last wish. I could have called the cops and gave those families closure but he'd wanted it to remain buried. It was his legacy.

I closed my eyes and I was down there again, bleeding from the head and seeing all of it for the first time. The smell was hitting my nostrils and making me gag. The photographs were crying out for help.

Some things were better left in the dark.

I stayed for a while longer until my knees finally came alive with pins and needles. I slid the rug back over, covering the door.

At the top of the stairs I wondered if the flashlight was still shining beneath the floor, illuminating the things in the shadows, but I supposed it had eventually died out.

Mike Jansen

Kevin Rodgers
The Scent of Jasmine

Beads of sweat blossomed on the forehead of a blonde-haired, middle-aged man while he strolled between the granite headstones of the Old Oak Cemetery. Pinwheels twirled in the grass next to the moss-covered walls of a mausoleum. Multi-colored balloons bobbed in the air near decorative vases and stone cherubs. Sweat stains formed around the armpits of the man's beige, Ralph Lauren dress shirt while he carried a bouquet of red roses in his left hand. He dropped his cell phone and car keys into the right pocket of his beige slacks with his free hand. He paused and bent his knees while he ogled the heart-shaped headstone of a woman named Elisa Bishop. A tear leaked from the corner of his left eye and crept into a forest of whiskers on his pale face. The man realized he had not shaved since Elisa's funeral two days ago.

"I moved all of your things down into the cellar, Elisa. Everything is packed and waiting for you. I decided to bring you some flowers," the man said.

He sobbed while he dropped the stems of the roses into a water-filled vase, which flanked a framed photograph of Elisa. He stared at the picture and admired Elisa's green eyes, auburn hair, and freckled face. In the photograph, Elisa wore a floral-print dress and pink, high-heel shoes. She leaned against an oak tree and smiled for the camera. The man remembered the perfume Elisa wore on the day he took the picture of her. He closed his eyes, inhaled a deep breath, and remembered the scent of jasmine. Yes, jasmine was her favorite perfume. The scent still lingered on her clothes, linens, and bed sheets.

A scratchy, masculine voice startled the man while he crouched next to Elisa's headstone. A slow, Southern drawl said: "I'll be closin' the front gate soon. You should be on your way, sir."

The man straightened his legs and whirled on his feet. He ogled a silver-haired man, who stood on the stone steps of a mausoleum. A red glow emanated from the tip of a cigarette while the old man inhaled nicotine and exhaled smoke. Grass stains covered the old man's torn blue jeans. Mud and sod plagued the soles of his brown work boots. Black, stenciled letters on his beige, pull-over shirt revealed his profession: OLD OAK CEMETERY CARETAKER. The man realized that the shadows of oak trees, stone crosses, and mausoleums had begun to stretch across the cemetery's St. Augustine grass.

"I apologize for staying too long, sir. I must've lost track of time," the man said.

"It's alright. I just don't want you to be locked in here all night," the caretaker said.

The man glanced over his shoulder and admired Elisa's headstone. The red roses seemed to glow in the gloom of dusk. The man strolled toward a narrow, cobblestone road, which formed an S-shaped path for vehicles through the cemetery. He walked toward a gray Toyota Corolla, which was parked under the moss-covered limbs of an oak tree. He plucked the car's keys from his pocket, unlocked the vehicle, and collapsed into the driver's seat. He closed the door, cranked the ignition, and felt cold air rush from air vents on the dashboard. He listened to "Kiss from a Rose" by Seal while he jammed the transmission into DRIVE, pressed the gas pedal with his right foot, and steered the car toward the cemetery's front gate. During the drive home, all he could think about were the crates in the cellar and the powerful scent of Elisa's jasmine perfume.

Two hours later, the man relaxed on a brown, leather couch in his living room while his left hand held the remote control of his 50-inch, Sony flat-screen television. His dog, a Jack Russell terrier named Beethoven, lounged on a green throw-cushion next to him.

The man scanned through the list of channels while Beethoven licked his right forearm. He located a documentary about Egyptian pyramids on the Discovery channel and tossed the remote control on a stack of magazines, which covered a mahogany coffee table. Images of Elisa's face formed in his mind while he leaned back and closed his eyes. Why did she decide to kill herself after a literary agent informed her that a publisher had accepted the manuscript of her debut novel? Why did she leave a torn piece of yellow paper under the windshield of his car, which failed to explain why she'd decided to take a bubble bath and slash her wrists with a razor blade? The man emerged from the early stages of sleep when he heard Beethoven growl. His opened his bloodshot eyes and focused on the terrier, which stood erect on the left arm of the sofa. Beethoven stared at a staircase, which provided access to the cellar.

"What's wrong, boy? What's got you spooked?" the man said.

Beethoven growled and snarled while he groveled against the man's chest. The dog's rigid stance and tense muscles terrified him. He'd never seen his dog behave in such a manner. The man hoisted himself off of the sofa, walked quickly toward a mahogany armoire, and opened one of the middle drawers. He seized a blue, plastic case from the drawer, snapped two latches into the open position, and flipped the lid up. A black, nine-millimeter Beretta rested next to a full clip of bullets. The man snared the gun from the case, jammed the clip into the weapon's handle, and pulled back on the barrel. A round slid into the gun's chamber. The man disengaged the gun's safety and tip-toed toward the staircase. He paused and gasped when the scent of jasmine drifted into his nostrils.

"Elisa? Are you down there?" the man said. He was startled by his own voice.

At the bottom of the stairs, the cellar door slammed shut. The aroma of jasmine dissipated gradually. The man held the Beretta with both hands and descended the stairs cautiously. He paused, glanced over his shoulder, and realized that Beethoven was standing at the top of the stairs. The dog bared his teeth and barked. The man shooed him away and said: "Stay up there, Beethoven! Go find a rawhide bone to chew on!"

The man gasped when he realized that the scattered pages of a manuscript covered the stairs near the bottom of the staircase. Rows of prose loomed under headers on dozens of white pages. The man bent his knees, ogled the 12 point Times New Roman print, and felt his heart thud beneath his sternum. The header at the top of one of the pages revealed: BISHOP/PARALLEL WORLD/145. The page belonged to Elisa's novel, which a literary agent sold to a publisher before her suicide. The man held the Beretta in his left hand while he seized the page with his right hand. Behind him, at the top of the stairs, Beethoven erupted into a frenzy of shrill barks and snarls.

"How did these pages get here? Who would do such a thing?" the man said.

The doorknob of the cellar door twisted and turned. Rusted hinges screeched while the door swung open slowly. Odd noises emanated from within the cellar while the man descended the stairs. Beethoven whined and whimpered while he watched his master step into a bright, luminous glow at the bottom of the staircase. The sounds of chirping birds and roaring waterfalls emanated from the other side of the cellar door. The man glanced over his shoulder and smiled at his dog. Then he stepped across the door's threshold and strolled into a parallel world...a world that Elisa described in the pages of her novel.

"My name is Zachary Harper. I don't know how long I've been here. My concept of time is blurred in this place. My watch doesn't work anymore, and it stopped keeping track of time when I entered the cellar. All of the crates are here. They're scattered on moss-covered rocks, beneath the limbs of oak and elms, and near the currents of fast-moving streams. Strange, exotic birds took flight from the limbs of nearby trees when they noticed me. I've never seen birds like these before. They're massive creatures with long, slender necks, multi-colored feathers, and blue, glowing eyes. It is dark outside and there's a full moon in the sky. I think I just heard a wolf howl!"

The man stopped writing his notes on the blank side of BISHOP/PARALLEL WORLD/145 and realized that his blue, ballpoint pen was running out of ink. He'd stolen it from Amscot earlier in the day after he obtained a five-hundred dollar cash advance to help pay his power bill and car payment. He'd jammed the Beretta into the waistband of his beige slacks. The gun's barrel felt cold against his lower abdomen. The weapon bolstered his confidence and made him feel safe. He folded BISHOP/PARALLEL WORLD/145 and shoved it into the right pocket of his slacks. The roar of a waterfall compelled him to hike southeast through the forest until his shoes kicked small rocks and pebbles into a deep, rocky chasm. In the distance, he watched oak and elm trees topple and crash to the ground while a huge, unseen creature charged through the adjacent forest. Zachary realized that the creature must've detected his scent.

Zachary glanced over his shoulder and gasped. A brick wall flanked the cellar door and rose from the forest floor. Earthworms flopped in fertile soil. Huge butterflies hovered in the air. Huge squirrels and giant owls clung to the moss-covered limbs of nearby trees. Zachary sprinted toward the cellar door, twisted the doorknob, and yanked on it with all of his might. The door wouldn't budge. However, Zachary heard Beethoven barking and yelping on the other side of the door. He twisted the doorknob repeatedly, but his efforts were in vain. He smelled the scent of jasmine when a strong gust of wind lifted strands of hair from his scalp and forehead. Zachary stepped away from the cellar's door and noticed a log cabin, which stood on a small hill deep in the woods. He yanked the Beretta from his waistband and hiked toward the hill. Behind him, deep in the forest, a feral monstrosity exhaled a loud howl. Frightened deer and startled rabbits scurried deep into the forest to seek refuge.

Zachary hiked to the top of the hill and strolled toward the cabin. He gazed upon the disemboweled, decapitated corpses of two lumberjacks when while he approached the cabin's door, which was slightly ajar. White maggots writhed on the bloated, rotten flesh of the shredded cadavers. The rancid stench of decay throbbed in the air. Zachary stepped onto the front porch of the cabin and found a dead, elderly woman sitting in a rocking chair. Huge, white orbs lolled in her eye sockets. Deep gashes crisscrossed her upper torso. Mounds of decayed intestines bulged from abdominal incisions. Zachary glanced away from her mutilated body when he heard a deafening roar near the cellar door. He bolted across the threshold of the cabin and slammed the front door. His shoes waded through pools of congealed blood, which had seeped from the butchered corpses of a skinny, dark-haired blacksmith and his obese, red-headed wife. They'd been slaughtered next to a fireplace in the den, where two plates of roasted pig and mashed potatoes remained untouched on an oak table. Zachary noticed a torn piece of yellow paper on the table near a pitcher of sweet tea. He gasped when he realized the similarities between the piece of paper and the one he'd found tucked under the Corolla's windshield wiper.

Zachary plucked the paper from the table, ogled the cursive handwriting, and read the message to himself: "My name is Elisa Bishop. There's only one way to destroy the beast. A piece of silver must penetrate the creature's heart. Where I come from, we call it a werewolf. I've identified the human form of the beast on page 145 of my novel."

Zachary reached into the pocket of his slacks and snared the piece of paper. Old receipts from gas stations, mounds of lint, and scratch-off lottery tickets accompanied page 145 of Elisa's manuscript. He tossed the unwanted items aside and unfolded the piece of paper. A massive beast rammed the cabin's door, which caused the structure to shudder. A loud scream erupted from Zachary's larynx when a giant claw penetrated a nearby window. Loud growls and shrill howls caused Zachary's eardrums to throb. He scanned the prose on BISHOP/PARALLEL WORLD/145. He experienced tightness in his chest and felt pain radiate across his chest and into his shoulders. He knew the identity of the werewolf. He knew where he could find silver bullets. He thanked Elisa for providing the information on page 145 of her novel. He watched the front door of the cabin explode into dozens of shards of splintered wood. The red eyes of the werewolf locked onto Zachary. Strands of saliva oozed from its massive teeth and huge tongue.

The prose of Elisa's novel enlightened Zachary to the truth: Elisa didn't commit suicide. She'd been murdered by the person who transformed into the werewolf. She died to keep the werewolf's identity a secret. Zachary stared deep into the werewolf's red eyes while the beast squeezed through the cabin's front door. He glanced over his shoulder and located the blacksmith's gun safe. The heavy, metal door was wide open. On the third shelf, next to a six-shooter, was a tray of silver bullets. The silver bullets were the reason why the blacksmith and his family had been slaughtered. Zachary sprinted toward the gun safe, but one of the werewolf's claws slapped him across his shoulder blades and knocked him to the floor. Zachary rolled over on his back. The beast stood on its hind legs. Its coarse fur brushed against the log cabin's ceiling. When the werewolf lunged toward him, Zachary detected the potent aroma of Elisa's jasmine perfume.

She knew that Zachary would die if she didn't intervene. She also realized that she was forbidden to breach the barrier between life and death. The scent of jasmine intensified while Elisa's image manifested in the cabin. She gazed upon the werewolf and remembered when the human form of the beast entered her house. She'd been soaking in the bathtub and reading a book. How did the man know that she knew his secret? Why had he decided to break into her house and confront her while she was vulnerable? She remembered the final moments of her life with frightening clarity...

The silver-haired man approached her while she sat at a table in a Barnes and Noble bookstore. She'd noticed him earlier while she parked her car. He stood near the front entrance and puffed on a cigarette. She'd noticed grass stains on his torn blue jeans. Her attention had been drawn to mud and sod on the soles of his brown work boots. And the image of black, stenciled letters on his beige, pull-over shirt was crisp in her mind: OLD OAK CEMETERY CARETAKER. The stench of cigarette smoke overwhelmed her when the old man leaned across the table to ogle the pages of her manuscript.

"You look very familiar, darling," he said. Elisa didn't like the serious tone of his slow, Southern drawl. "As a matter of fact, I think we've crossed paths many times."

"I don't know what you're talking about. Please leave me alone," she said.

"I'm afraid I can't do that, honey. You know too much about me. Yeah, you know where I go and what I do, don't you?" he said. His crooked, left finger pointed at the title of her book. "That's why you wrote a book about a parallel world, right?"

Elisa pushed her chair away from the table and stood up. She seized her purse and plucked her car keys from a pit of lipstick tubes and old receipts. The old man's left hand reached for her right forearm, but she sprinted toward the bookstore's exit. She sprinted into the parking lot, unlocked her red Honda Civic, collapsed in the driver's seat, and cranked the engine. The old man chased her. Her left foot stamped the gas pedal and the car sped away before he could catch up to her...

But she'd forgotten to gather the pages of her manuscript. She'd left them on the table at the bookstore. And the old man scanned through them leisurely after she departed. His eyes narrowed and a grin formed on his face while he examined chapter after chapter of eloquent prose. Yes, his suspicions about Elisa were confirmed while he read her descriptions of the parallel world. Yes, he realized that Elisa knew his true identity while he read her descriptions of the mutilations and murders. How could he allow her to finish the manuscript and send it to her publisher? There was a chance that a police officer or a federal agent would knock on his door. There was a chance that he'd be taken away in handcuffs and thrown in a jail cell. If that happened, he wouldn't be able to enter the parallel world and feast on the villagers during the full moon. He gathered the pages of Elisa's manuscript, walked out of the Barnes and Noble bookstore, and strolled toward his rusted, blue Ford F150 in the parking lot. He'd been stalking Elisa for a very long time and knew where she lived. He placed the manuscript on the torn upholstery of the passenger seat while he cranked the truck's engine. He grinned while he plucked a cigarette from a pack of Marlboros and jammed it between his chapped lips. He steered the truck through the parking lot and fantasized about slashing Elisa's wrists...

But he waited a couple of hours to confront Elisa. He parked the truck a block away from her suburban townhouse. He scanned through the pages of her manuscript while he sat in his idle truck, sucking the nicotine out of several cigarettes. Ashes gathered in his beard and accumulated on his clothes. Several people, such as a woman walking her Yorkshire terrier and a man pushing a lawnmower, glanced at him from time to time. But he waved off their suspicious glares and monitored Elisa's townhouse from a distance.

Finally, he turned off the truck's engine and opened the glove box. He plucked a switchblade from a stack of road maps and old, yellow papers. Yes, he decided to make her death look like a suicide. He'd slash her wrists and place the knife in her hand. He strolled away from the truck, crossed the street, and glanced over his shoulder. No one noticed him while he crept through the shadows, pushed open a fence's gate, and walked into Elisa's back yard. He used the switchblade to carve a gash in the screen of her back porch. He chuckled when he realized that the living room's sliding glass door wasn't locked. Within minutes, he located Elisa: she was soaking in a bathtub in the master bathroom. He grinned when he stepped into the bathroom and she gasped in shock...

Now he growled and snarled while he lunged toward her lover, Zachary. Rivulets of saliva careened from the werewolf's jaws while the beast leaped toward him. The idiot had somehow entered the parallel world and stumbled upon the blacksmith's cabin. And the foolish man had located the blacksmith's gun safe and stash of silver bullets. It would be a shame to rip him apart and feast on his bloody corpse. The werewolf exhaled a shrill howl while it loped across the cabin's hardwood floors and leaped through the air.

The scent of jasmine throbbed in the air. It intensified while the image of a naked woman shimmered and solidified near a fireplace. The werewolf snarled and growled while it gazed upon a naked lady, who held up her hands so the beast could ogle the deep incisions on both of her wrists. Yes, his switchblade inflicted those fatal wounds upon Elisa while she thrashed in the bathtub. Yes, his hard, callused hands forced her head under the water while blood oozed from her slashed wrists. Blood gushed from the open wounds and splashed on the hardwood floors while Elisa's ghost floated through the cabin. The pale orbs of her glazed eyes locked onto the werewolf and exposed the frail, elderly man who lurked behind a mask of coarse fur, huge claws, and sharp teeth. The wolf choked and slobbered when the scent of jasmine intensified into a potent cloud of noxious fumes. Elisa glanced over her right shoulder and smiled while she watched Zachary sprint toward the gun safe and locate the silver bullets. He removed his gun from his waistband, popped the clip, and removed his hollow-point rounds. Elisa's ghost used energy to hurl an oak table through the air. It pinned the werewolf against the eastern wall of the cabin. The noxious cloud of jasmine intensified when the werewolf slapped the table aside. The beast rocked on its haunches while it watched Zachary load the gun's clip with silver bullets. Elisa's ghost used her supernatural powers to topple a bookcase, which impacted the werewolf's lupine skull. The beast flailed and swatted the bookcase aside, which caused hardcover novels and leather-bound tomes to fly through the air.

"No more murders. No more victims. It all ends tonight," Elisa whispered.

Zachary jammed the clip into the handle of the gun. He yanked back on the barrel and smiled when a silver bullet filled the chamber. He disengaged the safety and aimed the barrel at the werewolf's chest. Then he lined up the sights, lapsed into a Weaver stance, and pulled the trigger five times while the werewolf leaped through the air.

"It's almost time for me to go," she said.

Zachary and Elisa held hands while they strolled through the forest of the parallel world. Moonlight filtered through an intricate network of tree limbs while they walked across a dusty, dirty path. Enormous birds with long, slender necks and multi-colored feathers roosted on the limbs of oaks and elms and monitored their progress. Deer, rabbits, and raccoons sprinted away from the trail. Elisa stopped walking and admired the white blossoms of a dogwood tree. Zachary leaned toward her and kissed her lips.

"I don't want you to go, Elisa. I love you and I'll stay here forever, if that's what you want me to do. We could be happy in this parallel world, couldn't we?"

Elisa craned her neck and located a gap between the tree limbs. She stared at the full moon and twinkling stars in the dark sky. She knew the sky's hue would change soon: it would transition from purple to dark orange. A new day was about to dawn and she would be forced to leave. She would never see Zachary again, and she knew he would be devastated. Her lips trembled while she turned to face him. Her cold, ghostly hands touched his face. His whiskers scraped the palms of her hands while she stepped closer.

"We're running out of time, Zachary. I'll watch the sun rise with you, but then I must go back. Hopefully I won't be punished," Elisa said. She wrapped her arms around his upper torso and kissed his left cheek. He hugged her and kissed her lips.

Robins and blue jays chirped from the limbs of nearby trees. They listened to the rush of water from the fast-moving current of a nearby creek. The massive orb of the sun peeked above the eastern horizon. Elisa and Zachary smiled while rays of sunlight penetrated the network of tree limbs and illuminated the forest floor. The scent of jasmine dissipated in the air while Elisa's image wavered and faded. Zachary exhaled a wail of sorrow while she slowly vanished. He hiked back to the brick wall near the log cabin. He twisted the doorknob of the cellar door and exhaled a sigh of relief. He twisted the doorknob, yanked the door open, and smiled. Beethoven barked and wagged his tail in the stairwell on the other side of the door. Zachary glanced over his shoulder and gazed upon Elisa's parallel world for the last time. Then he stepped across the threshold, closed the door, and went upstairs. He would never forget Elisa and the time he shared with her. He would never forget the caretaker and the werewolf he'd become. He sobbed while he reminisced about how he used to walk on the beach with Elisa at sunset and have candlelit dinners with her at ocean-side restaurants. But he smiled and felt a sense of inner peace when he smelled the potent aroma of her favorite perfume. He smiled because he realized that the scent of jasmine intensified whenever Elisa's spirit tried to comfort him. And he knew that the scent of jasmine would guide him back to the parallel world...a world that Elisa described in the pages of her novel...a novel that he hoped would sit on the shelves of bookstores and libraries someday.

Matthew Wilson
Video Nasty

Mom was dead, and James was sad.

Kelly Hybris was a church going woman. She did not care that she was portly and, since dad died twenty years before, she had no love in her life.

She gave all her time and soul to the church, organizing all their events including the monthly book readers club. James had few chances for pocket money when he was young; mom was kind, but what she did not put into the charity box she used to buy biscuits and holidays for neighbors children.

Mom was a people person. She had time for anyone who came to her with their problems. James didn't feel bad that other people took her time from him. Mom liked to help, and it would be wrong of him to be jealous that other people had their own moms and yet came to his.

Mom wasn't knowledgeable about matters outside the Lord's goodness. But she didn't need to be. People who came to her just wanted someone to listen to whatever bull shit problem was currently eating away their world.

Some free therapy.

Now mom was gone, and all that was left was her belongings.

"I won't be around forever," Mom had said, softly one afternoon when James had thought her sleeping. "It's a mom's job to look out for her child, and I've done a better job with other children than my own."

James felt his throat tighten. There was truth in this, but mom had raised him to be a gentleman, capable of looking after himself. The worst thing that had happened to him was when he caught a cold and coming downstairs, wrapped in a blanket, he had fallen down them.

A graze at most.

Five years before, Carla Mannt knocked on the front door at 11pm, weeping that her fourteen year old daughter had a miscarriage.

Now *that* was an emergency.

Mom invited her in, and did what everyone wanted.

Listened to her bull shit.

Mom never seemed to tire of listening to other people's problems, and when she had her own, when the illness took over, of course she only thought of others.

She told her son to sell all items, the furniture, the house, so she could finally make good on her promise of supporting him.

He could go on holiday.

James had taken her hand, informed her she would be around long enough for both of them.

But now mom was gone.

And all James had was her mementos.

Some things he could not part with, the photos and her jewelry, for they had greater sentimental value than an air plane ticket.

He found the videos on the fifth day after the funeral.

The house was too large without her, so he employed a neighbor to help him sort out the stuff in the cellar.

Later, he was glad *he* found the tapes.

Curious to look over old times, he exhumed the old VHS under the tangled Christmas tree, but instead of days on the beach and holiday at the fair '06, the worn tapes had names of people he half remembered.

Stan Blaydon.

James searched his brain for info. It took the better part of ten seconds.

Oh, yeah.

A neighbor known for arguments with his wife had finally had enough and walked out.

The talk of the street had happened some years before, and of course, mom had been there to talk to Mrs. Blaydon on the porch. Tell her it was not her fault.

Forget him! James had been too young to pick him out of a police lineup the last time he saw him. James just wanted to see mom dance at this birthday party.

That's what it was.

Mrs. Blaydon's birthday tape.

But it wasn't.

For a while, he watched the old man chained to the floor. He had to squint for the quality was low; the camera had been set up in a hurry.

"That's my fuckin' bike." James ejected with alarm.

Mom had bought it for his fifth birthday, and by the time he'd gotten too big for it, like all the other crap, it had collected dust in his cellar.

James nodded, satisfied at the location. Yes, he could see it now. The old save the church magazines that had not been moved since the 80's. There were even old biscuit boxes that had fallen off the crates, making handy homes for mice.

James watched, guts curling as mom came out from the

---

shadows. She wore very little, but kept her hands glued round the hammer in her hand. James had never seen his mom dance. She was too big to pull it off with any conviction.

But now she gyrated, seductively, in heat.

She moaned as she moved round the bound man. Mr. Blaydon seemed to snap awake from the sedative. He moaned when he saw what mom was doing.

Then he screamed, though briefly, as she bought the claw side of the hammer down on his eye ball.

All the videos had some variation of this trope, though the end was always the same. Mom would torture and mutilate the guy, particularly his genitals. Twenty videos. Twenty men.

Mom had found some time for love after all.

James vomited. He could watch no more.

All those years were a lie and he was glad she was dead. Gone somewhere she could not hurt people. All that comfort she'd dealt out was no consideration for the pain. She was evil and he wished the illness had eaten at her longer.

Vodka helped, and James' hate turned to self-hate.

Mom was right for having time for others and not him. He was too trusting, too dumb to notice what she really was.

Mom was superstitious. There was no charity in her going to church so often.

Being so old, she simply feared the next world and the twenty dead men waiting for her.

In her prayers, she asked God to stand up for her against the victims she had wronged. But God did not remove that evil need from her, so she believed it was her given right.

God would look after her.

So long as she interspersed these vile acts with some good. The men she killed were hardly worthy men. Mom felt a $100 donation and some quality bake sales at the church were sufficient to keep her soul in God's good graces.

The last tape hurt most: the one with his father's name.

No, Mr. Tanner had not died of natural causes. Biting his fist, James, needing to know, watched, and howled in agony at the climax as mom brought the hammer down on dad's head.

James contemplated suicide, but decided against such an act as he thought he might meet mom in hell. James did not go to the police. The man in each video was dead - and how - and what peace would it give to their families to know how much they suffered?

They'd hope that one day their disappeared love would return. The main point of course, was that James had to live here. If he told anybody what kind of demon his mother - no longer mom - was, then he'd have burning rubbish pushed through his letter box.

Let them think she was a kindly old woman who did great work for the church.

Let them think James still had a future.

For him, there would be no legacy. For the sake of good, he decided to let his blood line die.

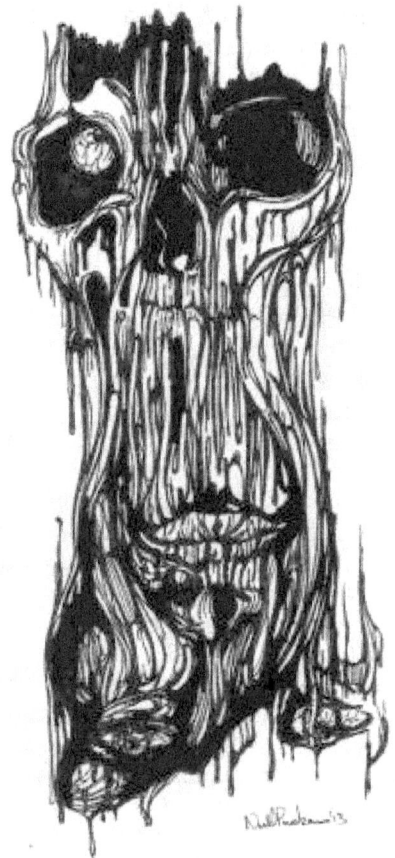

Niall Parkinson

Michael Randolph
Leannan Sídhe

"Are you listening to me?" Susan asked.

Timothy sat across the table, his attention directed at the store across the street. The worn sign, "Pellagra's," that hung over the entrance was the only indication a shop existed at the address.

"Hey!"

For a moment, he was sure an old lady was stopping to go inside, but she just readjusted her cane and walked by. He and Susan had been coming here for weeks and today was the first time he noticed the dismal shop. Thick mats of cobwebs trailed under the window eaves. He couldn't see anything beyond the grime covering the windows.

"I'm going to kill myself."

"That's nice. Get me another coffee," Timothy said, pushing his empty cup across the tablecloth.

"I burned all of your art." When he didn't respond, Susan curled her middle finger under her thumb, her long nail digging into her skin.

"I sold you to a serial killer, hope you don't mind?"

"That's a great idea," he replied. "Maybe we can talk about it later." He jerked backward, white-hot pain flashed across his ear. "What the fu-dammit," he yelled, covering the side of his head with his hand.

She smiled back with no hint of warmth on her face. "Ignore me at your own risk."

Timothy rubbed his ear, his hand coming away wet. He grabbed a napkin trying to stop the slow trickle of blood. "I thought you said you wanted to spend some time together today - quality time, not inflict pain."

"Stop ignoring me." Susan glanced at his ear, "You're such a baby, barely a flesh wound."

He reached up, gingerly touching the swollen area. A small flap of skin moved away under his fingertip. "Fuck, thanks a whole hell of a lot!"

"You're a prick, one fucking morning that's all!" Susan yanked her purse off the table, standing up she glared down at him. "Listen cockroach, I want your shit out of my apartment today!"

He reversed course, his lips twitching into a light grin, "Baby, come on. Sit down." She was always flying on the handle. He knew with a little sweet-talking, she'd eventually calm down. The last time, well last week...he'd spent hours begging her not to leave. That was after a counseling session they'd gone to and she's gotten pissed about a few remarks he'd made. It was evident she was still angry over that.

Susan stiffened her back, the top of her leather purse crumpling under her grip. He just caught her whisper as she hurried out of the restaurant; "Baby, my ass."

"Crap," he muttered, realizing everyone around him was staring, almost on the verge of laughter. "Who needs her any friggin way," he said loudly, trying to bluff his way out of being embarrassed. He sat back, rubbing his inflamed ear. Unfocused, with her glare in the forefront of his mind, Tim sat still a few moments before returning his attention back to the shop. *She'll cool off in a few hours.*

He dropped a twenty on the table, making his way out of the restaurant. He stood on the sidewalk staring across the road at the defunct store. *She loves antiques, wonder if that's what they sale?* Curious, he dodged in-between cars to the other side. "Screw you," he yelled, jumping past a canary yellow Honda as the driver blared his horn.

Tim walked up to the window, brushing the crime away with the sleeve of his shirt. He pressed his forehead against the glass trying to see inside, *shit.* He walked into the small entryway, grabbing the dirty brass door handle. He jiggled it. Locked, he was about to turn away when the door opened, a woman's pale face appearing in-between the widening crack. "Can I help you?" She asked.

His arm suddenly tingled at her abrupt appearance. He jerked his hand back, shoving both hands into his jean pockets. "Uh...just seeing...if open," he stuttered, gawking at her. He stood openmouthed, openly staring at her wide pale-blue eyes framed by long thick black hair. "Didn't mean to bother you," he finished before snapping his mouth shut. She blinked, her lips turning up into a small smile.

Surprised as she opened the door wider, he stepped back. A few inches shorter than him, he marveled watching her step out. She seemed to glide across the small entryway, the floor length black gown billowing around her.

His was mesmerized by the musical lilt of her accent as she replied, "Walter only opens up at nighttime." She pointedly glanced across the street at the restaurant. "Are you looking for a gift?"

Taken back, he leaned against the wall lowering his eyes to the ground. "Oh, you saw that?" He became suddenly aware of his stained jeans and t-shirt as he rolled his shoulders forward.

"She's quite beautiful..."

Tim peeked at her making sure the girl wasn't making fun. He relaxed, seeing the stony look on her face, "That's Susan." He straightened up, noticing a small silver pendant around her slender neck. "I'm Tim – Timothy."

"Gabrielle; come in and let us see if we can find something for your Susan," She said, gliding through the open doorway.

He followed her. A chill moved down his back as he crossed the threshold. Cold air swirled around the small shop as large brass fans hummed near the ceiling. A long display case filled with glinting jewelry drew his eyes. They walked across the deep red carpet, his eyes taking in the vast array.

Gabrielle faced him across the case. "What is her favorite color?" Ornate silver necklaces hung from small displays near the back, red and blue gemstones glinting under the white light.

"I can't afford this stuff," Timothy said. He frowned, glancing away. Jewelry boxes, porcelain dolls packed a table nearby. Full-length Victorian gowns hung from racks in the middle. He passed them, seeing a porcelain doll under a bell-shaped glass display case. "Wow," he whispered. Hopeful, Timothy walked over taking a close look at the doll.

He jerked as Gabrielle's arm brushed his. He looked back and forth between her and the jewelry, unsure how she had moved so close without him noticing. He turned back, studying the small doll, her white dress still in pristine condition.

His attention was riveted on the lifelike eyes.

They followed him as he moved around the corner of the table. Her light pink face blurred to a light red near the cheeks. Freckles dotted her nose. Long blonde hair fell down her back almost in the same style Susan kept. "Is this some kind of joke," he asked, his eyes moving to the brass nameplate on the stand.

"I don't know what you mean, Timothy."

"The doll's name is *Susie*! That's friggin creepy," he said, stepping back. His mom had one like this when he was a kid that sat on the mantel in the living room. It always bothered him. He used to play a game with it, trying to sneak past the doll without her seeing him. Every time he looked back, its eyes would be tracking his movements. He had decided an evil spirit resided inside the porcelain shell. One day to his mother's chagrin, Timothy had thrown it in the fire. That was the first time he had felt the touch of a leather belt.

Now, he faced the same doll from long ago, or so it seemed. It couldn't be the same one, couldn't be. He remembered the next day as he walked through the living room and an identical doll had been sitting in its place. So the game had continued. After his mother had passed away, his sister had auctioned most of her belongings to pay off debt. The doll had disappeared in the sale, bought by an antique dealer.

"Where did you get this?" Timothy asked.

Gabrielle pursed her lips, her pale eyes flicking to a door near the rear of the shop, "I got it from the cellar, down there. I don't know where Walter purchased it."

He glanced to where she'd motioned. A dark oak door stood at the rear of the short hall, opened just a crack; he flinched, seeing a wrinkled face peering at them. "Who's that?"

"Walter," she pronounced as if he was a simpleton. Gabrielle peered up at him.

She stood there, her eyes blinking as if she was a porcelain doll herself. His skin began to crawl, caught between the stares of a hidden stranger and this reflection of beauty. "Yeah, this is getting a bit weird. Time to go."

He froze as her long slender fingers touched the back of his hand. "Stay a while. I'm enjoying your company, Timothy. Are you not an artist?"

He glanced back to the door. The old man was gone. With her soft fingers lightly touching him, he thought of Susan for a moment and then discarded the image. *Well, she's the one that said get out.* Gabrielle's beauty was unmistakable, an alluring woman that oozed sexiness. Not in a trashy way, but in the way she held herself. Thinking back to a few books he'd read, the word regal popped into his mind.

A cross between lavender and roses floating on the night air filled his nostrils. Somehow, she moved within inches of his face with her lips turned up at him. He darted a glance at her mouth, the lushest dark red lips within reach, and no one in sight.

"To paint your portrait would be a gift from Heaven," he whispered, his voice turning husky with pent-up emotion.

"Stay a little longer, please," she pleaded.

Timothy no longer thought of anything, just this irresistible girl inches away. His world shrank into a space of a few inches, her eyes filling his vision. With the soft ruffles on her dress pressed against his chest, his mind blurred, everything fell away except them.

Her lips parted slightly. Flushed, Timothy leaned forward, her fragrance intoxicating. His eyes darted to the doll over her shoulder.

It smiled.

"Fuck!" He backpedaled away from the table, catching his foot as he fell to the ground. He let out a harrumph as he hit the floor, the hard edge of a coffee table smashing into the back of his head. The last thing he saw before the world blacked out was Gabrielle leaning over him, a smile on her lips.

He dreamed long into the night of a dark haired girl washing his face, talking to him as he slept. He lay on a strange sofa with his legs and arms bound together. Across the room a man with a hawkish nose sat. Emancipated to the point of being a skeleton, he looked as if he would float away on a strong enough breeze. His hard blue eyes never wavered with intense hatred that impaled Timothy. "Young lady, vermin such as him do not belong in your presence." He spat, his contempt evident.

"Hush, Walter, he has no home now. Be of the giving sort as once you were." Timothy lay still listening as he peeked through slit eyelids. His feet and hands burned from the rope. The soft glow of an antique lamp created a pool around Gabrielle and him as she sat on the edge of the sofa washing his face.

Morning sunlight streamed through a small window near the top of the wall, onto the rich dark furniture decorating the room. At the edge of his vision, dark red drapes hung in a line separating the room. The sharp hollow clopping of horse hooves grew as a carriage passed by outside. Long grey women's dresses passed outside while a boy's voice called out in an attempt to sale the London Times.

The man's deep voice filled the room. "I say be done with him and let the butcher have a whack."

Gabrielle's sharp intake of breath preceded her response. "Walter, must you be so cantankerous. Timothy is a guest and must be treated with respect."

Unsure of what was happening but firmly aware he was not some place he wanted to be, Timothy tried to stand up. He promptly fell off the couch, taking her with him.

Her scream of surprised startled him. Pain flared in his back as the man swung his cane overhead, connecting with a sickening thud. "Son of a bitch, dude," Timothy yelled, untangling himself from her. He struggled to stand but finally ended up on his feet hopping like mad to the bottom of the stairs.

"Timothy, come back, you have no place to run." She called after him.

He glanced back. She stood next to the man sitting on the chair. "Fucking mad, shit." Timothy struggled against the ropes.

Giving up, he wormed his way up the stairs. At the top, he grabbed the handle, pulling the door open.

Cobbled streets and tall redbrick buildings greeted his eyes. A long black carriage rolled past, the driver whipping the horse. *I must be dreaming.* He stared after the coach and the man wearing a long black coat and top hat against the chill in the air. Two women in thick puffy cotton dresses walked past, their heads down.

"Timothy," Gabrielle said, her light voice tugging at his heart. He turned. She was only a couple of feet behind him on the landing. "You're not dreaming, dear."

He had no success trying clear his head. Gabrielle caused his mind to turn fog. The pain in his hands returned. Gabrielle reached out, loosening the rope around his wrists. Needles flooded along his hands as the blood returned, "Fuck, why'd you have me tied up like a pig?"

"You're mine," she said, her tone leaving no doubt in his mind that she meant it. "Once you passed this door, you became my property." The ropes fell to the ground in a heap.

He studied the door even with his hazy mind he recognized the same worn pattern in the oak. "I didn't pass the door. You friggin kidnapped me."

"Please don't mince words, my beloved." She pulled at his sleeve, beckoning him to follow her. "Your head must be splitting, love, please be cooperative, and come back downstairs."

"Back there?" he shivered at the thought. "Why, so you can sale me to the butcher?" He glanced into the street, his mind unable to determine how he got there and for that matter why.

"You mustn't take his comments to heart. He was having fun with you is all." She clasped his hand, pulling him after her down the stairs.

This has to be a dream, fuck it, go with it." She led him back to the sofa, arranging the pillows so he would be comfortable. He sat, looking at the man across the room near the fireplace.

"Why did you come back?" Walter asked.

Timothy glanced away, seeing the porcelain doll on the mantle. "Gabrielle. Can't you get rid of that? Its freaky." Grey smoke began billowing up inside the glass cover as the doll slowly disappeared from view. On the front two words appeared in the smoke: *Timothy! Help!* Startled, he shut his eyes, refusing to admit he saw them. He grimaced, knots forming in his stomach. He must have died when he fell. This was payback for throwing her in the fire.

"You are not dreaming, dear. Susie needs your help," Gabrielle stated.

He chuckled and then shook his head. "This is nuts." He swallowed hard hoping the knots would go away, but they stayed. His heart raced, and sweat beaded on his forehead.

And Walter stared.

"Ha, you're stuck boy! Do what we want or off to the butcher," the man said. He leaned forward, jabbing Timothy in the chest with the tip of his cane.

"What's with you and the fucking butcher," he yelled. "Get that cane off me before I shove it up your ass!" He swiped at the cane.

Gabrielle glared at him. "Stop bickering, boys. Timothy dear, are you ready to listen?"

He glanced at the doll. No smoke was evident in the case, though it smiled openly at him. He grimaced, seeing the lips purse before it started blowing kisses at him. "Listen? Explain that little wretched piece of hell you keep."

"That's Susie, dear. How do you think we found you?"

"You're fucking bonkers." He stood up walking across the room to the window. A man passed outside trailing a small cart as he rang a small brass bell. An overflowing pile of old clothes shifted in the back as it hit a bump. He shook his head, turning back to the room. *What's really going on?*

His gaze shifted to her, sitting on the red velvet sofa with her black gown. An image he once saw in a book came to his mind. *What was that name? Lilith?* "What do you want from me?"

Walter grinned, leaning back as he scoffed at Timothy. "Ya have no heart, boy."

She turned her gaze to Walter. He smiled back, a knowing look crossing his face before slumping to the chair dead.

"I have assembled your studio, Love," Gabrielle said. She stood, exuding a primal call to him. She raised her hand, causing the curtains to separate. She beckoned to him. Unable to resist her, Timothy obeyed, coming to stand behind her, his body pressed close. Her fragrance pulled at his mind. Intoxicated, he drank in her presence.

His paintings lined the far wall, while an empty canvas waited for him. All of his supplies and tools were there. "No more distractions, my love. Let the world fall away, just you and I existing for all time." As if in a dream but knowing this was real, Timothy pushed all away, wanting nothing more than to feel her presence forever. Life surged within him. Everything vanished; no more Susan, nothing but Gabrielle and him remained.

A faint whisper within his mind beckoned: *I will be your inspiration.*

Niall Parkinson

Gary Murphy
Horrorwerk

Professor Roberto Klaus was coming to the sorry point in his long illustrious career when he simply couldn't continue due to age and increasingly bad health. He had been informed that he would die by the end of the month of heart and breathing complications, and did he wish to spend his remaining two weeks in hospital the offer was always there did he decided to choose that option. He had shrugged and casually said no, that he would spend it at home in the bosom of his family, where he was loved and, most of all, respected, rather than spend his few remaining days shuffling around on a ward looking at clinically-clean white walls and floors, counting down the hours. There was no respect in that. Although, he had said rather candidly to the doctors that when the time came he wished for it to be mercifully quick and painless and that he would much prefer to simply "black out" and fall flat on his face rather than seize-up in a contorted rictus, agonized and wretched or twisted out of all recognition. Professor Klaus longed for a graceful demise.

Smoking didn't help, and he smoked a pipe to boot where the nicotine level was much higher than that of a cigarette and he always chose to indulge in the finest and strongest, a lung-dissolving Bulgarian brand he could only buy via a special Internet website. Never without the pipe, it acted as a constant reminder of perpetual ill-health and his stubbornness not to quit. Not that it would make much if any difference now. The hangman's noose was already and had long since been around his neck and tightening with every minute and every hour that passed...

Professor Roberto Klaus had a special gift, however. More importantly, one that he urgently wished to pass down to a family member before it had the chance to evaporate when he died. He did not want this remarkable gift to simply disappear into the pale ether or merely rise and dissolve into the air as his useless and burnt corpse would do in the flames of the crematorium.

Professor Klaus believed his mental powers could somehow be passed on to his 12-year-old grandson by means of a simple blood-transfusion. Or perhaps something that was easier, like the digestion of his blood orally. Either way, young Harley Klaus was the key.

At his home near Leicester Square in an affluent London location, Klaus held a dinner party one evening for family members and a few close friends, just to explain his health situation, his impending demise and say his heartfelt goodbyes. Young Harley he stated would be the main beneficiary to his wealth, his home and his every last asset. But the Professor included he would also leave quite a sizeable chunk of his estate to his only son, George, and his wife, Andrea. He wasn't a heartless, soulless bastard.

George and Andrea never really ever knew of Roberto Klaus' sensory abilities or to what effect they could be administered by mere thought or profound concentration. They had never had reason to be told and the old miser was a private man who spent most his days lecturing at colleges and universities around the world, from New York to Paris, from Switzerland to Moscow. He was a Professor of Science, the Paranormal, and the Holocaust. In his time he had travelled millions of miles, either by ship or by plane, and he was proud to admit that.

However, due to terminally ill-health and his smoking habit, he was forced to mainly keep to Europe, and for the better part stuck to his teachings in London. It was his hometown, after all, and where his heart belonged.

The dark-haired and cherub-faced young boy approached him at the party. Harley said, "Granddad, are you really going to die?"

Roberto Klaus smiled warmly at his grandson. But he felt wounded when he replied, "Nobody lives forever, my boy. But I'll be with you in spirit always. Never forget that."

"I thought professors could work miracles."

Strange that, and Klaus replied, "No man should ever try to eclipse the work of the Lord, Harley. Not as a professor and neither as a human being. Miracles are there to be solely performed by God." He took the boy by the hand. "Come with me into my study, I need to speak to you concerning a matter of great importance."

The study was a large but cosy room adjacent to the main lounge. Entering it for the first time with his grandfather, young Harley was astonished, because for the boy it must have been not dissimilar to being the man who first set foot on the Moon. It was like walking into a world totally alien. Leather and rosewood and mahogany, an air of richness and affluence and seniority, the huge wooden desk and bookshelves that towered to the high ceiling, and the smoky aroma of pipe-tobacco and malt whiskey. It was dark and creepy but also heralded a fascinating adventure for a 12-year-old boy.

"I want you to drink this, Harley. Don't worry. It's only red wine..." He laughed, almost mockingly, and added, "...I started young, and so should my sole begotten grandson."

Harley accepted the goblet without argument and gulped it down like a sailor.

"Good boy," the Professor said and grinned, "Today I'm very proud."

Harley hiccupped and handed the goblet back. "Taste's nice," he said, smiling back, "Can I have another?"

Klaus laughed and held his hands aloft.

"Listen," he said in a low whisper, even if they were in a secluded spot, "We must keep this our little secret. "Mustn't tell mummy and daddy..." He put on a stern face, adding, "...If you do, I'll be very cross. And mummy and daddy won't like the idea of their young boy drinking alcohol, right?" He turned the boy around and playfully slapped his behind. "Now run along!"

As Harley scampered off Professor Roberto Klaus knew his work was done. He leaned back on his paper-laden mahogany desk and chuckled, knowing his legacy was strong and fervent and that his search for a successor was over and completed. Harley would discover his abilities without hindrance and accidently, just as he had as a youngster during the Second World War. Oh Mister Hitler, what you would have offered to possess such a magical ability...

It would have spread throughout the Reich like a disease.

Shortly afterwards, the boy and his parents observed the night was a cool one and said their farewells, saying it was such a nice night they would walk and return in the morning to pick the car up before work. A frail Roberto Klaus seen them off and wished them all the best. He watched the boy in particular as they departed along the street towards the main epicentre of Leicester Square. Harley Klaus looked back over his shoulder and scrutinized the ageing Professor suspiciously.

And it was not long before the trouble, and Klaus" legacy, went into immediate effect in the most corruptive sense.

"My God, Harley," George Klaus implored his son, as the boy stiffened on the sidewalk, "Are you all right, son?" He put his hands on the entranced youth's shoulders and shook him. "Harley! What's the matter? Are you okay? Speak to me!"

Suddenly the worried dad was forced to retract his hands, almost "unsticking" them, for the boy seemed more than just icy cold but at a point of freezing. Removing his hands, he turned to his wife Andrea and despaired. "He's freezing cold," he said. "My God, he's literally like a block of ice!" Harley had begun turning blue with this strange abrupt coldness. George shouted, "Harley! Answer me!"

The boy was in a trance. Until his eyes turned and fixed on George when they seemed to open a secret lock inside the man and switch fear for his son's disposition into a fear for his own mental stability. George and Andrea retreated backwards, for Harley suddenly took on a cold grinning persona and appeared grotesque, almost evil-looking. He took off running across the busy road. And stopped in the middle as a huge red London Transport double-decker bus threatened to run directly into him and mow him down, killing him for sure.

Harley raised his hand and "stared down" the huge scarlet shape approaching.

When he raised his hand, however, so did the bus, giving the appearance it was levitating. And when he cast his hand to the right, the huge bus traversed through the air to the right, flying and crashing into a series of parked cars. And because the bus was occupied, it would later be confirmed there was serious injury caused amongst its many passengers travelling through the Leicester Square vicinity during this time of night.

The Professor heard the racket outside and ran out onto the street, suddenly brutally aware of this night's shameful misjudgement, solely on his part. He was an idiot and a damned fool!

However, the incident occurring did not go undetected by the law in the area and because the vicinity was on high-alert due to a terrorism scare where the miscreants had threatened to bomb the place, and the deadline was tonight, officers were carrying loaded weapons and were decidedly edgy. When the bus transported through the air, they immediately drew their own conclusions, and were deployed to the area en masse, cars and vans and army vehicles flocking from all directions, sirens blaring amid a sea of blue flashing lights. Some of the officers and soldiers saw what happened and pointed at the boy who was currently scurrying down a deserted alleyway – a dead end. They followed, for they only could, because the world knew just as the armed forces knew, terrorists were getting younger by the day.

When Harley reached the dead end he looked around angrily and faced the incoming authorities closing in on him in the alleyway, as they blocked off the only route of escape.

They had him cornered like a rat in a drain.

Soldiers and police officers had drawn to a standstill and were there poised to open fire on the young terrorist if he displayed any sign of confrontation. Harley stood and stared at the people pointing guns at him. But no more was the evil or corruptive instinct. Just a frightened young boy trapped. Yet the boy was ready to kill and he knew just how...

"...Harley, my boy!" Roberto Klaus shouted, and pushed and shoved his way through the crowd of authority. They tried to hold him back but his persistence paid off and he got through without any serious fuss. It was as if they knew the old man would prevent them firing their bullets into a young 12-year-old kid. "He's my grandson! I know this boy...he's completely harmless...I can help you...trust me, I can help...!"

A passageway formed in the crowd and the Professor used it. He entered the alleyway and approached the nervous youth.

Harley's eyes welled with stinging tears. He yelled, "You did this to me..."

Professor Klaus implored, "I know I did, Harley, and I was a fool. An obsessive fool and arrogant and selfish, but together we can both be delivered unto greatness..."

Harley gritted his teeth to form a snarl and reached out a doomed hand.

He said, "I'm going to kill you, Grandad. And everyone else in your family."

The authorities appeared dumbfounded. But they were ready and more than willing to open fire at a moment's notice as the strangest occurrence took centre stage in the darkened alley. The two great psychic abilities had gone to war and the authorities hadn't a clue what any of it was about. To them it just looked like a young kid and an elderly geezer were pointing at each other. Even though secretly they guessed something much deeper going on. After all, that huge bus that flew through the air and the possessed screaming populace of Leicester Square scurrying around looking for shelter or a safe-haven from terrorists.

The Professor was far outweighed by youth and fresh perspective as Harley channelled his ability to disrupt the body"s internal nervous-system. The older man folded almost immediately, his heart and lungs shuddering inside their delicate ribcage as a burning fury seemed to fill his stomach and chest. It was like a claw within scratching and ripping its way out, as the same claw clutched vital organs and threatened to remove them and take them with it.

Veins sprouted across the boy's forehead and cheeks, opening and spraying minor sprinkles of blood across his face until it was awash with redness. His eyes bulged like they were about to explode. His lips had turned a cold icy hue of dark indigo.

It was payback time and Harley revelled in his newfound power of concentration.

Roberto Klaus attempted to open his mouth to perhaps plead for his grandson to stop but all that emerged with a thick regurgitated flow of yellowy puss.

The boy's extended hand suddenly clenched into a tight fist so it gripped his Grandfather's very soul, squeezing it relentlessly so that it couldn't escape his hold. But he felt his own pain now, for while he tried to finish the job, there was no room for any lack or drop in concentration. The older man was strong but not stronger and the battle of wits was closing. It now approached an end where there could be but one victor, one survivor, and one remaining dishevelled soul to continue this instrument of destruction's legacy. Whoever this proved to be, they would be afflicted so badly by tonight's confrontation that it would leave one tragically dead and the other grotesquely disfigured.

The soldiers opened fire on the boy as the elderly Professor Roberto Klaus fell dying to his knees clutching his expanding and shattered skull in agonized pain. When the old man hit the deck, his body was a mashed lump and his face unrecognizable. Harley Klaus" powers were not adept in magically assisting him to dodge bullets, and his young body slumped to his death in a hail of blazing firepower.

Nobody would ever really know what took place that night in Leicester Square. Professor Klaus" little experiment worked, that's for sure, but with an unforeseen circumstance that even he as a man of science and a man of the world would never have anticipated. It was like the old saying in America that he had picked up on his travels whilst lecturing there, "Everybody loves a hotdog. But they don't want to see how a hotdog is made..."

Adam Blampied
Buried

Three loud bangs on the cellar door. One. Two. Three. I close my fist around the cold metal key so tightly that its pointy bits dig into my palm and my hand hurts which I don't care about because I can't breathe because of the knocking and when the banging stops and I can breathe again I look down at my open hand and the key is glistening red and I'm crying but I don't remember doing that. And then the banging starts again. One. Two. Three. I'm. Still. Here.

Ever since Mummy and I moved into our new small house, I've known about the horrible thing behind the cellar door. We used to live in a big house in the city with New Dad, who I'm not supposed to call New Dad, says Mummy, but he didn't mind and smiled at me lots. We had to leave because we don't like him anymore, so Mummy drove us here and even though she was tired and upset she still said *Ta-dah*! The house is white and has hanging plant pots with yellow droopy flowers in them.

The whole place smelled of soil when we first walked in, and I started to panic but Mummy sprayed the purple mist around so that it smelled like flowers. The soil smell was coming from the cellar under the stairs. The door was open and the steps went down to this dark pit of mud. There wasn't even a floor, just the ground all brown and it smelled so bad that I screamed.

Mummy can't take me to the garden centre because I cry when I smell too much soil. I was only small when Proper Dad died. I'm still small, but I was smaller then and my uncles made me pick up soil from this big pile and throw into the hole on top of my Dad. *We're burying him,* they said. *He has to be buried.* I threw a handful in, then I grabbed another and another. After a while I got covered in soil and they had to pull me away screaming.

We have to go. I keep crying at Mummy. *There's too much smell and there's a horrible thing!* She closed the door and locked it. *See,* she said, holding me by my head to stop me as I cried. *It's closed, I closed it. Stop!*

But it's just behind the door, I cried. *It's still just behind the door.*

I ran out to the car and jumped on the backseat and did what I always did. I pressed my face so hard into the seat that it squashed my nose against my face. I cried and I cried, but Mummy didn't come out to get me. After I'd finished crying, my chest was sore, my throat and my head hurt and I was hungry so I came back inside. Mummy was sat in the kitchen. She'd half unpacked some mugs and was drinking out of one, with a big green bottle open on the table. Her makeup was smudged like a panda.

I can't sleep here, I keep saying but Mummy won't listen. Whenever I fall asleep I dream about the horrible thing behind the cellar door. It's banging on the door and the door is slowly breaking. Pieces of it crack and fall off and eventually it opens and I wake up screaming for Mummy, who has stopped coming. *Aren't you going to see what's wrong?* a man's voice will sometimes say through the wall. But she doesn't come.

She has given me the key, forced it into my hand and walked away, and every morning I put it in the keyhole and turn it to make sure it's locked. It always is, but one day it won't be. I know that as much I know anything. On hot days we have to open the windows and the wind comes through the house and you can smell the cellar from the kitchen. Yesterday morning at breakfast the smell was so strong. Mummy said, *just don't,* but I panicked and rushed to the hallway to make sure the door was closed. It was but I ran back to the kitchen crying, *please, we need to leave. Mummy, please! We have to go! Please!* Mummy, who was drinking from a mug, screamed. Not words, just a scream. I shouted *Get me a new Dad so we can go. You always do,* and she hit me in the back of the head and walked away. I got red on my neck because her gold ring cut my head and she wouldn't let me go to school. I just stayed in bed with tissue paper up my nose.

I don't want to make her angry. She's been so cross all the time since Proper Dad and I don't know what to say to make her not. Sometimes she's cross when I speak, sometimes when I'm quiet. I know we mustn't stay here though. The smell and the horrible thing will get us, I think, and I love her so I won't stop.

She came into my room and sat down on my bed. She hugged me close and I hugged her too. She smelt sour, like fruit that had gone off and her lips were stained red. She cried and rubbed my head and kissed me. *Don't say anything,* she whispered to me after a while, gave me another kiss on the forehead, and left me to sleep.

For the first time in days and days I didn't dream of the horrible thing behind the cellar door, but of me, Mummy and Dad, before holes in the ground, big empty green bottles or smells from under the stairs. I think of him most of all, and in my dream, he brushes the soil from his clothes and hugs me and he smells so clean.

I woke up. I'd slept the whole day and it was dark and I was warm and sticky in my bed. I went downstairs with the key in my hand to check the lock. It wasn't morning but it's just what I had to do when I got out of bed. As I went downstairs I could her a man say *you want I could ask them down the bar. Couple evenings work we could sort this all out,* and when I got to the bottom of the stairs and turned around, the cellar door was open. I screamed and I screamed. Suddenly a man stormed up the stairs from the cellar, hands covered with soil and I screamed even harder. He tried to grab me but I took the key and pushed it as hard as I could into face. The pointy bits tore the skin in a big line across his forehead and he started bleeding and let me go. Mummy came running and tried to help him but he pushed her down and ran out the door shouting, *you wait. You wait til I tell the fellas.* The front door slammed and Mummy threw a mug at me. It smashed on the wall and red and bits went everywhere. She yelled, but I ran into the kitchen, knocking over some bottles on the table. They smashed on the floor and Mummy grabbed me by the hair. Some of it came out and I got free. I ran into the hallway. She was yelling again so I kept running. I still had the key in my hand so I ran into the cellar, closed the door and locked it.

The horrible thing is behind the cellar door. Mummy is banging and banging and banging on the door and I'm sat on the soil, crying. In my dream the door cracked and opened and I know it will here too, so I start grabbing handfuls of soil. I'm covered in it and the ground stings against my hurt red dripping hand but I'm thinking of Dad and I dig as fast as I can, hoping that if I go through the earth, if I get deep enough through the soil, maybe I will find him.

Jason WolfgangGehler
Scarecrow Fields

The lengthy trip had gotten the best of Rory Ellison. The yellow lines on the surface of the pavement eroded to a single blur. It had been two and a half excruciating days inside his Civic with his girlfriend and her best friend. A fifty-five hour span of hollering, screaming, and exasperated chatter on where the hell they were headed. A few rest stops later, including an overnight stay at a Best Western [or two] lengthened the trip. Although Rory, a fairly intelligent twenty year old, with striking features for a freckled Irishman, knew full well this trip was doomed from the start. He replayed the thoughts in his head of never taking your girlfriend's BFF with you on any lengthy trip. A routine dash to the mall usually strikes the match between the couple. Rory's main problem stemmed from the fact that Janet's friends never liked him, or perhaps had kept their jealousy subdued over Janet's relationship. In either case, Rory's emotions flared.

They had left the Eastern seaboard a day before Hurricane Sandy had devastated entire area, leaving the shores of New York City, New Jersey, Long Island, and parts of Carolina gargling underwater. New York City's streets, tunnels, and subways had flooded forcing residents to fight for survival. No power. No food. Atlantic City, Coney Island, and other parts of the boardwalks drowned instantly. Rory knew they couldn't head back home. They were in a sense trapped inside this surreal road trip. A road trip that was *HIS* girlfriend's idea nevertheless.

Janet's idea to investigate a secluded town in the heart of Indiana, called Scarecrow Fields, prompted some abrasive chatter from Rory. The couple bickered on why they couldn't fly out to Indiana. Janet wanted to experience a road trip cross country, with this particular stop along the way. Her consistent affection for the weird, and mysterious had massaged her brain into taking this trip. Scarecrow Field harbored evil according to some eyewitness accounts, soon to become the hottest trending subject on the social media circus. A series of events painted in a brush of secrecy and lies even kept the local police away, forcing the townsfolk to cobble together enough strength to survive the night. A certain cloud of horror swirled inside that town, and it had caught Janet's curiosity.

Rory rubbed his eyes with the back of his right hand. The green painted mile markers cruised by on the shoulder of the road, in a reflective stare of dominance. The Civic's clock flipped to midnight, signaling another day had approached. Rory glanced a fleeting peek at the girls, and soon laughed as they were dead to the world. As hour fifty-six clicked by, Rory maintained his determination not to fall asleep on the road. The Civic remained the only soul on this darkened patch of pavement, with the exception of an occasional tractor trailer. Rory's CD collection exhausted, his I-Pod had decided not to converse with him through musical language anymore, left him to search his brain for entertainment. Not even the scandalous images of Janet's curvy body in purple and black lingerie with her dirty blond hair tied into a devil's ponytail could keep him awake.

Rory felt the car start to rumble and rock as the next sign approached. A loud whistle erupted from underneath the hood before a moan of exhaustion brought the fifteen year old Honda Civic, to a dead stop. Rory, with whatever ounce of coolness he had left, guided the car to smoother place on the shoulder of the highway. Janet stirred, chortling back a heavy snore.

"Where are we?" She asked, her small finger rubbed the crust from her eyes.

Rory grumbled an incoherent answer, as his left hand released the lever on the floor of the car, sending the hood springing open.

The night seemed decent enough for November in the Midwest. A slight breeze, mixed in a definite midnight glare of the darkness, forced Rory to work harder on fixing the problem. His distaste for the dark, or anything out of his comfort zone routinely lead to anxiety, or a firm drink of spirits. His hands worked with a fever pitch to secure the lamp on the hook to brighten his view.

The radiator whistled once more, steam built up with the chamber. Rory quickly removed his shirt, wrapped around his hand and released the cap, and titled his face away from the car, ready to scream in expected pain.

A deafening screech erupted from the night sky. The moon's crescent soon disappeared underneath a wave of black. Janet and her friend Savannah hollered from inside the car at the ominous sight outside. One by one the screeching hit the sign behind Rory like rocks on a metal sheet. A few glanced off the raised hood, pounding their heads against the vehicle's toughness.

Ping,

Ping.

Ping.

Rory fell backward, his burning hands waving in defeat, swatting away the approaching bats. Their fangs ripped at his wrists before the flying rodents disappeared into the night.

The radiator's whistling soon ceased, and Janet emerged from the car, her cries finally hushed from the sight of Rory on the ground, writhing in pain.

Her eyes followed the few dead bats sliding down the green sign, staining the white letters in their red blood:

Scarecrow Fields.

A dirtied, beaten to its rusted skeleton, blood red tow truck eased to an uncomfortable stop alongside the stranded, panicked trio of teenagers. It's headlights unevenly placed in their sockets, still yielded some amount of light. The bent, dim rays illuminated the blood splattered traffic sign, while the engine continued to cough forth oil and antifreeze.

The white spackled lettering on the passenger door had started to wear off from years of weathered abuse. The remaining letters, still caked in mud and rust spelled out the owner of the truck: S. LIVED CURSE TOWING.

A aged man exited the truck, his feet slow to shuffle across the highway. His steel toed boots kicked away streams of pebbles and small rocks, en route to the bewildered teens. The man's age not fully known, yet his aging skin displayed signs of arthritic conditions and several scars strewn throughout. His frame well suited for his business. A muscular man, his legs were the strength of his body, and had suited him well in this profession. His fingers flicked off a dying cigarette into the night. His face remained tucked beneath a maroon red San Francisco 49er cap with the rim bent in the form of a downward horseshoe. A silver pewter necklace hung snug around his pallid neck, with a cross dangling from the chain.

His ears swelled with their screams, especially the girls. The boy was down on the ground, his face splattered with red streaks and superficial claw marks. He knew what had happened. These specific parts were the breeding and hunting grounds for the town's bat population. His eyes researched the scene, taking in the disarray and moderate chaos. A disruptive smile cracked across his peeling lips.

"Sir, can you help us?" One of the girls yelped the question.

"Perhaps," the man's response was cloaked in a growl. His hands lit another cigarette. A brief orange hue brought his face to life, before it returned back to the darkness.

"We need a ride to town. Please?"

"Where you headed Missus?" He asked while he circled the car, keeping a haunting eye on the teens. "Yep, it looks like you have a flat tire back here." He plunged a knife into the rear tire before anyone could debate the issue.

"I thought it was a radiator problem." She seemed mystified by the news.

"Well, that may be the case as well." He slipped the knife back inside his pocket keeping it concealed from view. "But, you're not going anywhere on this flat. Its kissing the pavement," he paused. A muted sigh of discomfort exploded inside his mouth. The pain crept to a mild annoyance inside his chest. A cracked rib or two remained a strong possibility from his last encounter. A fervent twist of his head and another drag on the fresh cigarette had brought his senses back to normalcy. "Where you headed again?" He sucked off the last of the cigarette and dropped it to the ground with a victorious stomp from his blood stained boot. He approached rear bumper of the Civic and scraped off what resembled brain matter from the crevices of the sole.

"Now, I don't know where 'yer headed, but we have a nice town where you can catch your breath and shower up." He reached for his chains from his truck. "If you want, I'll be happy to drag this car there," he said with a meaty laugh. The kind that draws the nicotine from the lungs and coughs the laugh through the mouth.

"Yeah, that seems okay with us," she said. "My boyfriend's a bit concussed I'm afraid. The offer for a ride to your town would be greatly appreciated."

"Sure, hop in," he offered. His hands made quick work of the Civic, preparing it for the haul into town. "We have a crackerjack of a mechanic back in town. His fingers make love to these machines."

One by one the three teens entered the medium sized cab. A bit uncomfortable, yet they displayed a genuine graciousness for the ride.

The man revved the engine to life, engineering a coughing fit from the muffler. A quick swipe of the windshield wipers seemed to scrape away an odd mixture from the cracked window. "Ah, there we go," he said, satisfied by the clean window.

"What was that?" The boy asked.

"I hit a deer the other night, splattered the fuck all over my hood, the headlights, and the windshield. I even stepped in the remains during a routine check of the carcass."

"That sucks."

"Listen, we have a short ride back to town, but the residents are a bit odd."

"How so?" He asked.

"They abhor tourists, or non-residents," she chimed in.

"Janet knows everything about this town."

"Rory, you know it's a very intriguing urban legend," said Janet.

"I'm Savannah," Janet's friend introduced herself, her scrawny body scrunched up against the passenger side door. "What's your name, Sir?"

"I'd prefer not to divulge my name," the man replied with a harsh smack of his lips together. He needed a smoke in the worst way.

"How come?" asked Rory. "It's not a girlish name, like Madison, or Carly is it?"

The man peeled his eyes away from the dark road for a quick glance at Rory. The dank pupils retreated, then enlarged with a passionate distaste for this boy's humor. "No," he snarled. "I have sort of an acronym for a namesake." He returned his glare to the poorly lit road.

"Which is?" Rory prodded.

"Maybe he doesn't want to tell us," said Janet.

"Yeah," paused Savannah, "that's cool with us."

"My birth name," the man snickered, "was indeed 'girlish'."

Rory stifled a laugh. "I knew it."

The man placed his right hand on Rory's shoulder without removing his stare from the road. The entire cab knew immediately that the driver was in charge with a subtle terrorizing control. "My birth name was Francis. I've since changed it after discovering religion."

The three teenagers were in a mystified silence.

"Graham Orville Desmond." The man tugged at his cross around his neck with a set of mangled fingers. The fingernails rugged, ripped, and stained with dying cells and a tinge of cherry blood. "This road has been traveled by many, weary tourists before," his voice lowered as they entered the permitted if the town's border. "What makes you so damn confident you'll survive the night?" His hand unlocked the driver's side door. His feet hit the hard dirt with hammering applause.

Savannah, Janet, and then Rory with a slight huff of impatience, exited the dank cab of the truck.

Graham resurfaced once more, his left hand tapped the burning headlight his hand dusted off a patch of dead flies. He closed his distance between them. "Welcome to Scarecrow

Fields," his voice low and monotone. His maroon 49er cap soaked from the increasing rainfall, the droplets of water flew from the bill.

"Jesus, it's fucking horrible out here? Do you have place we can crash?" Rory hollered. "I have a crushing headache." He ran his fingers across his forehead to massage the throbbing.

"Yeah, there's a motel down the way," Graham said.

"Do you expect us to walk?" Rory demanded, his hands kept the girls at bay in a protective manner.

"Are you scared of some rain? This is where my involvement ends with the three of you. I'm dragging this piece of shit to the mechanics, and pray he'll be able to get you back on track by morning."

The next day yawned and growled on the trio through a splintered window at the local motel. Rory attempted a shower than soon ended rather abruptly after brown water cascaded from the fractured shower head. Janet and Savannah moaned in displeasure over the water situation and quickly splashed some Degree deodorant underneath their arms.

"This sucks, you know that?" Janet seethed.

"We're only here for another day, at most," persuaded Rory. "Just hang in there baby."

Janet huffed and refused Rory's advances. "Bite me."

Savannah just rolled her eyes in disgust. "Can we at least head into town? I'm starving."

Scarecrow Fields harbored its own dark secrets, yet Janet was pulled into the mysterious storm of uncertainty. The television shows and various books clawed at her brain, a methodical digging that exploded her fanaticism with the subject. Rory and her inner circle of friends simply brushed aside her thoughts and stories of what could've happened. *"Let's focus on reality."* That's what Rory would always say.

The three entered the diner shuffling their weary feet across the cloudy dirt. Rory pushed the door open with a gentle breeze of a touch, clanging the bell in a pattern of clangs.

The townsfolk leered at the newcomers with different glances, curious stares, and ominous chattering. Rory barely made out the conversations, the words seemed foreign to his intellect. The girls also failed to comprehend the clarity of the folk's gossip mill.

A booth sat all alone in the far corner of the small diner. A faint ray light illuminated the area, although a fraction of sun exposed the dirty, ripped, and soiled cushion of the booth. A tear down the center lifted the stuffing from underneath into clear view. A series of failed attempts with duct tape lingered behind, a grim reminder of the booth's previous encounters.

The waitress reluctantly took their orders and soon returned with a paltry offering of smashed eggs, broken slices of toast with the moldy edges cut off, and orange juice that swam in a sea of brown.

"We can't eat this," Rory said.

"Why not?" The waitress was clearly offended. Her pudgy fingers tapped the pen against her pad. "I have other orders to take. You'll eat this and be satisfied you've gotten excellent service here today."

"I'm not eating this shit," he roared back. "We are guests in your town," his words trailed off.

The entire diner rose to their feet and began to surround the booth. The waitress placed her pad down, but not her pen. She used that to puncture Savannah's neck. Rory and Janet froze in horror as their friend bled across the table. Her hands cupped a river of blood unable to prevent the gush. The waitress gripped Savannah and drove the pen further inside her skin, exploding another burst of red across the table, and her white apron. A few moments later the girl went limp against the back of the booth and slid dead to the window.

Rory felt a hard shot to the side of his face. Janet squirmed beneath the table attempting an escape. Her chances were cut short after a shotgun blast tore through her right knee, bringing her instant pain.

Rory had another crack against the side of his face from the butt of a shotgun that forced him to slam his head against the table and fade to unconsciousness.

The screaming penetrated his nightmare with hellish volume. His eyes blinked in a blurred reality revealing the center of the town beneath the glaring Arizona sun. In the center of the town protruded a large stake surrounded by an assortment of medium to large size rocks. Janet writhed to break free but was bound tight by rope that seared her skin with every failed attempt.

Rory's senses took a bit to return. His nose picked up the scent of blood, possibly his, or Janet's for that matter. His eyes returned to focus on a mangled body in the far corner nearest the barber shop. He wept with a quiet whimper as a pair of wild dogs feasted on Savannah's dead body. Their teeth snapping against her once soft skin, peeling away layer by layer until the moon white bone became visible.

"Ladies and gentlemen," the voice bellowed to the gathering crowd. "We are gathered here today to summon the Great Spirit, the entity of evil himself," the man paused once more. The cheering erupted. "The demon of the fields, the scarecrow himself!"

Rory's senses fully returned and the blood from his wound still trickled down his cheek. He yelled for Janet, but her mobility was muted by drugs, or some other intoxicating substance. He watched her head roll about in senseless fashion, welcoming her death with a confused stare.

It was him. Rory recognized the voice. It was the tow truck guy from the night before. Graham Orville Desmond. Rory's brain manufactured the name and broke down the letters. *GOD*. Rory's mind also flashed back to the truck's name on the side of the door that night. S. Lived. It was Devil spelled backwards. Jesus fucking Christ, Janet was right about this place. "You can't do this!" He screamed at Graham. His arms pinned back by a couple of the townsfolk.

"Why not?" Graham asked, his attire suited his role. A well-worn preacher outfit. His hands didn't embrace a cross. It was a golden gun that held firm on Rory's position. "This town embraces my vision."

"We're humans," Rory again screamed. "You killed my friend!"

"Ah yes, you are truly humans," Graham seethed. His cracked lips swelled with spit. "The worst kind. You come here thinking this is some sort of tourist attraction? You have no idea what are you about to partake in." He paced back and forth. "The girl over there," he said waving his gun, "she was flat out annoying and makes for perfect collateral damage. As it turns out my hounds have a fondness for her pungent, whorish scent. It fuels their rotten brains." He chuckled.

"You will be held accountable for this." Rory strained to escape, but the grip tightened on him.

"By whom?" Graham clacked his tongue. "I own this town. I deliver the justice by which is served by me. No questions asked. Your girlfriend over there, the pure virgin will make an excellent trophy for the Scarecrow."

"Scarecrow?"

"A legendary spirit that comes forth once a month for a year on feeds on the innocence of a young woman, until it becomes whole, and then it feeds on *everything*."

"Janet isn't a virgin," barked Rory. "I've fucked her every which way 'til Sunday."

"Not a virgin in the sexual verse," he paused, "although they are a treasure to find. No, no, she needs to be pure of heart."

"Why is that?"

"That way the Scarecrow's heart will be strong and vibrant, devoid of any malice, discontent, and injustice."

"I won't let you do this."

A faint rustling of the corn stalks could be heard.

"Ah, the demon arrives for his final gift. It's been a long process, but a worthwhile endeavor on his part."

The cornstalks snapped in succession as the spirit emerged and circled overhead.

Graham looked up at the swirling whirlpool of pure evil. "This is going to be fucking insane."

The Scarecrow swarmed over Janet's body and devoured her clear to the bone.

Graham raised his six-shooter and obliterated her skeletal remains across the pit. His prized hounds snapped up several of her bones and sauntered off to enjoy their reward.

Rory in a fit of rage slammed his head against the groin of his captor and struggled free. Graham pivoted in time to fire a shot at Rory's charging body. Rory collided hard with Graham, knocking the preacher to the ground. The gun scattered of reach. Rory's gripped Graham around the neck and choked him hard.

Gasping, Graham reached deep into his pocket and retrieved a small knife that he plunged in Rory's right forearm. "You won't win this battle," he fought for breath. "Look," he said waving his finger.

The Scarecrow soon materialized from the whirlpool of souls. A monstrous entity, standing well over seven feet, his grotesque faced swiveled with ease. A monster with extreme flexibility, his limbs stretched and groaned for something to kill. His black soulless eyes stared straight at Rory. A face birthed from his dead victims soon became pale beige, yet remained slimy and rancid in scent. A thin row of needled teeth grinding against one another still stained in Janet's fresh blood. A forked tongue soon cleansed the remainder of blood with a formidable lash. Its lanky frame approached Graham and Rory.

"Unleash your fury upon this wretched soul, for he deserves your wrath," Graham's words excited the crowd, and even stirred a dark growl from the Scarecrow.

Rory snatched up the idle gun. "You brought us here, for this reason?"

Graham smiled. "But, of course. It wasn't accident we ran into each other. I've been following the three of you for a while out there."

"Call off your bitch," Rory said, "and do the right thing."

"It's been done. I can't undo God's will." Graham rose from the ground.

"Forgive me Father, for I have sinned," Rory repeated the line. His finger pulled back on the trigger.

Graham teetered back from the thunderous shot. His hands reached out in defense. Another bullet exploded through his flexed fingers and dropped the preacher cold in his tracks.

The Scarecrow sauntered closer. It's head twisted and looked down at Graham's quivering body.

"Shit, I thought that would've worked." Rory felt a sledgehammer tear through his chest.

The Scarecrow ripped out Rory's beating heart with its spider like grasp and swallowed it whole. Rory fell to the ground, a warm rush of blood poured from the wound. The gun bounced off the dirt and spun out of control. A bullet whistled through the air gunning down the hefty waitress from the diner. A swift drill between the eyes and the woman dropped with a faint grunt of death.

The Scarecrow followed Rory's death with a menacing snarl as the townsfolk scattered in fear after witnessing the gruesome series of deaths. One by one the entity devoured the folk until only one man remained.

At the edge of the cornfield, Graham Orville Desmond stood rigid, his shirt caked in his own blood, his six-shooter tight in his right hand.

It's long fingers reached down and grasped the dirt for support. Its hind legs sprang from the ground, the Scarecrow soared through the air. The monster landed a few short yards away from Graham,

"I have a scripture for you ." He cleared his throat. "I refer to Ezekiel 7:8. I will pour out my fury upon you and spend my anger upon you." He smirked.

Graham raised his six-shooter.

The Scarecrow dashed for the sputtering preacher.

A deafening roar consumed the small town and a splattering of red washed across the still stalks of corn.

The truck stop was grimy at best. But he didn't care. His right hand still wrapped in gauze and bandaged rather tightly. He waved down a beaten down orange tow truck. The other hand clutched a newspaper he had gotten earlier from the vending machine.

The wheels groaned to a standstill. The driver opened the passenger side door and welcomed him in.

"Where ya headed?" the driver asked.

The man cleared his throat. "North."

"You have a name?"

The man thought for a moment. "Preacher."

"Okay, okay," the driver introduced himself, "I'm Vickers. Walt Vickers. I'm headed up to Tennessee to see my brother Tom."

"What a coincidence, that's where I'm headed." Preacher entered the vehicle. "A place called Carnie Creek. It seems there's some folk up there who need some enlightening." He grinned as he took out his six-shooter. His left hand soon pushed the bullets inside their chambers.

"I hear you're the guy who killed that monster back in town after it went ape shit on the townsfolk. You're a fucking hero my friend."

"It's all God's will Walt, it really is."

Walt glanced down at the weapon. "So, what's the gun for?" Vickers asked as he pulled back to the highway.

"It's for thinning out the crowd." Preacher laughed. His left raised the gun and placed against Walt's temple.

A roar filled the truck followed by a flash of light culminating in Walt's remains being plastered across the driver's side window and part of the steering wheel.

Preacher reached over and opened the driver's side door. He rolled out Walt's dead body to the desolate highway road and regained control of the swerving tow truck.

'Carnie Creek, here I come."

Author Bios

Essel Pratt has spent his life exploring his imagination and dreams. As a Husband and a Father, he doesn't always have as much time to write as he would like. However, his mind is always plotting out his next story and manipulating the plot. Someday he hopes to quit the 9-5 grind and focus on writing full time. Currently, Essel is building his catalog by contributing to various anthologies as he works on his first novel. He also contributes to www.nerdzy.com and www.infendo.com on an (almost) daily basis. Essel focuses his writings on mostly Horror/Sci-Fi, however is known to add a bit of other genres into his writings as well. You can follow Essel at: facebook.com/esselprattwriting and Esselpratt.blogspot.com and on twitter @EsselPratt

David Eccles writes the tales that prevent him from sleeping night after night. He feels they have a life of their own and deserve a full and long life, which is why he releases them onto the page. His stories are often tinged with sadness and a typically British sense of humor. His first collection of flash fiction and short stories, *Darke Times and Other Stories,* is well reviewed and available in all popular e-book formats. He has been previously featured on various blogs and websites, including BOOKSoftheDEADPRESS.com. His work can be read in another four of James Ward Kirk's anthologies, *Sex, Drugs & Horror, Serial Killers Tres Tria, Bones,* and *Ugly Babies,* and his Circuspunk story *Death of A Phobia: Pugwash Plus 2 and the Pasty-Faced Fuckers* is to be featured in *The New Whakazoid Circus – The Greatest Show on Paper*, edited by Charie D. Lamarr and published by Chupa Cabra House early in 2014.

Matt Cowan's love for the horror genre stretches back beyond his earliest childhood memories. At a young age he stopped having nightmares after beginning to enjoy them a bit too much. His primary literary influences are Ramsey Campbell, M.R. James, Algernon Blackwood, Fritz Leiber, and H.P. Lovecraft. "The Collective of Blaque Reach" was originally published in 2008 by Dead Letter Press as the bonus chap book story for those who purchased the anthology BOUND FOR EVIL: CURIOUS TALES OF BOOKS GONE BAD. It was also read on episode 90 of the Tales To Terrify podcast in 2013. His short story, "Here He Comes A Wandering", won the Pod of Horror

Christmas Horror Story Contest in 2009 and was read on episode #58. He's had stories appear in INDIANA HORROR ANTHOLOGY's 2011 and 2012, as well as INDIANA SCIENCE FICTION ANTHOLOGY 2011 and INDIANA CRIME REVIEW 2013.His short story "Christmas Wine" will appear in the forthcoming O LITTLE TOWN OF DEATHLEHEM charity anthology to benefit the Elizabeth Glaser Pediatric AIDS foundation from Grinning Skull Press. In addition to writing fiction, Matt produces articles highlighting some of the legendary names in the field at his new blog Horror Delve, which can be found at mattcowanhorror.wordpress.com. He lives with his beautiful wife Lynne and stepson Brett in Lawrence, Indiana where he works for the local water utility. He's currently crafting several more tales to fill the void left by his long lost nightmares. Sites: Horror Delve Blog: mattcowanhorror.wordpress.com Facebook Author Page: ttps://www.facebook.com/mattcowanhorror

Patrick Lacey is an Editorial Assistant in the healthcare industry. When he's not reading about blood clots and infectious diseases, he writes about things that make the general public uncomfortable. He lives in Massachusetts with his wife, his Pomeranian, and his muse, who he's pretty sure is trying to kill him. Follow him on Twitter (@PatLacey)."

K. Trap Jones is an award winning author of horror novels and short stories. Trap is known for his raw emotional and often depressive narrative horror dealing with the complications and conflictions of the human mind. With a sadistic inspiration from Dante Alighieri and Edgar Allan Poe, he has a temptation towards narrative folklore, classic literary works and obscure segments within society. His writing style has been described as "filling in the gaps" and "walking the jagged line between reality and fiction." His novel THE SINNER (Blood Bound Books, 2012) won the Royal Palm Literary Award. He is also a member of the Horror Writer's Association and can be found lurking around Tampa, Florida.

Neil Baker is a troubled man who believed for a long time that he was a filmmaker who occasionally wrote stories. Now he is starting to believe he is a writer who sometimes makes films. Either way, this doesn't bode well for his family.

Mathias Jansson is a Swedish art critic and poet. He has been published in magazines as The Horror Zine Magazine, Dark Eclipse, Schlock, The Sirens Call and The Poetry Box. He has also contributed to several anthologies from Horrified Press and James Ward Kirk Fiction as Suffer Eternal anthology Volume 1-3, Hell Whore Anthology Volume 1-3, Barnyard Horror and Serial Killers Tres Tria.
Homepage, : http://mathiasjansson72.blogspot.se/

Suzy Saylor is a freelance writer from the Philadelphia area. She enjoys the horror genre more than she probably should and is currently working on her first novel. A mother of two, much of her time is spent making happy memories with them, but encourages them to never be afraid of the dark.

Kevin Rodgers was born in Huntsville, Alabama on January 17, 1972. At the age of six, he wrote a series of unpublished short stories after his mother allowed him to use her typewriter. His family moved to Greensboro, North Carolina in 1984, where he penned longer, more complicated stories. In 1986, his family relocated to Orlando, Florida, which is where he currently lives. He graduated from Winter Park High School in Winter Park, FL in June 1990. He received a college degree from Valencia Community College in Orlando, FL in 1992. He graduated from the police academy at Valencia's Criminal Justice Institute in Orlando, FL in September 2002. He enjoys reading fiction in the horror, fantasy, and science-fiction genres. Over the last three years, nine of his short stories have appeared in various magazines from Pro Se Press. The list of stories includes *Slaughtership*, *Hellhound*, *Citadel of the New Moon*, and *Stargazers*. James Ward Kirk Publishing recently published his horror tale, *Evicted Tenants*, in an anthology called "Serial Killers Tres Tria". His first novel, CADAVER ISLAND, was published by Pro Se Press in March 2013. He recently completed the second installment of the CADAVER ISLAND trilogy, which will be called THE MASK OF BEELZEBUB. He is currently working on the final installment of the trilogy, which will be called THE PLAGUE OF CORRUPTION. More information can be found at his personal website, which is http://kevin-rodgers.squarespace.com and his Amazon Author Page, which is http://www.amazon.com/Kevin-Rodgers/e/B00CCGRIZU

Dona Fox has recently been accused of being a poet. She continues to maintain that she is actually an author. Her short stories and poetry have appeared in Eldritch Tales, Haunts, Thin Ice, Cemetery Dance (Issue #1), Beyond, and New Blood. Recently, her work has appeared in the James Ward Kirk Publishing's Anthologies - Bones and Ugly Babies Volume I.

Matthew Wilson, 30, has had over 100 stories accepted / appearances in such places as Horror Zine, Star*Line, Spellbound, Illumen, James Ward Kirk Publishing, Static Movement, Apokrupha Press, Hazardous Press, Gaslight Press, Sorcerers Signal and many more. He is currently editing his first novel and can be contacted on twitter @matthew94544267.

DJ Tyrer is the person behind Atlantean Publishing and has had numerous poems and stories published in the small presses of the UK, USA and elsewhere, as well as online. DJ Tyrer is the author of the novella **The Yellow House** and the critically-acclaimed poetry sequence **Our Story**. Most recently, he contributed three vignettes to **Sorcery & Sanctity: A Homage to Arthur Machen** from Hieroglyphic Press.

Michael Thomas-Knight haunts the local coffee shops of Long Island, NY, somewhere between a famous house in Amityville and Joel Rifkin's lovely home. His horror fiction has been published in Twisted Dreams, Infernal Ink, SNM Horror Magazine and Dark Eclipse Magazine. Michael's fiction has also been in numerous horror anthology books including: Shadow Masters, From Beyond The Grave, 100 Doors to Madness, O' Little Town of Deathlehem, and Miseria's Chorale. You can find Michael at his blog, Parlor of Horror, which deals with all things horror: movies, books, and articles for the horror enthusiast. http://parlorofhorror.wordpress.com

Dale Hollin is a failed socialite and working writer from Indianapolis, Indiana. He has works published and scheduled to be published by Lovecraftzine, James Ward Kirk Publishing, Danielle Rose Publishing, Melange Books, and Anytime-Shorts.

Mike Jansen has published flash fiction, short stories and longer work in various anthologies and magazines in the Netherlands and Belgium, including Cerberus, Manifesto Bravado, Wonderwaan, Ator Mondis and Babel-SF and Verschijnsel anthologies such as Ragnarok and Zwarte Zielen (Black Souls). He has won awards for best new author and best author in the King Kong Award in 1991 and 1992 respectively as well as an honorable mention for a submission to the Australian Altair Magazine launch competition in 1998. In 2012 Mike won awards in the SaBi Thor story contest, the Literary Prize for the Baarn Cultural Festival and the prestigious Dutch Fantastels award for best short story. In September 2013 he joined the Horror Writers Association (HWA). More recently he has published in various English language ezines and anthologies, among which several publications with JWKfiction.com, Encounters Magazine and others. A full list is on Mike's site: http://www.meznir.com You can also find him on Goodreads, Facebook and Twitter. Mike's debut novel, 'The Failing God', will be available, in English, from JWK Fiction, during 2013.

Gary Murphy is the author of numerous anthologies including the "Wide Awake and Dead" series of books, and novellas "BloodZone" and "A Twisted Love Story", and the upcoming "Hellish Redcap". He lives in Egremont, Cumbria in the UK, and when not writing full-time dabbles in antiques-dealing, in particular silverware, glass and ceramics. He was born 29th of January, 1969 and studied at St.Mary's Junior School in Cleator Moor before his move to the Whitehaven Comprehensive School aged 11, before leaving aged 15. His sole aim and ambition is to reach as many people around the world as possible through the medium of writing, and entertain, amaze and startle accordingly. He'll do this for as long as he's allowed.

Delphine Boswell expresses her fondness for writing with the words of John Steinbeck, "I nearly always write just as I nearly always breathe." For her, writing is not a job, not a career, but a passion that excites her more than anything else she has ever done. In the past thirteen years, she has written seven novels in a multitude of genres, consisting of suspense, mystery, psychological horror, and dystopian fiction. All of her writing has a dark tone to it, and it is not any wonder that one of Delphine's favorite authors is Joyce Carol Oates. In addition to novels, Delphine has had a multitude of her short stories published in online e-zines and several print anthologies. From 80,000 word novels to a Hemingway six-word contest in which she won first place, and to everything in between, Delphine cannot stay away from her love of writing. You can learn more about her works at: http://delphineboswell.com.

Adam Blampied: I am an actor, writer and comedian in critically acclaimed UK sketch group The Beta Males. I'm also freelance film reviewer for BattleRoyaleWithCheese.com, and, as a writer, have had my work aired on BBC radio 4 and published in two collections of short stories, one called Toast (published by Mardibooks and available at Amazon.com) and another Twelve Nights of Christmas (published by Poshrat Press). I was also a winner of Four Stories, a short-film script-writing competition curated by Roman Coppola and The Director's Bureau and my winning film, Eugene, directed by Spencer Susser, currently has over 3 million views on Youtube.

Robert E. Petras is a graduate of West Liberty State University and a resident of Toronto, Ohio. His poetry and fiction in various genres have appeared in more than 150 publications, most recently in Hello Horror, Inner Sins and Haunted Waters Press. Email: klydepetras@hotmail.com

K.Z. Morano is a writer, a registered nurse and a blogger. Her recent works include "The Baobab" in Popcorn Horror Presents published in August 2013 by Popcorn Horror, "The Other Child" in Ugly Babies: the Anthology by JWK Fiction in October 2013 (to be reprinted in Blood Reign Literary Magazine December 2013). Several of her stories will also be appearing in various forthcoming anthologies.

Jason Gehlert is the author of the werewolf horror series Quiver. Through his tireless promotions, Jason landed several contracts, resulting in the fan favorite, Contagion, his sensational South African jungle zombie novel. Jason has been featured in several news articles, radio interviews, and has done various book signings around New York. He also has his own website, www.jasongehlert.blogspot.com and has plans to expand his writing library, prolifically offering up work after work each year, including Ferrymen, Jeremiah Black and many new projects with JWK Publishing and Horrified Press. Jason also holds a Bachelor's Degree in Communication/Media from Suny-New Paltz.

Niall Parkinson: DARK AGE DESIGN: "surreal journeys through landscapes of the angry and abandoned, the lost and lonely and the weak and wounded. These are the realms of the Dead End Collective. Dark, Surreal and Conceptual Illustration Niall Parkinson is an Irish artist specializing in the origination of dark, surreal, conceptual and spiritual hand drawn illustration from which he explores the darker regions of the human heart and experience. His background is in commercial graphic design and he had spent over 20 years working in this capacity within the printing industry. Niall has also had success in the music industry designing cd covers and booklets primarily for European metal bands. His real interest now lies in pursuing his illustration service DARK AGE DESIGN from which he hopes to work in the realm of areas which incorporate horror and nightmarish themes and concepts such as magazines, book illustration and cover design with perhaps some comic book work. Niall is also available to work within more conventional areas of design including signage, logo design, crest and typography development and other areas of design and layout Niall can be contacted via email at neonangelus68@hotmail.com

Greg McWhorter is a pop-culture historian and teacher who resides in Southern California. Since the 1980s, he has worked for newspapers, radio, television, and film. He has been a guest speaker at several universities and the San Diego Comic-Con. Today, McWhorter owns a highly acclaimed record label that specializes in vintage punk rock. He is also the host of a cable TV show titled Rock 'n' Roll High School 101. Since 1985, McWhorter has been writing nonfiction music-related articles for print and has recently turned to writing crime and horror fiction. McWhorter's stories have appeared in several anthologies and magazines. He has published work with EC Comics, James Ward Kirk Publishing, Scarlett River Press, Rorshoq Books, A Raven Above Press, Schlock! Press, Source Point Press, Horrified Press, eFiction Publishing, as well as forthcoming stories for Static Movement, Phrenic Press, and 13Horror, amongst others. He is a member of the Horror Writer's Association and recently had a poem featured on their webpage. You can follow him at: http://gregmcwhorter.blogspot.com

David Perlmutter

Member, Manitoba Writers Guild
    SF Canada
    Fictioneers
    Writers Union Of Canada
    Society Of Children's Book Writers And Illustrators
    Organization Of American Historians
    ASIFA
    Society For Animation Studies
    Professional Writers Association Of Canada

Canadian Authors Association

PUBLICATION CREDITS
Short Stories
"The Hunter And The Game". Published at *Kalkion*.com, September 18, 2009.
"The Windigo Blows At Midnight". Published in *Ethereal Tales* 5, Oct. 31, 2009.
"A Little Egypt (Yin-Yang!)". Published online in *Broomstick Books*, Vol. 1, Spring 2010.
"The Redeemer". Published in *Christmas In Outer Space*, ed. By Jean Goldstrom (Whortleberry Press, 2009.)
"The Witch Of The School". Published in *Dark Gothic Resurrected Magazine*, April 2010.
"Below The Belt". Published in *End Of Days 2: An Apocalyptic Anthology*, ed. By Anthony Giangregorio. (Living Dead Press, 2009.) Accepted into Anthologybuilder database, June 2010.
"Cotton Picking Hands". Published at *Kalkion*.com. December 3, 2009.
"Pink Dragon Blues". Published in *Kings of The Realm: A Dragon Anthology*, ed. By Christopher Jacobsmeyer and Chris Bartholomew (Lame Goat Press), February 2010.
"All I Owe You Is A Good Story". Published at *Lame Goat Zine*, Issue 1, posted December 25, 2009.
"Press". Published at *Vast Horizons*.com. Posted January 31, 2010.
"James Brown The Serial Killer". Published in *Daily Flash,* ed. By Jessy Marie Roberts (Pill Hill Press, October 2010).
"Secrets". Published in *Strange Mysteries 2*, ed. By Jean Goldstrom (Whortleberry Press, 2010.) Accepted into Anthologybuilder database, June 2010.
"Partners In...Something". Published at *Kalkion*.com, February 18, 2010.
"Censored". Published in *Deep Space Terror*, ed. By Chris Bartholomew (Static Movement, 2010.)
"From A Desk In Ottawa." Published in *Letters From The Dead*, ed. By Mark Johnson (Library Of The Living Dead Press, 2010.)
"Wackyland Vs. America". Published in *Novus Creatura*, ed. By John Arthur Miller (Aurora Wolf, 2010).
"The Devil And Summer Schwartz". Published in *Dark Gothic Resurrected Magazine*, Summer 2010.
"Pandemic". Published in *Inner Fears*, ed. By William Wolford (Static Movement, 2010.)

"Tzedakah". Published in *Diamonds In The Rough*, ed. By Chris Bartholomew (Lame Goat Press, 2010.)

"How Tomboy Came To Be Involved In The Superhero Business." Published at *Freedom Fiction*, Issue 7, Volume 2, 2010.

"Motor City Wolf". Published in *Night Of The Wolf*, ed. By Anthony Giangregorio (Living Dead Press, 2010.) Also published as an ebook by Untreed Reads Publications, 2011.

"Vengeance". Published in *Dark Gothic Resurrected Magazine*, Summer 2010.

"Interrupted Newscast". Published in *Daily Bites Of Flesh*, ed. By Jessy Marie Roberts. Pill Hill Press, December 2010.

"The Dispute". Published at *Swordreaver.com*, May 2010.

"Mana From Heaven". Published in *Free Range Fairy Tales*, ed. By Jean Goldstrom (Whortleberry Press, 2010.)

"Summer Schwartz Vs. The Middle School Vampire". Published in *Fem-Fangs*, ed. By Jessy Marie Roberts and Ty Schwamberger (Pill Hill Press, 2010.)

"Bloch's Parent". Published in *Dark Valentine* #2, ed. By Katherine Tomlinson. (October 2010).

"American Animation Oral History Interviews: Punkin Pye". Published at *The Fringe*, November 2010.

"Video Diary Of A Tall Soldier". Published in *Cup Of Joe: Coffee House Flash Fiction*, ed. By Jessica Weiss (Wicked East Press, December 2010).

"My Gym Partner And I: A Sticks And Bones Investigation". Published in *Pulp Empire, Volume Two*, ed. By Nicholas Ahlhelm (2010).

"'Toons Bite Men". Published in *Daily Flash*, ed. By Jessy Marie Roberts. Pill Hill Press, October 2010.

"The Ink In Her Veins". Published in *Caught By Darkness*, ed. By Chris Bartholomew (Static Movement, 2010.)

"When The Frost Is On The Pumpkin". Published in *Thriller! A Young Adult Anthology*, ed. By Chris Bartholomew (Static Movement, 2010.)

"Hot House Flowers". Published in *Were-What?*, ed. By Chris Bartholomew (Static Movement, 2010.)

"Radio Interview". Published in *Daily Bites Of Flesh*, ed. By Jessy Marie Roberts (Pill Hill Press, December 2010).

"Murder's Not Cool". Published as an ebook by Untreed Reads Publishing, January 2011.

"A Brighter Shade Of Darkness". Published in *Ghosts And Demons*, ed. By Chris Bartholomew (Static Movement, 2010.)

"Got A Match?" Published in *Ethereal Tales* No.9, October 2010.

"Cut And Run". Published in *Dark Gothic Resurrected Magazine*, October 2010.

"Black Magic". Published at *Dark Valentine*, October 17, 2010.

"Professor Bambury's Medicine Show". Published in *Cosmic Catastrophes*, ed. By Chris Bartholomew (Static Movement, 2010.)

"The Freeze: An Investigation Of The Jakobson Middle School Safety Patrol". Published in *Pulp Empire, Volume Three* ed. By Nicholas Ahlhelm (2010).

"Challenges". Published in *Peace On All The Earths*, ed. By Jean Goldstrom (Whortleberry Press, 2010.)

"Hard Work". Published as an ebook by Books To Go Now, LLC, October 2010.

"Down In Hollywood". Published at *Roar And Thunder*, fall 2010.

"Tip And Alice". Published at *The Fringe*, fall 2010.

"...Princess Marvel.." Published in *Trunk Stories*, ed. By Chris Bartholomew (Static Movement, 2010.)

"The Uninvited Guests". Published in *Unquiet Dead*, ed. By Chris Bartholomew (Static Movement, 2010.)

"Shooting A Star". Published in *Bounty Hunter*, ed. By Chris Bartholomew (Static Movement, 2011.)

"Cloning Death". Published in *Something In The Attic*, ed. By Chris Bartholomew (Static Movement, 2010.)

"Tofurkey Theft's Not Cool". Published in *Strange Mysteries 3*, ed. By Jean Goldstrom (Whortleberry Press, 2011.)

"Bisons". Published in *Closet Monsters,* ed. By Chris Bartholomew (Static Movement, 2010.)

"The Redhead, The Brunette, The Blonde And The Blob". Published in *Something From The Attic 2*, ed. By Chris Bartholomew (Static Movement, 2010.)

"Won Great City". Published in *Something From The Attic 2*, ed. By Chris Bartholomew (Static Movement, 2010.)

"The Pups". Serialized at Metahuman Press.com, Oct. 2010- Feb. 2011

"Character Assassination". Published in *Uncanny Allegories*, ed. By Eric Beebe (Post Mortem Press, 2010.)

"Shake It And Break It". Published in *Serial Killers*, ed. By Chris Bartholomew (Static Movement, 2010.)

"Throw Back The Little Ones". Published in *The Psyche Corrupted*, ed. By Garrett Starlen (Shade City Press, 2011.)

"One Fine Day At Universal City." Published in *Something From The Attic 2,* ed. By Chris Bartholomew (Static Movement, 2010.)

"Two Cats With The Blues". Published in *Dark Things 2: Cat Crimes* (Dark Car Press, 2011.)

"The Thing That Went Viral" Published as an ebook by Books To Go Now, December 2010..

"Suicide Mission". Published in *First Cut*, ed. By Heather Wildman (Paper Cut Press, 2011.)

"...The Space Scouts..." Published in *Powers: A Superhero Anthology*, ed. By Jay Falkner (Static Movement, 2010.)

"Jody Ryder And The Martian Marxian Invasion". Published in *Pulp Empire*, Volume 4, ed. By Nicholas Ahlhelm (Metahuman Press, 2011.)

"Ool Ya Koo". Published in *Halloween Hell-O-Ween Anthology*, ed. By Jean Goldstrom (Whortleberry Press, 2011.)

"Mixed Blood". Published in *Dark Deeds In History*, ed. By Dorothy Davies (Static Movement, 2011.)

"Human Nature". Published in *Pulp Empire, Volume Five,* ed. By Nicholas Ahlhelm (Metahuman Press, 2011.)

"The Camera Never Blinks." Published in *Adventures In Other Worlds*, ed. By Chris Bartholomew (Static Movement, 2011.)

"The Old Man And The Vampire". Published in *Short Sips*, ed. By Jessica Weiss (Wicked East Press, 2011).

"The Right To Refuse Service". Published in *Road Trip*, ed. By Chris Bartholomew (Static Movement, 2011.)

"Swing Your Vampire High". Published in *Ruby Red Cravings*, ed. By Brianna Stoddard (Static Movement, 2011.) and *Vampires Aren't Pretty* (May December Publications, 2012.)

"The Modern Adventures Of Wilson, Du Bois, McLuhan and Seldes." Published in *Jake's Monthly: The Final Anthology*, ed. By Jake Johnson (ebook collection, 2012.)

"Dead, Free, Black". Published in *Flashonomics*, ed. By Garrett Starlen (Shade City Press, 2011.)

"Town Hall Tonight!" Published at *The Fringe,* February 2011.

"With A Gun." Published in *The Seventh Sin*, ed. By Garrett Starlen (Shade City Press, 2011.)

"Angie." Published at *The Fringe,* February 2011. Also published in *Wolf Craft,* ed. By Ron Koppelberger (Static Movement, 2013.)

"Aspie Vampy." Published in *Dark Gothic Resurrected Magazine*, July 2011.

"Baby Bark Bites The Bullet". Published in *Science Gone Mad,* ed. By George Wilhite (Static Movement, 2011.)

"Water Hazard". Published at *Dark Valentine*, March 2011.

"Nothing About Us Without Us". Published in *Weird City*, ed. By George Wilhite (Static Movement, 2011.)

"Elf Insurance". Published in *Alternate Dimensions*, ed. By Chris Bartholomew (Static Movement, 2011.)

"St. Michael's Day." Published in *Summer Thrills*, ed. By Dorothy Davies (Static Movement, 2011.)

"The Boy Who Could Really Fly Like Superman." Published in *And I Swear This Is True,* ed. By George Wilhite (Static Movement, 2011.)

"The Milwaukee Incident". Published in *Daily Flash 2011*, ed. By Jessy Marie Roberts (Pill Hill Press, 2011.)

"Joseph Barbera." Published in *Tribute To The Stars*, ed. By Chris Bartholomew (Static Movement, 2011.) and *Daily Flash 2011*, ed. By Jessy Marie Roberts (Pill Hill Press, 2011.)

"Wack Whack." Published at *The WiFiles*, Fall 2011.

"Speedy And The Buck." Published in *Make A Wish*, ed. By George Wilhite (Static Movement, 2013.)

"How Not To Break Up With An Animated Cartoon Character". Published in *Monster Gallery*, ed. By George Wilhite (Static Movement, 2011.)

"To The Devil, A Daughter." Published in *Strange Valentines*, ed. By Jean Goldstrom (Whortleberry Press, 2012.)

"...Womyngrrl and boyman." Published in *Jake's Monthly Science Fiction Anthology*, ed. By Jake Johnson (ebook anthology, 2011).

"The Doc And I." Published in *Science Gone Mad*, ed. By George Wilhite (Static Movement, 2011.)

"Victory Over The Garden." Published as an ebook by Untreed Reads Publications, 2012.

"Up To Me." Published in *Weird City 2*, ed. By George Wilhite (Static Movement, 2011.)

"The Power." Published in *After The End*, ed. By Shane Collins (Static Movement, 2011.)

"Wack Whack." Published at *The WiFiles*, June 2011.

"Chez Jefferson." Published at *Kalkion.com*, May 2011.

"Summer Schwartz And The Crazy House." Published in *There Was A Crooked House*, ed. By Jessy Marie Roberts (Pill Hill Press, 2011.)

"A Zinger Must Die." Published in *Midnight Movie Creature Feature*, ed. By Denise Brown (May December Publications, 2011.)

"Summer's First Trip." Published in *Dark Gothic Resurrected Magazine*, summer 2012.

"...Zombie Killing Machine..." Published in *Zombies: The Other Fright Meat*, ed. By Matt Nord (Norgus Press, 2012.)

"The Doll House." Published in *Urban Nightmares*, ed. By Dorothy Davies (Static Movement, 2012.)

"The Fish". Published in *Thadd Presley Presents Murder* (Thadd Presley Presents, 2012.)

"Octopi Bleakly Corners." Published in *Masked Mosaic: Canadian Super Stories*, ed. By Claude Lalumiere (2013).

"She-Dog." To be published in *Super* (Static Movement, 2013.)

"The Meeting." Published in *Spring Fever* (Static Movement, 2013.)

"Terry The Turtle And The Watermelon Of Death." To be published in *Shithouse Tales* (Alter Press, 2013.)

"Just A Little Miss-Understanding" To be published in *Dark Light 2* (CCHB, 2013.)

"Tooned Out." Published as an ebook by Untreed Reads Publications, 2012.

"Please Don't Talk About Me When I'm Gone." Published as an ebook by Untreed Reads Publications, 2013.

Novels and Stand Alone Books

The Pups. Fiction. Published by Twisted Library Press, fall 2011.

America Toons In: A History of Television Animation. Non-fiction. To be published by McFarland and Co., 2014.

The Singular Adventures of Jefferson Ball. Fiction. To be published by Chupa Cabra Press, 2014.

Non-Fiction Articles

"The Unknown Stars". Published in *Tribute To The Stars*, ed. By Chris Bartholomew (Static Movement, 2010.)

"The Optimal Mode." Published in *Nameless Magazine*, Issue 2 (2012).

www.ingramcontent.com/pod-product-compliance
Lightning Source LLC
Chambersburg PA
CBHW070009260626
47159CB00005B/1730